pink
water
dawn

BILL GREEN

A Hodder & Stoughton book

This edition published in Australia and New Zealand in 1996 by
Hodder Headline Australia Pty Limited
(A member of the Hodder Headline Group)
10-16 South Street, Rydalmere NSW 2116

National Library of Australia Cataloguing-in-Publication data

Green, Bill, 1940-.
Pink water dawn.

ISBN 0 7336 0271 1.

I. Title.

A823.3

Printed in Australia by McPherson's Printing Group

Prologue

Below them the moon created a shivering path of light across one of the world's largest inland salt lakes. The size of the lake was something of a secret because it drained from Victoria's western plains and was saltier than the ocean. It was destroying the land around it.

Robert Evans liked the way the country hid its lake systems. Travelling by road across the state, you were unaware of the water. From the Bell UH-1 chopper speeding to his homestead another fifty kilometres west, the country looked like an inland sea. Evans liked secrets. Nurturing them was the way he made his money.

Beside him was the Indonesian general, who affected the latest dark glasses from Los Angeles. The glasses had indented the flesh of his head. He had grown fat while wearing them. He had removed them once during the flight and the hollows of his eyes had been swimming in sweat, the pupils looking dull, as if they had been cooked. He sat awkwardly, as if he was balancing the mantle of power, not wearing it. Next to the pilot was Major Richard Stephens, a man who had decided to bring Robert Evans and the general together for their mutual benefit and, of course, his own.

Evans was wondering how little he could pay Stephens for the introduction to the general. He stood to make millions from the deal, but Stephens seemed the sort of creature who liked a good social life, and the things that went with it. Evans found it easy to bribe public servants. You simply introduced them to a life they had never experienced but had always lusted after. Invite them to parties where celebrities deigned to talk to them, and give them a day in the company box at the races and seats at the tennis, and they were in your pocket, at a minimum outlay for catering and a tiny dent in the company's expense account.

The general was a problem. He had already hinted at the size of the kickback if he placed this order, and it was considerable. Evans had brought them out to his stud farm to show the general he was a man of considerable substance, and to avoid the possibility of American or Australian security services overhearing conversations.

The chopper dropped down onto the front lawn of the homestead as the moonlight faded behind the dark purple of an approaching cold front. The homestead was well lit and as they walked from the smell of aircraft fuel up the steps to the front verandah of the bluestone mansion, they met the smells of pastries and sauces. Evans was glad he had had the foresight to hire the catering team.

The women joining them for dinner would greet Evans like old friends. He had often used them for cementing deals. They enabled the contracting parties to bond on major issues. The women were helpful and fun, and sharing them lent a camaraderie that transcended contract details.

Evans turned for a moment on the verandah, touched the general on the arm and pointed to the lights of the small town in the distance. It was a magnificent rural sight across the park-like paddocks of the stud. The huge oaks at the bottom of the four hectare garden were still, giving the scene an immeasurable sense of security.

The dinner was a success. The general got pissed quickly and made piggish advances to several of the women. He couldn't believe such beautiful women were so accessible. The women were working to Evans's command, like sheepdogs rounding up a recalcitrant sheep. The general was deposited in the study, where Evans and Stephens waited with the contract. He was in a high state of titillation. The goods were only referred to as 'the product'. The actual strength of the product was not alluded to in the contract, giving Evans some satisfaction in knowing he could supply them with the cheapest of materials. Evans had no idea where the product was going to be used, apart from the fact that he knew President Soeharto of Indonesia had warned that his country would not cease its expansionist policies until the year 2010. Presumably 'the product' would be used to subdue the small countries it desired.

The general signed the contracts. The two women he had chosen were urging him with their eyes to hurry up; they were eager. He signed and immediately left the study. Moments later his trousers were around his ankles and his ego and his flesh were being tended.

The major was dissatisfied. It seemed to him that he had put in the hard work and he deserved a larger percentage of any profits that were generated by the deal. After all, it had been his idea, and he had brought the general into the country without fuss. Even the new defence pact between Indonesia and Australia wouldn't entirely exempt the general from some token observation by security, but the media had no idea he was in the country. In the major's mind, the small percentage he stood to make had grown in value to thirty per cent. Evans was firm. That amount was out of the question. Evans had to make the 'product', maintain secrecy, organise transport and finally deliver. Bureaucrats didn't realise that the money in any deal always took the majority share of any profits. It was the way things were. An idea is only an idea unless there is money to support its development.

Now the major was being cagey. He wouldn't name his final figure. It irritated Evans, made him see the danger the major represented. Because of his other deal looming, in the shadow of this one, the major might become a considerable concern. He also had to pay the third man, the person who was going to protect him locally from government curiosity.

The major was roused out of bed early in the morning. One of the women from the previous night delivered breakfast in a flowing satin morning robe. When she had finished with him, he was told that he was scheduled for an early morning ride. He laughed. Hadn't he already had it? He began to feel optimistic. Evans was recognising his worth.

Evans joined him for the walk down to the stables. When they entered the old stone complex, the major was surprised that there were no saddled horses. A rather slim man walked towards him in the traditional strapper's gear of jeans and solid boots. He was much surprised when the strapper performed a whirling somersault ten metres in front of him, more surprised at the weapon that appeared in his hand as if by magic, and then he was surprised no more. He didn't feel the steel enter his brain, didn't even hear it.

'Why do you have to jig around like that?' Evans said to the tall strapper, who was looking down at the growing puddle of blood spreading out beneath Evans.

'Makes it interesting,' the strapper said, looking up at Evans. His eyes were smiling happily in accord with the rest of his face, and then they closed down, the steadiness of the gaze surprisingly cold and calculating. To shake off the need to shiver, Evans strode out into the morning sun. The paddocks were peaceful. He liked the country. Behind him he heard a pleasant chuckle. It reminded him of the son of one of his station hands who had been on a rabbit shoot and had covered himself with hundreds of dead rabbits, burrowing through the furry pelts, laughing, enjoying the sensations. Evans decided he would have this one killed off at an appropriate time. The bastard was becoming unstable.

One

A man's body had begun baking in the intensive care ward of a city hospital. Small fires had broken out deep inside living tissue. His body was smoking as he died. The smoke hovered over his body, unmoving, emerging like fog in cold air from the warm earth. Because of this man, I would have to leave the farm and my horses for a week or so. I had been promised a sweet bundle of money to investigate the chemical company the bloke had worked for. Last night Willa Buchan called me. Her voice was that of a concerned mother on the phone. Resonant, full of the life she was enjoying. And she wanted me.

I tried to remember the woman I had known behind the voice. She had been a girl, really. Perceptive, quick, a handsome brownish red colour in summer, a skin that smelt of summer days and tasted of salt fresh from a swim.

The voice still hinted of that sort of girlhood. We hadn't got very far into a relationship. I had been frightened of her wealthy background. It hovered between us, nebulous, but with a power to alter my life, alter me. She could do anything she wanted, pick up any time and leave——she spoke of lengthy pleasure trips overseas; something not only alien to me, but something I couldn't afford—and I had nothing to offer her, apart from a raging libido. Once our drunk friends had burst into the bathroom on one of those hot summer nights of drinking and playing; they didn't believe we had rushed under a cold shower to fuck.

I remembered accompanying her to the airport for her plane to London, and she was happy to leave, confident I would follow her once I realised the void she left in my life. My lack of money had meant nothing to her. She just imagined that it would quickly come to me and I would follow her.

As she talked I listened to the echoes of those summer nights so long ago. She was explaining the death of a man she had never met, a cousin-in-law, who had died writhing in pain. She suspected the medical staff had killed him with morphine because they could do nothing about the agony. She went along with the death. It was the accident she was interested in, and why it had happened.

It sounded as if a scientist was needed, but Willa said their sympathies would be with the chemical company. She had contacted me because of the fuss I'd made about chemicals and pollution over the years. I had never thought my interest in the environment would earn me the sort of money she mentioned. Exactly the opposite, in fact. Several of the stories I had written had been in small magazines under pseudonyms, for my own protection. The manufacturers of chemicals had a great deal of influence in media circles, and in those days I had needed employment.

These days I was braver. I had found financial independence. Like most thoroughbred breeders, and a few journalists who race horses for a hobby, I run experiments in racehorse breeding. I study the breeding lines and decide how, on a limited budget, I can breed champions. That should bring a smile to the faces of the odd knowledgeable racehorse breeder. Stallion fees in my price range vary from around five thousand to twenty thousand dollars. And although I had two stallions on the stud, I needed finance for fresh blood. It was supplied by individuals like Willa who wanted their mysteries solved.

I would have worked on this investigation for nothing, just for the memories of that summer. After the call, I brewed coffee, and sipped it, looking across the paddock to the lake. I wondered if she had ever regretted leaving me.

Willa was running a refuge for women who wanted to get their lives in order and learn to how to fight their husbands and a variety of bureaucracies. When I had knocked around with her, she had been a lawyer who hadn't wanted to practise law because for her justice was an absolute. No partial justice for Willa. She realised she'd be a misfit in the profession. My use to her that summer may have been as a way of letting go her ambition, tasting another sort of life. But now she was a woman who had made a life for herself, knew the score, and could be dangerous to do business with. Her need of me now was for something else entirely.

The story around the death so far was a hairy one, and many influential people wanted to put a cap on it. Politicians had been silent about it in question time in Parliament, and so far none of it had reached the press.

It had all started with the victim being thrown into a chemical vat by his mates at the Abidex chemical company. They had thought it was full of the allegedly harmless herbicide 2,4-D. The poor bastard had been making a noise for weeks about the chemical's effect on the environment, animals, people, everything that was included in the food chain. The other workers believed the company's statement that chemicals were okay, completely harmless, and they were paid a lot to believe that—less these days, though, as jobs became scarcer. So they were irritated when a lone voice among them began to agitate against the use of chemicals in agriculture.

They grabbed him one night after his shift finished and hauled him to the vat. It was a lot of fun. Problem was, as he fought to keep out of the tank, he had sliced his back on sharp metal scaffolding, and scraped his ankle as he went in feet first. His mates were joking, of course, but they had also been firm. When they pulled him

out, he was in a state of collapse. That had
alarmed them because chemical tank dunking had
once been a form of initiation when new blokes
came to work at the plant and nothing like the
collapse had happened before, although blokes
who were allergic to the stuff usually never
returned to work.

The bloke had recovered in hospital. He had
been washed down, given antidotes and anti-
allergy shots and was thought to be on the way
to recovery. Then he had caught fire.

It turned out the chemical hadn't been 2,4-D
at all, but had only smelt like it. No one knew
what chemical concoction it had been. The company was still saying it was 2,4-D, and was
claiming the hospital dressings on his wounds
must have been flammable. The government research centre had come up with a variety of
chemicals in his tissue, but had concluded none
would have caused his death.

His widow was a young cousin of Willa's from
the poor side of the family, and the dead man had
been twenty-eight, without work for most of his
life, and had been anxious to start bringing in
the reasonable money that workers could make
around chemicals. He had a degree in economics,
but so did many cab drivers and ditch diggers.
He'd had to hide his education in his job appli-
cations. He was proud that he could afford a few
things that could get him and his wife out of the
house on weekends.

The widow thought the research centre hadn't tested for enough chemicals, and came to her cousin for help. She had chosen well. Willa felt guilty that she hadn't looked up her young cousin before, and she was tough when it came to fighting company bureaucracies.

The cousin's husband had stayed alive for a few days after the first fires. The medicos thought he would live because it had only been his wounds that had caught. Suddenly, though, he was screaming as smoke rose from the sheet. It was as if it were steaming. This time the smoke was from fires deep inside him.

Everybody scrambled to deny everything. His widow had tried the cops, but they had been met with denials from the chemical company and their scientists that bodies could catch fire spontaneously. The hospital and the health department were anxious to exonerate themselves, too.

Finally, Willa had thought she would try my style of reporting. Naturally, I'm not the sort that has a permanent position with a paper or a television network, and who is pointed in the direction of a story by a well-connected chief-of-staff or news editor. Reporters like me have to keep a low profile because we require total anonymity to assemble the evidence when we move into new areas of corporate, factory or sporting life. We're a rare breed in this country. In Europe we're respectable, and American schools of journalism use texts with titles like, *Muckraking*, and

Covert Media Investigations, mostly published by Pennsylvania State University Press. Muckraking became hugely respectable after President Nixon lost his job over the Watergate break-in.

In Australia we're barely tolerated. Here the media lies very close to the politicians, and often in the same bed. They do each other favours, and you don't have a job too long if you begin to dig into the murky stuff supporting the country's powerbrokers. A friend of mine turned up dead, while investigating corruption in the customs department. It was labelled a suicide because he had been having relationship problems and it had been his own gun. So, why dig any deeper? For the simple reason that the truth was being hidden. I could feel it.

I made it into the coolroom with a photographer. The cop on the door was an old friend; he knew corruption, saw it destroying the people he worked with. He leaked information to take revenge on those he saw as bigger crims than those they chased. He often rang me about those who took up temporary residence in the coolroom.

To my mind, no one who knows guns shoots themselves in the belly, the most painful of all deaths. We took shots of the cadaver and left.

My story on his death was slagged by his friends and my colleagues. They said he had died for love, wanted to believe that. But I knew somebody killed him. A muckraker never kills himself if he's got a good story running.

I chased those I thought responsible. But by then they were powerful enough to escape justice. You don't dislodge entrenched people with evidence their own corrupt kind have to examine. When a state has succumbed to the force of money on every level, muckraking rarely wins.

Nothing identifies the true muckraker as a legitimate reporter. Those elevated to muckrakers in America are just the reporters who would have been the traditional investigative reporters, living on a good salary. In this country, rarely can muckrakers use a network or newspaper's name; we tend to create too much trouble. But these days I have developed an ability to fix the problems before they require media exposure. I can blackmail, threaten and cajole with the strength of any capitalist attempting to save his business.

For instance, I imagined this current case was the sort of problem Greenpeace would finally take off my hands if I could substantiate the evidence I had collected. Insidious chemicals being manufactured close to the waters of Port Phillip Bay was something for them to run with.

Starting out for the city down the dirt track in the early morning as the birds were waking across the silver water was an exquisite sensation. The lake was teeming with bird life. The swans were close in to shore, their necks gracefully unfolding from their backs, their soft calls a reminder of the gentler moments of life. Further out across the water the air was hot with the sound of more-raucous birds. The horses were playfully snorting after a gallop along the muddy edge to warm up. At least they'd show form on wet tracks next winter, confident of their balance in the heavy going.

A flotilla of pelicans slit the metal surface of the water as I closed the gate to the farm. I glanced about to make sure there was no impending emergency I should take care of before I left. The big American race mare, Shy Bride, was down on the bank of the lake still sleeping, dreaming as the water lapped less than a metre away from her. She was rapidly approaching twenty and probably shouldn't have been in foal, but she was and I worried about her. Her huge belly was slung off to one side as the foal moved to face the sun that penetrated the womb. I was intrigued by this habit, only recently discovered by curious veterinarians with new hi-tech toys. I'd need to be back within a week to make sure she birthed without trouble.

The road to Linda Lectrof's place ran south of the lake. The bush here was rarely still. The country was rolling plains interspersed with timber hectares, and draining water had established a lake in the dip between our houses that spread over ten thousand hectares. Linda was acting stud master when I was away. She had turned up some months ago, just moved into the area, and had an obsession with racehorses. Her ambition was to train. There are no official qualifications for getting an owner-trainer's licence, apart from a knowledge of horses, and that's impossible to gauge. You have to run a clean establishment and your horses have to look good when the stewards call to examine your residence.

She had a chance. She had already asked if she could train some youngsters of mine, and had applied for her owner-trainer's licence. Unlike the professional trainer on a full licence, she would have to have some equity in the horses she was training. With the horses she leased from me like that, she would take two-thirds of the horse's winnings. It sounds a lot, but with only about five per cent of the thoroughbreds born ever making it to the racetrack, it wasn't much at all. Training horses would take six hours of her day, barring accidents, and the work on my place amounted to another four.

Linda was out of a relationship and had come to the country for a decent house and stables on dole money. Hundreds of properties had old houses left by departing employees as the rural life became tougher. A diligent person could turn them into something worthwhile at low rent. I had been thinking of asking her to live-in on my place but I was fully aware of my motivation. I

knew that she too was aware of the carnal tremors she caused me.

I pulled into Linda's place to discuss the activities for the next week. The house was a
weatherboard that was slowly returning to the
earth, but she had arrested the process, giving it,
and the stables, several coats of white paint. It
was a two-bedroom place and the back windows
looked over the lake to my place. It had verandahs
all around and they were covered with grape
vines. A passionfruit grew over the tank at the
back of the house.

Her kitchen light was on as I drove up. I
walked to the verandah and she opened the wire
door. The spring on it protested. She was showered and dressed. A handsome woman who pulled
her hair back when she was working, she had a
fine forehead and cool grey eyes, and she wore
jeans that I had to stop looking at when I talked
to her.

'Heading off again?' she asked, hooking her
thumbs into her belt and leaning against the door
jamb.

'Yeah, something's come up.'

'Okay,' she said, turning back into the warm
kitchen. I wanted to stop her.

'Apple and Art Shy are working so well,' I
called from the car, 'you could probably finish
them hard over the last two hundred. Four hundred next week. Depends how they pull up.'

'They're better than you think,' she said, anxious to close the door. It was probably the cool morning, but I felt she had a visitor. 'I'll get a coat,' she said and disappeared. The two colts we had been talking about had been in work for ten weeks and showed no sign of shin soreness; unusual for two-year-olds. Give them time, I thought.

The spring creaked as Linda opened the door again. Her body was slim and hard from the riding and the physical work, and it was tanned through winter, one of those cinnamon complexions that keep you young into the forties. I liked her, often thought of calling her up in the evenings to ask if she needed companionship as much as I, but I never had. She stood beside the car and we talked about the foaling season coming up. She didn't want to have to do all the work. She had other things to do with her nights. 'God,' she said. 'I've got eggs in the pan.' She sprang onto the verandah and was through the door. I reversed the car and pulled up close to the verandah. 'I've gotta go,' I said. She gave me a backwards smile as the screen door closed.

It was flat, boring country, the roads avoiding the lakes that I knew were hidden away. The timber country close to the Western Highway was refreshing. The smell of the eucalypts, the flash of bright parrots, and the intimate backroads where you had to drive slow enough to see things always inspired me. Close to Geelong a quick descent took me through an industrial workers' suburb to the freeway. I drove to the music of J.J. Cale, his big beat preparing me for the city movement. 'Cocaine' sounded its heavy base as I approached the Westgate Bridge.

I was into the pulse of the big metropolis, was even capable of changing its beat occasionally. I knew all the trails scam merchants hit because I had their instincts. It was part of horseracing. Calculating the odds meant taking into account the venal natures of owners, trainers and jockeys, and gauging how they would jump given a fast or slow horse. I applied these lessons to my more profitable work. I knew if you wanted to win in any field, you had to dirty your hands, find out how everything ticked.

I wanted to take a sample of the chemical from the vat at the Abidex plant close to Williamstown. Security would pose a small problem, but I don't have the patience of the greenies when I know people are being shoved around. If I had my way, I would turn up at greenie protest sites with a chainsaw to use on the company executives. But senior executives never confront protesters, so finding them had to be done behind the scenes.

I drove down to the Williamstown foreshore. I loved it here. It was where I spent my time when I worked in the city.

I wanted to check the advance of pollution in the water surrounding the tongue of land that jutted into the bay, Point Gellibrand. There was a good story building about the bay. It had history, too, the first sheep landed, a hated gaol governor killed on this beach last century, prison hulks anchored close to the old jetty.

The area of land at the tip of the point, the most beautiful in Melbourne, had been sold by the state government for a carpark. Protests against this are ongoing, but as this area has been treated as working class throughout its history, governments of all political persausions have been determined to keep the western suburbs an industrial area. Worse still, they have been allowing the bay to be killed with chemicals. One day I would have a hook to hang a good bay story on. The governments claimed a clean E-coli count meant harmless water. But that, like E-coli, was total shit. It was the heavy metals they didn't test for that would finally kill the bay.

The sea was as clear as the day was windless. Down near the structure of the old time ball the water swirled up to rocky foreshore. I clambered across the rocks and reached into the chill water to squeeze a few handfuls of sand close to the surface. An off-coloured slick rose on the water. An oily chemical. If this stuff was in the sand, it was in the food chain. An international oil company had vast storage tanks for benzine—a serious carcinogen—three hundred metres away. They were also careless with their tanker-to-land transfers.

I returned to the car and drove west towards Altona. Abidex was on the fringes of Altona and it was never without the sweet, foul smell of herbicides. One of my farmer mates couldn't smell 2,4-D without an involuntary bowel response. He had been using it for years on variegated thistle, although it was practically useless against the meaty plant, but then one spring the sweet smell of clover milk that it gave off registered foul to him and his body lost control.

I turned my old Impala convertible into the guard gate. When it's necessary to get things done quickly and you know it's going to be a hassle, I always believe in telling the truth and being up front. It makes you feel more confident. So, when the guard asked me to identify myself and the individual I had come to see, I said, 'Jack Speerman, and I just want a small sample of the chemical in the open vat near the lunchrooms.'

The guard smirked. He was a bloke in his mid-thirties, safe in his grey guard's uniform and his little security control centre, still confident of his physical impact, despite easing off on his training a decade ago. 'You're not going to get past that,' he said, pointing to the lowered pole that prevented entry and exits. 'Now piss off.'

I slipped the automatic into neutral and the old thing chunked. I revved the engine. He turned back into the guard box, thinking I was reversing. I rose from behind the steering wheel, stepped over the door onto the guard house steps, and followed him through the door.

As he turned I removed his dark glasses, dropping them on the floor and crushing them underfoot. I waited for him to do something about it. I had a decade on him, but there was no gut on me and I ran three kilometres a day before putting in eight hours breaking horses and cleaning stables. I understood his thoughts: I get five hundred clear a week to stop serial greenies? It's not enough.

'Raise that fucking thing or I start feeding it to you,' I said.

He raised the black and white pole and I stepped out of the little guard box, into the driver's seat of the convertible and drove on.

'You fuckin' prick,' he yelled as I drove through. 'You won't get out.'

The stench closer to the complex was overpowering. There were kilometres of piping winding around in the style of a car radiator, but as large as a city block. I didn't want to know what the plant did just now. I knew it would depress me.

I drove down the side of a huge corrugated iron shed to where several large, squat vats stood. I stopped at the one closest to the huge shed entrance, took bolt cutters, a vacuum flask and syringe and climbed the ladder on the side of the vat.

Obviously it had taken quite a few blokes to dunk the victim, because there was only a small manhole in the top of the vat and they would have had to keep his legs close together. I cut the padlock on the manhole and swung it open. The foul exhalation very nearly stunned me. I gasped for air, held my breath and looked down. The sides and bottom were shiny steel. There was a few centimetres of chemical catching the light way down. There was an internal ladder, but there was no way in hell I was going to risk being overpowered by the stench. I didn't want to end up in the stuff.

I jumped down from the vat, walked inside the building and took a broom from the cleaner's office. No one about. I wrenched off the broom part, took gaffer tape from my car, attached a syringe and 16 gauge needle to the bottom of the pole and tied some string to the plunger handle. I quickly lowered the syringe into the chemical and pulled up the plunger. I only inhaled again when I was halfway back down the ladder.

I was lucky that most manufacturing plants no longer have dozens of workers. No one had moved to stop me. I drove around the building towards the gate and then I saw the trouble.

Six men waited, probably the entire working staff of the place. I drove my car to within three metres of the boom gate. To avoid the workers—who didn't look too enthusiastic anyway—I walked over the back seat, across the boot, opened it, admired my farm workshop—no poncy four-wheel drives for me—and unstrapped the Stihl chainsaw. It started first pull. I walked towards the boom through the blue smoke clouding from the saw. Men were standing near the guard box now, and I watched them as the chain bit into the pole, wood chips flying to the ground. I could feel the give as the boom prepared to fall.

The pole bounced on the road with a 'donk' and then ran across to the gravel on the verge.

There was no aggression from the men. One of them was laughing, although if the guard had been allowed a gun he would have shot me. I slipped the saw into neutral with the motor slowing, and placed it in the passenger seat.

When I turned onto the highway, I switched off the Stihl and motored towards Williamstown. No one was following. I guessed the police had been called; if I stayed on the highway they would have to meet me as they came from the Williamstown police station on the waterfront. I needed a detour.

I turned off on a dirt road around the sportsground. It led to a small holiday fishing hamlet where Kororoit Creek entered the sea. I pulled in behind the tea-tree there, just behind the fishing club. There were twenty shacks here, each with little verandahs fronting the creek where the occupants sat on summer evenings, looking out across the creek and the wild ground to the sea beyond, or dropping a line in for bream. I watched an old-timer pole a small clinker-built boat across from his bait ground on the opposite shore.

The day was beginning to warm up. The groundcover across the creek was a sanctuary for native birds and reptiles. It was part low flood ground and stunted mangrove beach. Walking there was out of the question. Tiger snakes thrived, as well as the unnamed brown snake whose venom had been found to act faster than that of the taipan. The new snake had been discovered in central Victoria some years ago and for some reason had not been named. No one had been bitten yet so the media hadn't been inspired enough to give it a decent name. Occasionally when the tide was running out, the fishermen, whose boats were moored at a boardwalk along the bank, would see a snake coming down with the swift water and shotguns would appear and they'd blast it to sausage meat.

The boats were mostly old clinker-built or bondwood ones in immaculate condition. The members of this fishing club were workers from Brunswick and Coburg. None of the smart new dashing hulls here. There wasn't a boat over eighteen feet.

This little fishing hamlet with its ancient boats was about to disappear. Abidex wanted to run a pipeline along the side of the sanctuary, and some of the council, mostly made up of men who lived within a block of one another—no regional representation here—were given campaign money by the oil companies and free trips to various parts of the world.

I waved to the fishermen, who wondered if I was a local lad come down to try and score some outboard motors. One walked over to me. He was fair-skinned but hadn't stayed out of the sun. His face was peeling away from the hairline. I got out of the car and shook his hand. 'Jack,' I said.

'Clive,' he said.

'Beautiful down here,' I said.

'Yeah.' A police car with siren went past on the highway.

'Quiet,' I said.

He grinned. 'Quiet?' he said. 'One of me mates was headin' out this mornin' and there was a mist at the entrance. He saw a few rocks and thought, they're not s'posed to be there. Then he saw they was Viets after shellfish, right. It's illegal. He put a few loads into the air and the shot come down pitter patter all round 'em like rain. He reckons they really moved.'

'How's the fish running?'

'No bloody snapper again this year. They haven't come into the bay.'

He pointed to the convertible. 'What's she got, a five litre V8?'

'Yeah,' I said, 'something like that.'

He grinned. 'Not good for the environment.'

I took field glasses from the glove box and looked towards Abidex. Nothing was happening there. The cops had already pulled out and were heading in the opposite direction, to the freeway. They had my licence number. In a week or two the cops from Colac might call out to my farm, and then again they might not. No one was injured. The timber might have been worth twenty dollars. I hadn't threatened anyone with the chainsaw. On top of all that, they had been attempting to detain me against my will. I had a better case than they did.

I nodded to Clive and reversed the car across the gravel and crawled down the potholed road. Now I had to see Willa and the widow, Ann Hough. I was meeting them at ten, down at one of the sidewalk cafes on Nelson Place, where you can look through a small park of giant elms to the sea.

Two

Williamstown is the only Melbourne suburb that makes use of the bay the way Sydney makes use of the harbour. Houses and restaurants nestle down on the waterfront. As I drove through the roundabout, I looked for Willa and her young cousin at the tables outside Hobson's Choice. The tables were empty.

I was there five minutes, sipping a flat white, watching the desultory traffic and absorbing the sunshine. I was thinking how I was much like the sparrow that was hopping across the outdoor tables making a living from the crumbs of the civilised, when I saw Willa and Ann.

From the other side of the road, they looked to be about the same age. Willa was dressed with some elegance, though, clothes that flowed, their movement revealing the long, firm legs, the broad shoulders and the sloping breasts. Ann was into Gothic grunge, fingerless gloves that I couldn't imagine being pulled on in a serious fashion-conscious way even if you were in mourning. Behind them was a man, allowing them to lead. He looked uneasy, his white suit too flashy for a day's browsing in the western suburbs.

As the women stepped onto the roadway a ute that had been approaching, seeming to be searching for a parking spot, accelerated, swerving towards them. Willa sensed it, grabbed for Ann and pulled her back between parked cars, stumbling into the man behind them. He fell onto the boot of a parked car. I saw the driver of the ute clearly—dark hair, beard, and a neck that met his shoulders with no space in between.

The ute rebounded off a nice new Japanese job, leaving the side torn and flattened, and headed off. It kept accelerating, too fast for the roundabout, mounted it, left it on two wheels and headed west towards the sea.

I ran for the convertible, sprang over the door, and jammed the key in the ignition, hitting the motor as I watched the ute disappear. I gunned it out of the space, motor roaring on the change, and spun the car into a U-turn, doubling back to meet him somewhere north. He had headed towards the centre of the suburb; it was surrounded on three sides by water and that meant I would be ahead of him. The road he had taken west and then north would stack time on his distance. A bit like cutting him off at the pass.

I watched the traffic on the Altona Road, sitting out close to the new housing going up on the old rifle range, but I didn't see him. He was either a local and was already sipping coffee in his kitchen with the ute in the garage, or he had taken the freeway, some four kilometres further away. After several minutes of aimless driving I headed back to Nelson Place. I had the number but also knew it would have been useless to check. The ute would be stolen.

Willa, Ann and their companion were standing next to a table, waiting for me—still too anxious to sit. I double-parked the convertible and joined them.

Willa was a tall beautiful woman of forty-five. Linen suit against unfashionable tan, she looked as lithe today as in the summer of seventy-eight. She tossed a swathe of fair hair away from her face. A strand of grey looked chic against the thick mass. Her eyes were blue, flecked with tawniness, and spaced wide apart. Her nose was straight and balanced, lips deep red. Her forearms were firm with muscle. She crossed her legs the same way, tight, as if she were trying to hold herself under control.

Ann had a soft neck with a pulse beating there. It was years since I had seriously looked at a woman so young. The skin was incredibly smooth and soft. Her dark eyes were set wide apart, a family trait, and I saw she wasn't too ready for a discussion of any sort. She was still strung out with grief, her eyes barely registering anything, just wandering. She was only here because Willa had brought her along.

Willa introduced her companion, Peter Bresler, a man who had obviously been very pretty in his youth and had all the confidence that attaches to that. Now he was handsome, although only a short way from the seediness age sometimes imposes on the pretty boys who have indulged too heavily in the good things. He was a moist person. His skin was firm, his hands shiny, but with a cool clamminess when we shook. His eyes were expressionless, but I knew the sweat was from fear.

His clothes were expensive and suited him. A dark blue shirt beneath the suit, gold-rimmed dark glasses and a gold and platinum watch. He spun a chair outwards on one leg. It was amusing. He seemed to think spinning the chair was an impressive physical gesture. He looked at me to gauge my reaction. I smiled at him. I had a feeling he was not to be underestimated, though.

I knew Bresler by name only. He was a very big owner of good racehorses. His friends owned hotels and had interests in many casinos.

'My God,' Willa said. She nodded to Bresler. 'Peter said it was a drunk driver. Are they drunk at this time of the morning in these suburbs?'

'No,' I said. 'He was trying to kill you.'

'Ridiculous,' Bresler said.

'What's ridiculous?' I asked.

'He was trying to kill you,' he mimicked me. 'That's ridiculous,' he added, emphasising the last word almost threateningly.

'The driver wasn't drunk,' I said. 'He was determined.'

Bresler shook his head, looking at Willa: this is the sort of individual you're dealing with? It might have worked in a Toorak restaurant where Willa and he felt safe, but here, where their world had very nearly been removed from them, it was different. Willa knew that I had lived close to the edge in many situations, understood that I knew exactly how things were.

'Are you some sort of authority on Melbourne crime?' I asked him. He laughed at me. I followed that up. 'Do you know who ran this suburb for three decades?' I said.

'Willa, let's go,' he said. 'He's one of those appalling people who threaten you with sensationalised information.'

'And you're one of those people who still try and dominate the thoughts and actions of women,' I said. 'Let her make up her own mind. No need for the hostility.'

Willa brought the dialogue back to earth. 'Who would do this?' Willa asked, coming down on my side.

'Whoever wants it covered up.'

'Cover up, cover up. Journalists use that phrase to sell papers.' His voice was rising.

'You're a bit hysterical over this,' I said. 'I know these things are a shock . . . ' I smiled at him.

'Who do you work for?' he demanded.

'I work for Willa,' I said.

He quietened. He thought he would use this for leverage—he imagined I wasn't a real journalist, hired by a real news organisation. 'He's the worst piece of scum,' he said. 'No serious organisation would hire him.'

'Willa hired me,' I said.

I looked at Bresler. 'You missed the mark, mate. We've got work to do here. If you don't like me, you can fuck off.' I leaned across the table and grabbed his upper arm, squeezing it and giving him a little push.

'And if you stay, I'm leaving,' I said. I looked at Willa. It meant I was letting the ten thousand dollars slide. I needn't have worried, he was already up when I looked back at him, and she didn't ask him to stay.

'I'll see you later,' he said. 'I'll ring you,' he added, shaking his mobile. He turned and walked across the road.

I looked at Willa, but didn't say anything. She gave me an ambiguous nod, but it wasn't enthusiastic.

'Is he your lift?' I said.

'We came in separate cars.'

'I think we should move.'

I left my number with Miles, the waiter at Hobson's who had reported the incident to the police. The police could get the witnesses at the restaurant. The women needed to be off the street, I told Miles.

I piled them into the convertible and drove them to my apartment. My mansion was an old funeral parlour that now had eight shops on the round floor and the former funeral director's apartment on the first. I lived on the first during my city sojourns. I got it at cheap rent because the locals wouldn't have a bar of it. They called it the morgue, or the works. It also had ghosts. I had an easy-going relationship with ghosts because I didn't believe in them. Light refraction, I told myself, although the beige pants suit the woman wore created a few problems with that theory.

I parked the convertible in the courtyard and entered through the back door, past the door that once led to the blood room—later called the embalming room—but which was now a nail shop, called Hot Tips. Up the old marble stairs where the air was cool and slightly musty, and into the hallway where at different times three distinctly different ghosts had been seen. I had seen two. Both women. A friend had seen a man in a long tweed jacket with raglan sleeves, obviously from a different era. The place had been built in the twenties.

The kitchen was a vast expanse that looked over the roofs of three shops, the carpark, and the supermarket to a large Victorian building with a fabulous facade that faced away from us. There were different perspectives here. Willa slipped off her linen coat and tossed it over the back of a chair. Ann sat on a stool, looked down at the floor as if at any minute she might like to rest there, and then tried to pull herself together and looked out the window. I pointed at the coffee percolator. Willa nodded, sliding onto a bench behind the table. 'Ann?' I asked. 'Coffee?' She shook her head.

Willa asked what the hell would happen now? Would the police give them protection?

'What for?' I asked, cynically. 'No one's been hurt.'

'Someone died,' she said.

'In hospital,' I said. 'If they can't find the reason, they'll call it natural causes.'

'It's painfully obvious that they tried to run us down.'

'Just a bad driver,' I said, mimicking a cop. I added, 'You'll have to look after yourselves. You've shown your willingness to make trouble, and that was more than just a threat today. He was really trying for you.'

'What about you?' Willa said.

'You're paying me to investigate this thing.'

So far Ann hadn't said a word. 'I think it won't be any good,' she said now, looking at Willa. She swivelled on the stool, but the movement had no energy. It was as if she were aware that if she didn't move she might stay here forever.

'What won't be any good, Ann?' I asked.

'Trying to find out things.' She was very young, very frightened. 'I don't want to,' she said. 'I want it all to stop.'

Willa touched Ann's arm, 'Yes,' she said. She looked across at me, nodded slightly.

'That's fine, Ann,' I said. I saw then how completely broken she was. I felt as if the only thing I wanted to devote my life to was protecting her. The worst of it was that I knew I could never be able to help her with an offer of emotional support. Her plight might make me suffer, but when I attempted to approach wounded people, I usually found they drew back.

It was almost as if I were Victor Hugo's laughing man. He would sway people with his sincerity and care for the unfortunate but, as he spoke, the surgery that had been performed on his throat to make him a child clown, would make him laugh, so that his audience would imagine they were participating in a joke.

'Ann,' I said, 'you can move beyond this. There is always new life.' She looked at me blankly, aware I could never experience her loss.

'This is an incredible place,' Willa said, shifting to a new subject. 'These walls are reinforced concrete.' She touched the white walls. 'They're so cool, and it's been hot for four or five days.'

Turning my attention from Ann, I started to explain my place. It was better than Willa thought. I was hooked into the internet here, and my library was an extensive resource. These days of commercial and covert agents working for multinational companies to prevent information reaching organisations like Greenpeace, and spiking the latter's chances of protesting by destroying their vehicles, ships and followers, it was best to have extensive resources. You never knew whether you were dealing with a country's government or security. You needed to know the difference, and the difference between their policies. I stocked terrorist literature and the favourite methods of various groups—the PLO, the Syrians, the Israelis—even a huge stock of stuff from Che and Fidel, rushed out in the late sixties and early seventies to cash in on their fan clubs.

'You offered me money to work on this,' I said quietly.

'That won't be a problem,' Willa said.

I had wanted to cement my position, wanted to know Bresler hadn't affected my standing.

Ann had moved away and was just gazing into the foliage of a large fern. It was as if she would have liked to have been smaller, able to crawl into the secretive plant, lie on the warm earth there.

Ann visited the bathroom. I turned to Willa. 'You should take Ann somewhere safe,' I said.

'The bastards will have to pay' was her reply.

'It'll be difficult to make them pay.'

'I mean expose them,' she explained. 'I'm not going to have Ann sue them. Losing the money doesn't hurt them. I'm sure they'd have insurance and they'd just blame his mates.'

Mates, I thought.

Ann joined us again, without looking at either of us. She was a very frightened woman. Her pulse was beating too quickly; her dread was apparent on the surface of her skin.

I drove them back to their car parked near the sparkling water of the marina. I waited until they drew out into the traffic and followed them, about three hundred metres back. I had a sawn-off shotgun, double-barrelled, clipped under the dash. Only two shots, but very forbidding. The spread of shot was likely to take in strolling sightseers, so it was best for working in close. Cradling the gun, I felt ready for the return of the madman in the ute.

I dropped way back on the Melbourne—Geelong Road, watching for anybody attempting to follow them. A pursuer trying to keep close to Willa's grey BMW driven at breakneck speed would stand out. Willa took the ramp to Footscray at the last minute, moving across two lanes in the traffic to do it.

She turned into one of those barren Footscray back streets, no trees, single-fronted dwellings with a bit of lawn, some hydrangeas, or a single row of roses. Ann slipped out of the car and Willa walked back to me. 'She's going to stay with me, I'm in a security building.'

'She's frightened,' I said, watching Ann walk quickly to the front gate of her semi-detached. She passed some stunted rose bushes and a threadbare lawn. On the verandah there was some Victorian ironwork. I wondered how it could ever have looked like a place to breed hope. The area had no spirit. 'She's not going to take the pressure,' I said to Willa.

'She loved her husband,' Willa said. 'They had lots of things planned.' Her eyes flooded with tears and she turned away. She began walking back to her car. And that was the moment I was struck by a feeling of horror.

I looked in the rear vision mirror. The street was still, not even the sound of passing traffic. I watched Ann walking to the door. She seemed to be travelling in slow motion. I had pushed open the car door and was backing out of it, the gun held in front of me. I must have yelled something because Ann turned towards me for a moment.

She pushed the door and a second after she entered she was blown backwards towards the street, and then she was covered by the front of her house and a portion of next door's. The scene played over and over, smoke and dust a moving blur as it exploded across the street. The noise was overwhelming. I watched as a piece of weatherboard twirled high into the air and then slipped down, catching an air current as if it had been dropped on a sloping slide of air. It disappeared into the smoke. Fire was licking at dry timber.

Willa and I ran into the smoking rubble. It had spilled out over the footpath into the street, debris piled against the gutter. The windows of the BMW were gone. I ran through the hanging front gate and it bounced away from me onto the front lawn. I began pawing through the wreckage, my eyes burning, running tears, from the smoke and dust I guessed. It was light stuff, all timber and plaster, and flaming. Willa was screaming, 'Ann, Ann, please Ann.'

We found her torn body a few minutes later, and I was careful removing the wood-backed plaster over her head. There was blood from her nose and mouth, but it had already stopped running. Her body was warm. She reminded me of a small, dead bird. The pulse was gone, and she probably wouldn't have wanted to live anyway with what had been done to her chest. There was nothing left to attempt to activate except a heart quivering, partly missing. Willa put her head down close to Ann's, sobbing.

I went to Willa's car, retrieved the mobile phone, and rang for the police.

I stepped cautiously through the debris, looking for anything that vaguely resembled a front door. There were only splinters left, but the charge had blown outward, the very top and bottom of the door pretty much intact. It was one of those booby traps made by guerillas in Third World dictatorships.

I found scatterings of cardboard twirls. They were as thin as feathers. This bomb had been a mixture of potassium chlorate and sugar placed in a cardboard tube balanced on the door knob with a small twist of tape. A glass phial with a few drops of sulphuric acid had been stoppered with paper, and the paper end inserted into the mix. When the bomb fell from the door handle, the acid hit the paper, dissolving it in about a second, hit the mix and exploded. The tube had rolled away from the door and when the door opened the blast would have caught her full on.

Three

'I think', I said to Willa, 'that you need to think about surviving.'

She stopped walking around my kitchen and looked at me with such devastated eyes, it appeared surviving was the last thing she wanted to do. I scooped the coffee into the plunger. She pulled a mobile from her bag and rang her office, but clicked off without speaking. I put my arms around her as sobbing racked her body. I could feel the line of her hip and leg against me. I held her until the sound and movement subsided. I placed her on the sofa and sat holding her hand. Her touch was barely with me. She was exhausted. I suggested that a doctor might help her. But she mumbled something into a cushion and appeared to fall into a deep sleep.

She woke about half an hour later. Now her face showed no anxiety at all. I took coffees up to the front room and she took a cup and walked to the window and looked out over the bay. 'This would cost a million in New York,' she said, looking up at the high ceilings, the floor-to-ceiling art deco windows. She walked to the balcony door. And like those people who think they can ignore their grief and get on with their life, it struck her like a cutting scythe. 'Oh Christ,' she said, caught so hard by emotion that she fell against the wall, the coffee missing a table she had aimed for. 'She was a child,' she said. 'I didn't know her.'

I held her around the waist, but she shrugged me off and walked out onto the balcony. I followed her out. I watched two men running around in the street below. One was in an expensive suit, and the other in a big-shouldered sportscoat in cotton, a camera with a tele lens around his neck. It took me a moment to realise they were looking for us, wondering where we had disappeared.

'People don't look up, ever,' I said, pointing them out to her. 'I can call out to people in the street and they have no idea where it's coming from. They just refuse to look up. Occasionally an intelligent dog looks up.' One of the men was standing at the edge of the carpark, and the other raised his arms in a helpless gesture: we've lost them.

'They'll wait at your car,' I said. 'They know you'll have to pick it up some time.'

'Stuff them, they can wait all night,' she said. Her tone was changing.

'I'll get a cab,' she said. 'I'll leave the car.' She turned around to me. 'I want those people caught,' she said. 'I don't care how you do it, I'll pay.'

I looked into her eyes. She realised what she was asking me to do. Through the tears and the redness, they were hard.

'I don't just kill people, you know,' I said.

'Not what I've heard.'

'I've had to save myself occasionally, that's all.'

Her lips tightened. She didn't believe me. Didn't want to.

'I want to know why it happened and who did it. I don't care how it's done. They started the killing. Ann was a child.' She bit her lip and the sob turned to a curse. 'Fuck them. Fuck them all.' She began breathing deeply to ease the tension.

'What do you expect to pay for what you want?'

'Whatever it costs.' She had regained composure, and turned to face me.

'It's not your style.'

'It is now.'

Willa's request was plain, and I needed to think about it. I walked around the corner of the balcony, looking at the ferns and small gum trees in tubs. They all needed water. She followed me around the corner and looked over at the Old Vic hotel displayed in its heritage colours. I wondered who had told her about the deaths connected with my investigations. I didn't like it. There must have been someone taking a tally. Obviously too much had leaked out from the job on the bird smugglers in Far North Queensland. It had been several years since that bloody fiasco. Time tends to loosen the tongues of people involved in spectacular happenings.

'You're a lawyer.' I called back to her. 'Whatever happened to due process?'

'It's not working.'

The sun shot the bay green as we talked. I needed to know her commitment, needed to know if it would dissipate with her grief. Across the water to the east were the industrial wharves and then the city. Running from that was the everlasting beach that seemed to stretch thirty kilometres to the south, until it was blanked off by the Williamstown marinas and the old tug wharf. The last was now where the frigates were being turned out for the navy.

Finally, she went to her bag for her cheque book and I went to my computer to discover the Abidex directors, but the Australian Securities Commission was not yet hooked into the Internet. I rang a stockmarket player who had his own data base for such information.

'Christ,' Roly said. 'You must be the only bugger in the country who doesn't know that.' Roly was a financial journalist who used all his privileged information to further his own interests. I liked Roly. Regardless of whether he might get caught and jailed for promoting stocks he held, he would still be the same irrepressible bastard.

'Yeah, okay,' I said. 'Well, tell me.'

'Shifty Evans is the managing director,' he said. 'Our own Robert Evans, the shameless bastard who promoted that fraudulent timber company in Malaysia. He said he had thousands of hectares of forest to woodchip, but it was only an understanding he had with the government. He missed on the freehold and a licence to cut. He only avoided being indicted because he claimed he could have had the timber if he had been prepared to pay bribes to Malaysian officials.'

'I didn't hear about it,' I said. Willa came into the study and slipped a cheque to me. She was about to leave. 'Hey,' I said, covering the phone. 'Part of this deal is I tell you how to keep out of trouble.' She put her bag under her arm. She was anxious to go. I tuned in again on Roly.

'There wasn't much in the papers. He has a lot of media mates. You wouldn't have heard the gossip because you've exiled yourself out in the sticks.'

'So has Evans,' I said. 'He's bought a stud near me to drop some income tax. The thoroughbred industry pays fuck-all tax since they decided to give the last prime minister racing tips.'

Roly laughed. 'Is that why you're in the game?' he said.

'No,' I said. 'I'm in it for the money.'

Roly laughed. 'Didn't know you were in in such a big way. A neighbour of Evans.'

'We call anyone neighbour if they live within a twenty-five kilometre radius,' I said. 'That's just the country way.' In fact, Evans was thirty kilometres away, but we shared the same back lane, a dirt track that was the only thing passable when flood waters rose.

I heard Willa's restless movements behind me and quickened to finish the conversation. 'Anyway, we'll have to catch up, mate. Soon,' I said.

'Fuck you,' Roly said. 'I hate the country.' I had known I was safe. He was an information junkie. He hated leaving his machine. I hung up.

'Stay here,' I said to Willa. 'You can't just go wandering off.'

'The police said they'd contact me,' she said. 'I'll have to be at home.'

I touched her arm. 'The cops aren't going to solve this one,' I said.

'They will. They'll link it to Abidex. It's obvious.'

'There's a difference between your knowing and the cops proving it,' I said. 'That bomb was made out of primitive material. Anyone who knows bombs will spot it as third world styled stuff. Very dangerous for the maker and the bomber. Its success depends on the individual maker's skill. It won't look like Abidex, for a start. They'd do it a hi-tech way.'

'I don't feel I can just stay around waiting. I have to do something . . . ' She ran her fingers up and down her forearm as if she were trying for new sensations. She was distracted, filled with that edginess that comes with questioning your life, being on the edge of changing major beliefs.

'Hey, come on, I'll knock you up a pasta. You can rest here. Sleep for a while. You need food.' I didn't bring the blood on the collar of her jacket to her attention. She obviously hadn't looked in the mirror.

'Good,' she said, but she didn't put down her bag.

Seeing death makes me hungry. It doesn't affect some people that way. They'd rather drink. I had once been horrified watching a policeman eat a pie as he stood five metres from a family that had been burnt to death in a bushfire. It had horrified me then. Now I saw it as just bad taste.

The greengrocer was around the corner in the same building. He always had good basil, wide, thick leaves. Walnuts. There was parmesan cheese, garlic, oil and pasta in the pantry.

Through the greengrocer's window, over the boxes of fruit, I saw one of our pursuers. He was searching the faces of people passing by. They gave him a wide berth. It reminded me of a recent bank hold-up in Williamstown. One of the gunmen had stood on the pavement next to the getaway motorbike and ordered everyone onto the opposite side of the road. This bloke wanted to do the same thing. He wasn't about to give up. I watched him walk around the corner. I followed him. My doorway often confuses people because it looks as though it could lead into either the dentist's on the right or the travel agent's on the left. He was looking at it. I back-pedalled around the corner, placed my purchases on the dentist's doorstep and waited for him to take things a little further. I wanted him to walk through the courtyard where the shop owners parked their cars.

He looked into the beauty shop, the nail shop and the travel agents. He walked through the courtyard entrance and I sprinted after him. I was filled with an intense rage for Ann Hough. The rage was totally compelling. I couldn't have stopped what I was about to do if I had wanted to.

He was standing looking up to the roof tennis court for possible ways to climb to the roof of the first storey. At a run, I punched him hard over the kidneys. He went down with a grunt. If he wasn't pissing blood by tonight, I'd stay away from this work forever.

He looked around at me, surprised, the pain no more than a flicker across his face. He was dark, had brown eyes and a huge jaw. His elbow had split his jacket. 'If I see you around here again,' I said, 'you're meat.' He was dazed, but feeling for a weapon. I smashed down on the side of his jaw and caught him with a heavy left before he hugged the cement. I took a Ruger .22 from his jacket. There was a professionally made silencer attached. I dropped the weapon down the neck of my shirt, left him, and went back for the basil and walnuts. I picked up the bag

feeling ridiculous. With a need to murder flickering through my heart I could still take care of
domestic routines?

There were only a few people looking for
bargains in the window of the opportunity shop.
They didn't look at me. I was breathing hard and
it wasn't from the slight exertion. My adrenalin
was coursing through me, signalling full alert.
The outrageous wounds to a frightened girl were
almost too much for me to contemplate. I wanted
to go back into that courtyard and kill him.

Upstairs I filled the Browning shotgun with
shells, jacked one into the breach, and hung it
over the door at the top of the stairs. To get the
feel of the Ruger, I fired a couple of rounds into
the *Yellow Pages*, propped up in the hallway at the
bottom of the stairs. The lead didn't make it
through. There was barely a sound. Willa certainly
didn't hear it.

I dispensed with the low velocity bullets and
filled the magazine with Winchester hollow
points. I kept a round in the breech of the Ruger,
and topped up the magazine. I placed the weapon
in the small of my back and gaffer taped it. It
was above any area that was usually searched, but
would take exactly half a second to shoot. Willa
came out into the hall to look for me, and I
grinned at her.

'Do you want to ring your friend?' I asked her.
My opinion of him was obviously showing,
because she defended him.

'He's from a different world,' she said, and then I saw her hesitate, because she realised he wasn't. 'Well that's not really the thing. But he does things differently, diplomatically.'

'That's exactly what you need,' I said. 'A diplomat.'

'You mentioned food,' she said.

I know some people say that the basil should only be ground with a pestle and mortar but I use a Mixmaster with chopping blades. I pour in 200 millilitres of oil, follow it through with thirty or forty basil leaves, washed and damped dry with a tea towel, and then add some good walnuts, 140 grams, half a handful of parmesan, and then the garlic—if it's for a hangover, a lot of garlic. And the feel of putting a recipe together is calming.

At the refectory table in the dining-room, we made pigs of ourselves with the pesto sauce and the pasta. Another bottle of wine was required.

Four

We decided I should stay over at Willa's place for the night. It was a nice penthouse, she told me, with full security arrangements and an underground carpark. If anyone followed us there, I didn't see them. We bowled out of my apartment, walking quickly to the car. I had the gun in a florist's cardboard box. Over the Westgate Bridge we turned off at the service station on the left, took the road to the river. Only those few locals who travel to North Melbourne know the route. We didn't see another car, but to be safe I doubled back onto the freeway, and then exited to hide in the heavy traffic of Beach Road.

I took a left turn into Fitzroy Street, St Kilda, and pulled over in front of some flash restaurants there. Then, up Punt Road to Toorak Road and the secluded little street, heavy with trees.

It was a strange night. Willa and I lay on the same huge bed. She told me how talking with Ann had affected her. Ann had been as close to her as a daughter. She had opened up to Willa in a way that was overwhelming. She had held nothing back. It was as if Ann had let her see how she lived life, how she kept her secrets, her ambitions, all neatly formed and planned for. There had been a sweetness, a generosity to everything she did. Willa had felt privileged to be offered these secrets. As a consequence she now knew more about herself and how she should regard herself and the world. I was sleepy, but asked what that meant in practical terms?

Nothing to do with anything practical, she said. It was a thing of the soul. I was only vaguely interested in this because half my mind was searching for all the tie-ins that Abidex would have to make to have Ann killed. I was also very tired.

In the early hours of the morning I sensed that Willa would have welcomed any advances that were forthcoming. I made no moves and drifted off to sleep. Much later I felt her move against me, then slip away the shoulder straps of her nightgown and trail her breasts across my chest. Everything she did to me was a caress. I tasted her lips; they were used as if she were in a trance: generous, warm, slow. They were replaced with a wicked tongue and desperate breathing. The heat that flowed through me defeated any inhibitions. We ravished each other as if it were our last night on earth. Her breasts were thrust into my mouth, dragged away, replaced with her hot tongue, and while her arms were feverish and demanding, her legs were smooth and languid. We were driven by a need for those freedoms released by lust. Her body was so pliant, so determined to feel extremes.

I was out of bed at five a.m. The dawn sky was pink and grey, the clouds so clear and bulky they could have been heavy. I knew that the insidious carriers of industrial waste always wanted to be well away from the city before commuters begin to wonder exactly what the unmarked truck in front of them is carrying. I always wake early in the morning. It's the only time I can think with any depth. After that the day moves quickly and any thought is purely reaction. But I knew this investigation all hung on the chemicals, where they originated, where they were held, and where they were going. If I could get samples at each of those places, it would go a long way to placing the chemical that had caused Ann's husband's agonising death.

At around six I was parked 600 metres away from the Abidex factory, scanning the place with my field glasses.

I laughed to myself as I saw a nice shiny tanker emerge from the factory gates. It had come from a rear roadway and along behind some trees planted to make the chemical plant look innocuous and safe. The larger tanks at the back of the plant were in nice pastel colours.

To my surprise, it didn't head into the country but down Kororoit Creek Road towards Williamstown. I almost didn't follow, thinking it must be an empty truck that had discharged chemicals at the chemical complex, but it was riding heavy, the suspension low and the engine howling a little as gears were changed, blowing heavy black smoke as it accelerated to cruising speed.

I put down the glasses and followed at a distance. It missed the main shopping centre and turned down through suburban residential streets to the bay.

The tanker entered the Newport power station and I turned down beside the park, where I could keep it in view through the trees of the park to the south. After only moments at the gate house, I watched it move onto the cement apron at the back of the turbine housing.

Across the parkland towards the Yarra, I saw fishermen lining the banks of the Warmies, so called because the sea water sucked in to drive the turbines was pushed out hot into a manmade pool about thirty metres wide and four hundred metres long. The fish loved it. There was a slight steam rising from the pool this morning. And if I wasn't mistaken those fish were about to run some chemical waste over their gills.

I took the Pentax camera and fitted the telescopic lens. The truck was stopped in the centre of the apron and the driver was crouched down screwing bulky pipes to the outlet valves. He was joined by two men in overalls.

I put the lenses on them. They were joking, talking about football, or their weekend. I flashed off some shots as they moved up a small tractor with a mini-crane and winch to move the steel lid off the drain.

I needed shots of the registration plate while the truck was at its work. I had to leave the car to walk fifty metres around past some fishermen with rods over the river proper. Huge mullaway had been caught here in the past and there were some hopefuls about. I kept the camera down by my side because the lens really was lengthy, but I had to show it when I was in position. After two shots the men saw me and turned their backs on me. 'I got you on film, you arseholes,' I yelled. They pretended not to notice at first. The truck was no more than forty metres from the cyclone fence. How the hell they thought they could do this stuff without some greenie coming down on them, I had no idea. Then they panicked, taking the flexible pipe out of the sewer before the pump had stopped, and the chemical spewed about. This was too good. I shot some film and ran back to the car as the truck hit the trail, a pipe still bouncing.

At the car I took a syringe, ran back to the fence, scaled it, and ran for the spill. Two men sprinted from the turbine complex, heading for me. I used the classic ruckman tactic, running for them, a hand out to brush one away as I sank the shoulder into the second. At the spill the muck was about two to three centimetres deep and spreading over the apron around the sewer cover. I sucked some into the syringe.

I turned as the two men approached me warily. I held the syringe at eye level to give them some idea of the threat they faced. I kept it out in front of me like a knife. 'Okay,' I said, 'I'm employed to track down these infringements. If you want trouble, that's fine by me.'

There was a problem. I had to get over the fence with the loaded syringe fast enough to avoid their grabbing my legs. The tall one was the one who had joked and laughed, prompting the others. Now he was very serious, looking around the immaculate grounds of the power station for a weapon. The shorter one was heavy around the shoulders and he walked with his arms and legs wide, as if he was thick with muscle.

'I rang the cops as soon as I saw you blokes. You're on film, right.' I knew I sounded a bit too defensive to be really threatening. I uncapped the needle on the syringe. 'You probably don't know what this shit is,' I said. 'But once it's in your blood, you begin to burn. If you get it on your skin you get irreversible liver damage.'

'Bullshit,' the tall bloke said.

'Try it,' I said. 'Just a little bit. Come on.' They stopped, looked at each other to acknowledge each thought something had to be done. They decided to begin slowly.

'So, how much do you want?' the tall one said. He had one of those big faces that men get when they feel they're right with the world and can begin to enjoy it. He'd have heart trouble in a couple of years.

'You're smart,' I said. 'But it's not going to cost you a thing. I'm not after you. I'm after the company. Abidex. They're loaded.'

They relaxed. 'Aaaah shit,' said the talker. 'Why didn't you say? We thought you were one of those fuckin' greenie pricks.'

'Yeah, well I go to them if I don't get the money.'

'I reckon he's havin' us on,' the short one said. He's a fuckin' greenie. Look at him. He's got that look like he's never drank piss in his life.' He was very wrong.

I had been backing away towards the fence, but now I stopped and pulled the Ruger out from under my coat. I knew this upped the ante. A syringe looks like nothing at all from a distance, but a gun with a long barrel and a silencer is unmistakable, and one of the fishermen at the Warmies had only to use his mobile phone and the special operations squad would be involved. 'This look like a greenie?' I said. 'We're both breaking the law here. Do you get the picture?'

'He fuckin' yelled at us, right?' the short one said to big face, wanting trouble. It was very close too; I was begining to feel I had to give explanations. That's the time to act.

'Let him go,' Big Face said. Handguns and silencers. Had to be criminal. They walked away as I quickly stuffed the Ruger in the back of my strides. At the fence I capped the syringe and tossed it over the fence. I went over quickly, picked it up and walked to the car.

I headed down to the Kororoit Creek, hoping that the truck had returned to Abidex. There was nothing in sight on the road ahead. I parked on the gravel road that led down to the hamlet on the creek and watched the Abidex chemical plant through my field glasses. No one around. I should have followed the truck. I drove to the Victorian government laboratories to have the chemicals tested.

Reception was unhelpful. They usually received their samples for testing through doctors or vets. This was wasting time. I drove to a vet at Werribee and explained the situation. I had bought a property and these chemicals had been left behind. I wanted to know how to dispose of them without hurting the environment. He was suspicious. After all, I hadn't brought in an animal. He was a rotund little bloke with fair receding hair and bright blue eyes. He was the sort who joked around to try and establish where you're coming from. 'Hey, farmers know they can't be hurt by ag chemicals.'

'I know I'm okay,' I said, fitting in with him,' but I've got some valuable animals. I don't want to dump it in my lake and kill my stock, maybe my neighbours'.'

'Where's your place?'

'A hundred kilometres west. Small thorough-bred stud.'

'Haven't got a local vet?'

'Sure, one who'd pour this down the drain and tell me the labs rang and said it was okay.'

He took the syringes, labelled them with my name and address, an identifying code, and said it could be at least a week.

'I want it tested until they discover which chemical, not just a run through the main culprits.'

I left him and headed back to the funeral parlour. I drove down the back lane to the back entrance to the courtyard, parked the convertible in the garage and locked it in.

Inside I rang Willa. Her voice had that no frills intimacy that exists between two people who have experienced a great deal together. In a sense we had, although it had only been spaced over twenty-four hours.

'I'm up,' she said, 'and I have no idea what I should be doing.'

I thought of the smooth shapeliness I had encountered. I wanted her body turning again slowly, knowing she didn't want to lose one sensation. She should be taking it easy, I thought, but the best women are always as restless as the men.

'Have you spoken to the cops?'

'They're coming later.'

'Will I see you later?' My voice faded a little. Jesus, I thought, over forty years and I'm as vulnerable as an adolescent.

'No, I don't think so,' she said. 'I should be working.' Her voice was uncertain.

'Hey, you're in a hell of a lot of trouble. Forget your work. You can't go on as if nothing has happened.'

As I was speaking to her I was looking out the balcony door towards the bay. Suddenly the light flashed. It had the quality of a giant speed camera. A moment later there was a cracking sound—a *karumping* over the suburb. It was louder than rolling thunder, or an overhead lightning strike. It had a horrible, ominous feeling to it; the windows didn't stop rattling for over half a minute, and dirt rose from the street while the sound continued. As the main explosion faded, echoes travelled back and forth. Then came the smaller explosions, sharp explosions that had sting in the sound.

'Hear that,' I said.

'I hear it,' she said. 'What is it?'

'I've got to go. Sounds like a tank farm going up.'

I rushed up to the roof tower. Black smoke was pouring out of a ship on the bay. Flames from the forward area leapt at least as high again as the height of the ship, and then spurts of the stuff rocketed up a hundred metres or so for seconds at a time. An oily green smoke poured off in a massive maelstrom. Putting the glasses on it, there was an evil dynamism to the way the smoke rushed into the sky. Anybody on the deck would have been instantly incinerated. And, as the flames were spreading, the deck appeared to ripple as another explosion blew the stern away.

I ran down the stairs to the phone. I rang the Harbour Authority. 'This is Nigel Harris here from the Bay Emergency Service. I want the destination of that ship and all of its ports of call faxed through to me instantly.' I gave him the number of my fax machine and hung up. You had to strike while minds were frozen by panic. There is no way thoughts of a cover-up descend on a lazy bureaucracy quickly. I couldn't think of a reason they wouldn't send me the information. Not when somebody, anybody, was about to take some responsibility.

Once, as a police reporter, I had stood in a control room listening to a tank farm foreman report as a fire raged in a split tank. It had taught me a lesson. The foreman had wanted to talk rather than fight the fire. He spilt his guts to the manager about a faulty safety valve and the fact it hadn't been checked. I wrote the story and it made the front page. The oil company threatened the paper with sanctions on their advertisements. From then on, tank farm accidents went unreported, or received page ten treatment.

Now I watched the bottom of the street filling with black green smoke. I was thinking of evacuating but I saw the breeze was from the west as it pushed at the potted trees on the verandah. The smoke would eventually be blown back over the water to the city.

The fax rang a few minutes later and the *Dana Rose's* shipping schedule came through. The ship was bound for Djakarta. It had loaded at Coode Island. The shippers were Abidex Our little investigation was heading into the stratosphere.

Five

Throughout the day on television and radio a spokesperson from the shipping company, Cargo East, said how good it was that the ship was on fire. It meant there would be no fuel left to pollute the bay. Nevertheless, they tried to put it out.

Eight crew members who had died in the explosion had been Indian seamen, on what an Australian sailor would regard as starvation wages. Three Australian crew members were missing. No one was yet asking the owner of the fuel to please explain.

It was one of those days when the wind comes out of the south-west, high up. The wind, combined with the fierceness of the fire, meant the black smoke went way up and over the city in a high curve. I spent time watching the ship through the big glasses. It was out of control and at the whim of the currents and the tides. The crews on the tugboats pouring thousands and thousands of litres of foam over the blistering hull wore fireproof suits and masks.

Occasionally the temperature became so hot the tugs hit reverse and their screws boiled water as they backed off. There was no possibility of them getting close enough to manoeuvre the stricken vessel. In the first hour, columns of flame periodically headed skyward and dropped burning chemicals on the surface of the bay, where they ran for a while in front of the breeze. Small amounts of flame were beached at Port Melbourne and had to be foamed at Station Pier where they began to eat into the wooden pylons of the wharf.

Finally, the ship came to rest south of St Kilda beach, off the marina. Fishing on the bay a few weeks back, I had seen seals and penguins there. The current from the ocean pours through the Heads straight up the bay to Point Cook, Altona and Williamstown and then turns east across the mouth of the Yarra to Port Melbourne and the beaches south. The drifting fuel would destroy the beaches on the east side of the bay.

There was something eating away at my mind, but the sensational visuals were not allowing thought. I found myself tracking back with my glasses, imagining the damage that would have been done if it had blown under the Westgate Bridge. I had also covered the Westgate Bridge disaster. A span had fallen when under construction, killing more than thirty workmen. That was close to the depths of uneasiness I now felt.

I swung the glasses further upriver to Coode Island. The answer burst on me. From the tower, I could see up the river mouth to Coode Island, only about four hundred metres from the bridge.

It was a chemical warehouse, a cocktail of the most hazardous chemicals that industry was capable of producing. That was one thing, but it had gone up five years ago. Some weeks before it happened, I had been asked to write a story for a political newsletter on how Coode Island was a disaster waiting to happen. I had been castigated by influential Labor Party members, and then, two weeks later, it had gone up. It had burned for three days and the chemical fallout was still being experienced by those who fought the fire and those who lived locally. Recently there had been an increase in soft-tissue cancer in the city, almost an epidemic, some medicos claimed, but of course it couldn't be sheeted home to the carcinogens that burned during those days. No one had bothered to collect the data.

So this was an unlucky little corner of the bay, the responsibility of bad politicians, bad bureaucrats and neglectful commerce.

I turned from the view and headed downstairs. I took a tape recorder and camera and drove to Coode Island.

The island wasn't really an island. It was surrounded on three sides by water. To the south, the Maribyrnong River, now a turgid industrial waste stream that flowed into the Yarra River to the east. To the north, the ground had been dredged for another loading dock. From early in the century to the nineteen sixties the island had been a storing ground for molasses and sugar, but as the population increasingly required more sophistication in their service products—glass disappeared in favour of plastic and synthetic foams—it became a lethal chemical mix. Chemicals that didn't like each other were stored side by side, separated by little more than a centimetre of steel and three metres of comparatively fresh air.

I turned east onto Footscray Road and then took a U-turn at the lights over the bridge and I was on Coode Island.

At the south end of the island there was a checkpoint. In large letters it indicated that those unauthorised persons found beyond it would be fined $2000. I slowed the car and looked around. To my right was where the last Coode Island fire had started. It was an abandoned hulk of burnt tank foundations. The gate was wide open and I turned in.

I parked the car in a cleared space and then walked towards the cyclone fence that bounded the river. Beyond was the loading dock. It was still the subject of huge criticism. It was a rough wooden extension of the bank no more than twenty metres long, but it contained thirty-six outlets and safety valves for loading the most appallingly toxic chemicals. A turning ship, or even a smaller vessel that lost power, could have carried away the structure with barely a nudge. A local pilot had said it was the only wharf in the world where instructions to the manoeuvring helmsman included, 'Steer for that other ship'.

I looked across the river at what appeared to be a fish canning factory. Some Vietnamese workers were eating lunch out on the wharf there. I climbed over the cyclone fence and walked down to the chemical loading dock.

Two blokes were standing beside the small shack at one end of the dock, looking at the smoke over the bay. I walked towards them and called out so I wouldn't startle them as I got close.

'Bit of a fucking mess,' I said, nodding back at the rising plume of smoke that now dominated the sky to the south-east.

'Too fuckin' right,' the thinner one said.

'Load here did she?'

The older man, heavy around the gut and obviously the senior, cringed a little in his gestures. He saw an awful chasm stretch out in front of him. He pulled a hand across his forehead. 'Get lost,' he said, with a pitiful show of aggression. 'There was no trouble loading.'

'Didn't say there was,' I said, walking towards him. 'But it would be good if I could see a copy of the manifest. You know, check to see if the wrong chemicals were loaded next to each other. I mean that's not your problem, is it? It's not your job. You just connect the pipes.'

'Who the fuck are you?'

'A reporter,' I said.

The thin bloke backed away towards the shack. I stood at the entrance to the small dock. If I walked into their territory they'd feel threatened and I'd have nothing from them at all. 'I tell you what I want to do,' I said. 'I want to lay the blame where it should go.'

The thin bloke had backed around one side of the building and offered me his profile as he looked out over the river. He was pretending I wasn't there. The big bloke was undecided. 'What I reckon', I said, 'is that they'll blame the blokes who actually put the chemicals into the ship. That's what they usually do, blame the small people. They don't want an inquiry into the safety of the whole system. I mean, look at this piece of shit you work on.'

The big bloke pulled some rubber gloves on. 'Can't talk to you,' he said. 'You're caught here, you're in shit.'

I walked out of the thin man's view and took my card from my wallet. I dropped it down beside the fence.

'Okay,' I said. 'But it's a pity. My story will be about the unsafe practices on the island here. Bad policies, not about the people who were told what to load.'

I walked back the way I had come, beside the pipes on the bank.

From the car I rang Abidex and asked for the names of the chemicals on the ship. They were ready for the query. All manifests were carried on the ships, they said. There is no secret about the manifests; they are public knowledge. It's just that there are very few copies made. None in fact.

The night scene was beautiful. The fire raged skyward and the sea looked as if a midnight sun was rising from it. The hoses on the fire were giant fountains of orange. Great arcs of colour that, from my tower, obliterated good portions of the coast like a fiery wedding cake. I sipped a red as I watched it. I couldn't bring myself to eat dinner. I was feeding off emotion. I could have been listening to violin music, although it wasn't Rome burning. But I understand Nero. The view was sublime.

I took the call while I was watching the display. The voice was low and carried fear. 'Jack Speerman?'

'Yes,' I said.

'You want the manifest.'

'Absolutely,' I said. 'Do you want to come here? Or can I come to you.'

'I'm in the back bar of the King Alfred in Port Melbourne. I'll be here for an hour.'

'How will I know you?'

'You'll know me,' he said. 'I'm from the dock.'

The phone clicked. I rolled my shoulders, trying to loosen the fear. This was the worst sort of rendezvous. I didn't know the area well and I didn't know the pub. Port Melbourne pubs tend to be trading places rather than social meeting houses, and the patrons mind their own business. It sounded like the classic setup. But you always had to show. One of the trials of a muckracker.

Port Melbourne is a bad area that is rapidly being done up by the children of wealthy parents. The kids have just begun their careers and their parents want them nicely set up. They buy them their first little houses from the elderly vendors who lived there for fifty years and can no longer afford the rates or the transport. The larger pockets of criminal activity remain in the unrenovated pubs.

I drove the car a half a block from the King Alfred and parked. There was some activity in the main bar, but the conversation stilled when I entered. Strangers in these bars tend to be undercover cops looking for handouts.

The main bar had a big screen showing the trots. There were blown-up shots of legendary footy coaches from the thirties until today, and the hard liquor was still in shelves high over the bar. The best thing about the place was the brass footrest that ran the length of the bar.

I walked through to the back bar. No barman, just two big blokes nursing beers. The nearest was in a shearer's singlet and his muscles flexed as if to threaten the entire space. The other one was smaller, but not much. He was the talker. 'You looking for Joe Edfield?'

'Nuh,' I said, but I thought, maybe I am.

Making their strategy clear the bloke with the shearer's singlet moved around behind me. There was nothing I could do about it. To have turned to watch him would have been a signal I had entered the game. I wasn't ready for that yet, and I knew they had to be certain I was here to meet Joe Edfield.

'Joe's a friend of yours, then?'

'No.'

'Who are you waiting for then?' the talker said. 'You can tell me, I mighta seen him?'

'I'm having a fucking drink. Are you the fucking barman?'

The shearer's singlet grabbed me by the shoulder. 'You fuckin' watch who ya fuckin' talkin to cunt.'

'So, you're the barman?'

He shifted his weight, about to punch, but he was one of those muscle-bound dolts who have lifted so many weights their flesh works against itself. I sidestepped and brought a heavy glass ashtray down on his skull.

I looked at the talker as the hulk fell across a bar stool and slipped to the floor. He was looking down at his friend. 'Who's Joe Edfield?' I asked.

'You don't want to know,' he said.

'Yeah, I do.'

I turned slightly and stamped sideways at his knee with the sole of my boot. I heard the crack. He grabbed at the bar so he wouldn't fall. Pain had distorted his eyes. 'Joe Edfield?' I asked.

'He's fuckin' gone,' he ground out. 'and you'll fuckin' follow him. The fuckin' freak couldn't keep his fuckin' mouth shut.' I looked around the bar. It would only take one of his mates to come through the batwing doors and I was a goner.

I ran out the back of the bar and into a small courtyard not yet converted for summer evening drinks. I stepped onto the middle piece of timber that held the corrugated iron fence and vaulted over. I hit the garbage piled there, rolled off it and sprinted down the cobblestoned lane towards my car.

It was then I saw Joe Edfield, the heavy man from the chemical dock. He was lying propped up close to a light at the rear entrance to a house. They obviously wanted him found. His face peered owlishly, as if he might be watching closely, but his focus was unchanging. Beside him was a bottle in a paper bag. I looked behind me. No one was following yet. I grabbed him by the jacket and pulled him upright so I could get into his pockets. His limbs were loose and dead. It surprised me he was still warm under his coat. A thought flashed that it didn't matter if he was dead or alive, it was never going to change anything, that my death would have the same significance. Bullshit, I thought. I'm going to make it matter. His pockets were empty and so was his wallet. His hair was matted with blood, his skull fractured. Whoever picked him up would assume it was an accident. Not the first time a drinker had cracked his skull on the cobblestones. I heard voices and began to run again.

I could smell burning fuel in the air. The breeze from the sea was no longer cool. I ran out the end of the lane and across the road, then slowed to a walk as I neared the corner that would bring me out into the street the pub was in. I stood close to a tree and looked towards the lights of the pub. No figures crossed the lights. They weren't searching for me.

I drove back over the Westgate, the radio on, listening for news flashes. There were three survivors from the crew. They had staggered up on the beach, having been missed by searchers in choppy water.

Six

The field glasses were old, with whacking great lenses that made night viewing easier than those small modern ones with sensational magnification. I could see the black smoke cracking away from the flames like silk in a high wind. The fire drew the tugs in closer, their hoses now pouring in many thousands of litres of foam. There were booms off to the south, cupping in chemicals that had begun to float away untorched.

I was entranced by the sight. While the wind held from the south-west, Williamstown and surrounding suburbs were in no danger from poisonous smoke. According to newscasts, it was blowing high over the more affluent suburbs. If the city was lucky, the fire would be out before a predicted wind change in two days' time. It wasn't the hazardous fumes with which I'd have to contend. Ann Hough, an innocent and traumatised woman, had been killed because she was a nuisance. She had been snuffed out with a bomb used by guerillas in Third World countries to throw any suspicion off those involved in hi-tech industries. The bomb had been a favourite of that great consultant of guerillas, General Bayo, who had trained the Cubans and Che

Guevara, and whose methods had found their way to the Middle East. Willa and I would now be targeted. We posed a bigger threat than Ann Hough, and obliteration on suspicion was the usual policy when such high stakes were involved.

I took stock of the building. Was it a safe refuge? The steel-reinforced concrete was practically bombproof, unless they wanted to blow the pub next door as well, and the roof was only assailable using grappling hooks and climbing ropes. Even if they made it to the roof without me hearing them, the steel door from the roof to the apartment would take an oxy-welder to penetrate.

The doorways from the street were also metal. Obviously the original funeral director had worried about his assets. Intruders couldn't get in and the cadavers couldn't get out. By the time anybody made it into the place, I would be armed.

The advantage I had in the survival stakes was that I had no fixed routine. They would have to come inside. Willa, however, was vulnerable. She was a workaholic. She would leave the safety of her security penthouse every day to work at her office in Fitzroy. I had to lead them away from her. Show them I was the greater danger.

Downstairs I dialled the weather to see if there were any predicted wind shifts in the night. I was told they'd had hundreds of calls already about the smoke. 'If you're in the western suburbs,' she said, 'you'll be fine.' By implication, others wouldn't be quite so good. Despite the assurance, I taped the sides of the bedroom windows and the door with gaffer tape and kept the radio on for news reports.

It's strange that people can live so close to a disaster without freaking out. It's the old story of frogs being slowly boiled to death because they don't notice the rising temperature. I'm no fucking frog. Living within a kilometre of a benzine tank farm, I keep an industrial mask in the bedroom cupboard. It's a North R 313, and its refill cartridges are labelled that they shouldn't be used 'in highly toxic atmospheres where there might be a deficiency of oxygen'. Nothing's guaranteed.

I rang Linda. I needed to know the farm was running smoothly, that the phone was ringing close to the stillness of the lake. It was a fast escape from the hell the city was turning into. She was quick to answer.

'What the hell is happening down there?' she said.

'I'm not sure,' I said, not wanting even to think about the inferno on the bay. 'How are the horses?'

'They ate up. Didn't leave a skerrick. The work's not hurting them a bit.' I shut my eyes, thinking about the horses in the paddocks, dozing by quiet water, the frogs around the lake quiet now the temperature had dropped a bit.

'The boys, alright?' I asked, meaning the stallions.

'Sure,' she said. 'They galloped around a bit this morning, but they settled by the afternoon, stopped calling out. Typical males,' she said.

'What?'

'You know, rowdy as hell while they're marking out what they think is their territory.'

I'm not up to anthropomorphic discussion, I thought. 'I just hope the grass is still sweet this late in the season,' I said.

'What about the ship on the bay?' she said.

'Everybody's ignored the danger for years, and now it's happened,' I said. 'Everybody's running for cover.'

'Are you involved?' she asked. Her voice was surprisingly soft. I was moved by her concern.

'Not really. Just trying to find out what the chemicals were.'

'Why?'

'To publicise them.'

'People are angry here,' she said, 'and they're not even close. I mean why aren't people campaigning down there.'

'They're in shock, and some of the media owners are in chemicals. They don't want to alarm people unnecessarily.'

'Jesus,' she said.

After she hung up, I sat in the big chair near the phone, looking at the deepening of the flame reflected in the glass of the balcony door. I imag-

ined her brisk walk, all her emotion in the movements of her body. Marvellous. Working around
the farm, her stride was loose and casual. Indoors
her movements were feminine, as if she were
no stranger to high heels and other arousing
textures.

I woke about two-thirty a.m. At that time of
the morning the streets below me are still. I knew
the instant I woke that someone had cut his
engine and was still rolling over the asphalt of
the street. I moved the curtains aside. The fire
was not so intense. Was that good or bad? Were
the chemicals still burning up, or were they
escaping? It was strange that there was no noise
from the fire, but then twenty or thirty ships a
day moved down the bay, and unless you are
closer than fifty metres there is no sound from
their engines.

The baker was already at work. I saw the light
in his shop down from the post office and, as I
eased the window up, I smelt hot bread.

I crept out onto the balcony to see where the
car had parked. There was nothing in the street—
Williamstown had no through road to anywhere
else, so the shopping area was empty by about
eleven p.m.——and that meant the car had moved
across the supermarket carpark behind the building. I went up the stairs to the roof with my
racing glasses, carrying the Browning automatic,
with extra shells poking from the fingers of my

left hand for quick insertion, and another half dozen in my pocket.

On the stairs, I saw Mona. She was a nebulous being at any time, and she always turned her back to me. She has a beige suit with bell bottom flairs from a style that was in around twenty years ago and is on its way back. It occurred to me that if she ever allowed me to see her face, I was about to die.

I definitely don't believe in ghosts, so I know there is a perfectly rational reason for her appearance. I just haven't found it yet. 'Get moving,' I said to her. 'It's bloody dangerous around here.' She stayed with her face to the wall. The closer I got to her the more translucent she became. Not that I could see through her. Perhaps diaphanous is the right word: I could *almost* see through her. I called her Mona because occasionally she made noises in the night.

It came to me as I moved out on the roof that I saw more of the ghosts at times of high sexual activity in the apartment. Perhaps she had misjudged this time.

On the roof there is a studio, a collection of cul-de-sacs, and an open-ended play area with two toilets and a washbasin for those who played tennis on the roof in the twenties. There is also a structure that once had a crane attached. From below, it looks like a hangman's gibbet against the night sky. I stood beside the structure with the butt of the gun on the parapet and leaned forward

slowly, until the courtyard below me was in full
view. A four-wheel drive was in close to the
recessed wall under the tennis court. Two men
were at the rear door. I put the glasses on them.
The lights from the supermarket's carpark were
a great help. The detail was plain.

It was a bomb they were assembling. Another
primitive one. A Bayo special. With a difference,
the explosive was a plastic. The bomber was a
fast craftsman. He constructed on site. This meant
that if he was searched he would never be in
possession of anything that could be spotted as a
bomb from first glance, and it meant he wasn't
going to blow himself to bits before he made it
to his victim's location. I was in close on his
hands, the lenses fogging a little though, with the
moisture in the night air, or a smearing chemical
that was hovering. He poured the acid into the
glass phial and stoppered it with paper. This was
the detonator that would be pushed into the
plastic and rested upright. When movement dis-
lodged the plastic, the acid would eat through the
paper in about two seconds. The paper was there
to stop any acid accidentally dropping on the
explosive. Not a great safety device. The explosive was to be rested inside the car and I'd blow
it when I opened the door, or turned the wheel.
I was so focused on the bomb making, I almost
missed the third man trying to open my car. It
should have been very easy to do, a knife through
the convertible canvas, but then if I saw the slit

in the tonneau in the morning I'd know something was going on. He was taking his time.
Didn't want to make any noise.

'And just what the hell do you think you're
doing?' I asked, leaning back out of sight, but
having my voice boom off the walls below. For
all they knew, I could have been standing next to
them.

They slammed home the tailgate of their vehicle and leapt in. I heard the motor fire, and the
tyres spun with smoke as I ran across the tennis
court to catch them as they accelerated away out
the back. They had to ease down to cope with a
buckle in the gutter and the roadway distorted
by the heavy supermarket delivery trucks.

I whacked one shot into the boot of their car
and dropped to the roof behind the parapet. I
watched through a small drain in the parapet.
The first explosion blew the back half of the
vehicle away. The velocity of the air thrown back
through my peephole seemed to burn my eye for
a second. The vehicle kept going, slowed to a
crawl, but was definitely not abandoned. The fire
was only spluttering as they turned the corner,
the engine roaring.

I walked across the tennis court and, pretending the Browning was a tennis racket, made some
nice forehand strokes.

Once at the top of the stairs to the roof, I
knew there were others in the house. The door
at the entrance to the apartment suddenly

slammed shut. It only did that when the front door to the street was opened, causing the draught to move like a gale.

There is a cool fear that sweeps through the body when you know you're being hunted. A prickling that begins in the back and moves up through the scalp. All that confident speculation on the coming violence had fled. They were here. Now. Do something.

I went down the stairs from the roof quickly and silently. For a moment I thought of retreating even further, taking the next flight down and then shooting out the door of the blood room, but I knew they would have all exits covered.

Stepping onto the soft carpet of the hallway was a challenge, but the light from the pub on the corner lit the place well. With the Browning out in front of me, I felt I could do it. I'd fire on the slightest movement. I ran down the hallway without a sound. Carpet on reinforced cement is as soundless as you want it. No creaks at all. Only Mona made noises here.

The door at the top of the stairs was still shut. But it looked ominous, as if it would burst open at any moment. Fuck it, I thought, and blew a hole in it. That'd keep them thinking.

I grabbed the phone from the desk in the hall leading to the long balcony and dialled the cops. It would do no good in the long run, but a cruising cop car can delay things for minutes. 'Cops on their way,' I yelled. Silence. They would now know that they had to move fast. The cops could be here in minutes.

I left the door and ran for the balcony. I eased over it onto the shops' verandah roof. I pushed my head over the side and waited for them to leave the street door.

Three came out the door in a rush. I couldn't lean over the pavement canopy to shoot because I would have fallen to the street. Two ran to the front car. They had left the engine running and the doors open. They slammed the doors and the car screamed around the corner, accelerating away down the street. The third man had to unlock his door and he was having trouble. For him it was a nightmare of fumble. I knew what he was feeling. I jumped the three metres to his car roof as he was shutting the door. I rolled off and pointed the Browning at him, flicking the barrel—get out.

'Fuck you,' he said, reaching for something on the dashboard. I bunted him in the side of his head with the butt. Opening the door, I dragged him from the car, across the pavement and into the foyer. He was groggy, but I made him walk.

My workshop beneath the stairs had everything I wanted. I bound and gagged him with gaffer tape and stowed him in the workshop. I took a blunt nose .38 special from his ankle holster. I left him to think about his predicament. If his mates came back, I had a hostage; if they didn't, I had a potential source of information.

The door had been opened with a small ram. I hadn't even heard it, but then I had been a flight up and on the roof at the end of the building. Using a drill, I bolted a piece of two by four across the door. In the morning I'd have someone come in with serious locks.

I went back to the stairway cupboard and flicked on the light. The bastard was curled up on the ground and looked at me with an easiness, despite the gaffer tape mask. His casualness enraged me. This bastard had come to kill me, scared the shit out of me. He was one of those who were out to kill a lot of people. I grabbed him by the hair and it pulled from his scalp. It was a wig. I grabbed him by the collar and hauled him upstairs, his legs bouncing.

The kitchen had a long art deco window that looked over the roof of the bank, the greengrocery and a dental clinic, to the carpark. I pulled the gag from his mouth. He had been waiting for this and turned his lips inwards so they wouldn't tear. He had experience.

He was English, sounded like a north country accent. What hair he did have was shaved. He was a big man, though, with young jowls and cheeks that were very large and red and squeezed his eyes to slits. I looked for a wallet. Nothing in his pockets. 'Sit down,' I said. He sat.

'Who wants me dead?' I asked.

'Fook you.'

I brought my elbow down on the side of his face. He grunted. But he was still a long way from his pain threshold. I stood in front of him. I had the image of Ann Hough in front of me. The smooth, young skin, the eyes that were filled with fear. 'Two people have died,' I said. 'I don't want any more going the same way. Ann Hough was only a girl, and they're still picking up parts of her in front of her house. I want you to tell me who I have to see to stop it.'

He laughed outright. I slashed at him twice, hurt my fists, ignored the pain, turned away from him. I wanted to kill him. When I looked at him again, I saw he was unconscious. I grabbed a vase with water and dead roses in it and threwe the contents over him. The large thorn of a rose caught on his cheek, and the rose stayed there.

I knew I was losing it. It was becoming one of those bizarre situations that build because you don't know the compulsions that drive you. Every small thing engorged my anger. The rose thorn hooked into his face increased my urge to shoot him The trickle of blood reminded me of the mess after the explosion. I looked away from him and focused my mind again on my need for information. I removed the rose from the side of his face. Hold on, I told myself; hold on for Christsake—control it.

I grabbed the back of the chair and pulled it back against the wall so it wouldn't fall. I began flicking his face with the backs of my fingers to wake him. I realised he was back when he began flinching in time to my rhythm. He didn't bother to waste his energy turning away. I stepped back. 'Names, mate. That's all I want.'

He didn't say anything and his breathing was shallow and quick.

'I don't need you,' I said.

He opened his eyes. 'Yeah,' he said. He was unimpressed; almost smirked. I don't know what it is about me, but I'm always underestimated. If they could see life from my side of my eyeballs, they wouldn't be so dismissive.

I opened the kitchen drawer. I took the Ruger out and shot him in the calf muscle, well back from the artery. I didn't want a little fountain of blood pumping out over the floor. I pushed the pile of newspapers under the slow leak.

He was focused now.

'Give me a name,' I said.

'I don't have one. Jesus Christ, I'd tell you if I had.'

A brain shot can really bleed. It can damn near pump out every drop of blood in a body. An old mare I shot after she broke a leg pumped an arc of blood for two metres. I went to the drawer where I kept the garbage bags and took a roll. I put on rubber gloves and taped six of them together. I spread them out on the floor in front of him like a rug.

He knew what they were for.

'Look at it this way,' I said. 'I don't need to kill you. I really don't. If I let you go, you're not going to the police. You can't tell them a thing without implicating yourself. And you won't be coming to get me again because you won't be able to.'

'Why not?' he said.

'Because you will be out of it.'

'Yeah?' he said.

I leaned down and put the Ruger to his left ankle and then to his right. 'They could probably work miracles with one shot to each ankle,' I said. 'Surgeons love jigsaw puzzles. But two shots to each ankle, that's a different matter.'

I left my final intentions vague.

He stared at me, realising what I was made of, fearing me at last.

'Of course you only get to be crippled if you talk. If you don't talk, you die.'

He was silent, chewing his bottom lip, holding something back. 'It's Abidex,' he said.

'Who at Abidex?'

'I don't get to know that. It's just what I've picked up. They were trying to protect the deal they made.'

'What sort of deal?'

'The ship deal. That's all I know. It's what I've heard.'

'Come on; the ship deal? You reckon that's an answer?'

'They think you know about it, know where it was going.'

'Where was it going?'

'I don't know that.'

I believed him. He was one of the soldiers. He was paid to do what he was told, not to know why. But he had to know something about the number of people he was hired to kill, and to what lengths he had been paid to go.

'How many others like you?'

'There's people watching you we don't even know. They're fooking us up. We can't do anything while they're around.'

'Who are they?'

'Bloody wogs, that's who they are. They do things different.'

'What cars are they driving?'

'Blue Holdens, white Falcons.' He was going to give me nothing more. At least I knew to look out for the most common vehicles in Australia. I moved the gun barrel towards his ankles. He squirmed. 'Jesus,' he yelled. He wasn't going to tell me anymore. My rage had gone, doused by his fear. He was safe. I ripped the leg of his trousers, stoppered the wound with gauze and bound it. I cut the tape and gestured him off the chair. He was easy on his leg. He was a powerful bastard, though, so I kept back from him.

I locked the doorway at the top of the stairs. It was there I saw he was setting himself for a grab at me. I planted a foot between his shoulder blades and pushed him down the remainder of the flight. I jumped after him, punching him hard in the chest as he tried to rise. He fell back.

'You get up, arsehole, and you walk. Any more horseshit, I cut your throat and toss you into the street. They don't give a fuck about people dying around here.' In fact, they didn't. A pub patron had been stabbed four times outside my door and the cops hadn't even been bothered to interview me. They never got the culprits. Worse, an old lady had been bashed to death in broad daylight a street away and they upped the cop presence in the suburb for a few days and that was the end of it. Cops and politicians are only dedicated to the appearance of law and order. They no longer have the capacity to develop local knowledge. I would take advantage of this developing lawlessness.

I pulled off the piece of two by four to get out, leaving the wooden door open. I locked the lacy alloy outer door. On the empty pavement, I pointed him towards the entrance to the court-yard. I gestured to my car. 'Open it up, hero,' I said. He cowered. I kicked him hard. 'Open it up, shithead, there's no bomb.' He didn't believe me. He wouldn't touch the door handle. I knew then he was working with those he called the wogs. He knew their devices.

'You're with them,' I said. 'Who are they? Who the fuck tried to bomb my car?' I bent him over the boot. 'Listen,' I said, close to his ear. 'I can shoot you and dump you off the end of a wharf, or I can take you to hospital. Your choice.'

'They're Muslims, Syrians. Nasty bastards. They're tied into the deal.'

I drove him to the Footscray Hospital's casualty entrance and watched him limp through the glass doors. As all gun wounds had to be immediately reported to the cops, he would be detained. In the short term, it was as effective as killing him. He'd have to make up a story about a shooting accident. He wouldn't open his mouth about me.

I drove back through Footscray and along Arden Street, on a short cut over the Maribyrnong River, to Carlton. No one followed. I was the only vehicle for the length of Arden Street. I took a room in a cheaply renovated motel in Lygon Street. It had the advantage of all the rooms looking out over the carpark and the stairways. If anything moved, I'd have it covered.

Seven

My night was restless. My part of the world was growing bigger. An investigation into toxic chemicals had grown wings. In view of Australia's new defence pact with the Indonesian military, fuel and chemicals bound for that country made sense. We were helping our neighbours to oppress those who wanted independence. But it was also third rate hit squads from the Middle East's Islamic countries. It didn't make sense. Not yet, anyway. I desperately needed more information.

I woke with a clear thought. It was time to bring a politician into the investigation. Usually they're totally unresponsive, but if you have an edge on information that is seriously going to interest their electorate, you can usually gain their attention for five minutes. That's about the depth of their commitment. If you have information that they can recognise as devastating to their chances of re-election, their cooperation is marvellous to behold.

The bloke I had in mind was not only the federal member for Port Phillip, the area that surrounded the bay, but his constituents were becoming so concerned with the environment that in a recent poll, they had placed it above unemployment, and the electorate had seventy per cent unemployment among recent school leavers. That was marking a big turn around. The stuff I had for him was dynamite, considering his party was now in government.

I went down early for breakfast. Orange juice, muesli and then eggs and bacon on buttered toast. I knew one half of the breakfast was healthy. It would probably be another decade before dieticians finally decided which half. Cholesterol, they have discovered, often prevents major strokes in those inclined to have small brain bleeds. It doesn't mean you binge on cholestrol, but it does have a purpose. Feeling pleased with myself that I was no longer paranoid about the food I ate, I rang Willa to alert her to my day's activities. She was paranoid about everything. She was also misdirecting her anger.

'How can you go on?' she accused me. 'I have to arrange a funeral,' she said, her voice catching. 'You do what you want. I just want it over.'

I left the silence alone for a few moments. It seemed a mark of respect for the murdered. 'I'm going to need your help,' I said.

'I can't believe it,' she said, ignoring me. 'I woke up this morning and I was certain it was a bad dream. I don't know what the hell you're doing.' Her voice was bitter.

I decided to let her have it. If she was going to confuse her motives and blame me, she could go back to her boyfriend. 'The wealthy always think their disasters are bad dreams,' I said.

'Christ,' she said, the rage at my insensitivity boiling through her voice.

'Willa,' I began in a reasoning tone, 'I know it's bad for you. I know it's you who have to get through it. But I think you'll be really angry if you let this go. You're going to get over this.' I paused for a moment. 'And I'm sorry, but you won't be able to go to any funeral; they'll be waiting for you. And you won't be able to stay at your place for much longer. They'll be able to get through the security after a bit of planning.'

She was silent for a long time. I could hear her anxiety in her breathing. 'Alright,' she said at last.

I asked her to meet up with me immediately, but she begged off that and arranged to meet for dinner. She was regretting some of her dealings with me. 'Willa,' I said, 'for Christsake, realise that you can't walk around the city as if nothing's happened.'

'I'll be alright,' she said. 'I'm organising the office. They can do without me anyway, but there's a few things to clear up.'

'You can't go there,' I said.

'I'll do it on the phone,' she said.

I was at Nick Harris's electoral office before he was. I parked the car fifty metres away and listened to the latest on the ship. There was a tower of black smoke heading east over the city, but I thought they would have something more than I had seen as I had driven from Carlton. The one interesting point was that they were running short of the foam they were pouring on the blaze and had to send to Sydney for more. The state wasn't geared for these emergencies, despite the Coode Island lesson.

I liked Nick. For a politician he was a moderate liar and truth shifter, and he *had* discovered that the study on asthma in the western suburbs had been manipulated to make it appear they were only slightly above average and so the chemicals released into the atmosphere were relatively safe. He had pestered the statisticians for their procedures and then revealed that they had included the western suburbs asthma figures in the numbers used to get the average asthma rate for those suburbs across the river to the east. Naturally it made the figures for the west look relatively good. Having the guts to take on the bureaucracy like that meant he could be of some help here.

I saw two of Nick's staff members turn up at nine-thirty, and he turned up around ten. I called out to him and began almost immediately to change my mind about using him. My doubt started with his appearance. He was wearing a beautiful suit, double-breasted with a superb texture. Cloth like that they only tailored. He was trying to look like a prime minister. He saw me coming and, smiling, pretended he wanted to get inside in a hurry. It was a funny move—and I smiled back——but it was also a message that he didn't want to see me.

'Hey, Nick,' I said. 'Have you got the manifest for that?' I pointed to the black plume rising above the shop fronts, seemingly only a hundred or so metres away. It was actually about four kilometres.

'You're joking,' he said. He pushed his way through the heavy glass door with his shoulders, his briefcase in his other hand. I followed him into his main office past his staff. 'I can't get that sort of stuff,' he said.

'Those manifests are supposed to be available to the public.'

'They're not, though,' he said. 'They get lost, copies aren't made, you know the game.'

He tossed his briefcase onto a chair and slid behind his desk. 'Coffee, please,' he called to his staff. He rubbed his face, which was getting too chubby for television, and said, 'What the fuck are you doing here so early?'

His staff were in his employ for the long term; they wanted careers in politics. They were quick with the coffee. The first woman was round and good-natured. But her eyes were steely and her shoulders too set for me to believe her good-natured chatter. 'I wasn't sure we'd be here this morning.' She nodded towards the smoke plume visible through the window. The second woman, bringing in the mail, wasn't going to respond to me in any way whatsoever until she gauged the attitude of her boss.

'What's it like working for a political has-been?' I asked them. They showed alarm, like curious birds sensing danger. It was my turn to nod to the window. 'If that's not solved to the satisfaction of Nick's constituents, he won't get pre-selection next month,' I explained.

I turned back to Nick. 'Some people work for a living,' I said, hating to drop a cliché on him, but that was all his sort of politician understood, a sort of jolly, jolly bullshit approach to life.

'I often remember the old days,' he said.

'Yeah,' I said. He was older than me and he meant the sixties and seventies, the years when he rose to prominence as an organiser. I had been a teenager who had marched, that was all, but I remembered that protesters can change anything they want to if they're passionate enough. I once talked about it to him, and after that he had begun to remember me as a colleague from back in those times. I didn't disillusion him.

'It was those protest marches that made me realise I had to go into politics,' he said. He had been in the first rank of some of the Vietnam moratorium protests. He had felt at home. He was one of those who felt his life couldn't be about protests any longer unless such activity gave him more power and prestige. Unfortunately, protests don't usually do that.

I told him about Abidex dumping chemicals into the river and that it was Abidex's chemicals on the ship, that I felt the burning man in the intensive care ward, his murdered wife, and the murdered dock worker were all tied in.

'If I'm going to raise that in Parliament,' he said. 'I want proof. If it's right, we'll do something about it.' He looked strong and determined.

'Now, don't bullshit me, Nick,' I said. 'You blokes do fuck all. Coode Island chemicals were going to be moved, remember, the city was in constant danger, bullshit, bullshit. All I want you to do is begin passing the word to your colleagues that there is something going wrong here, and that they'll get blamed for it.'

Nick's face didn't change. That's one thing I find uncanny about politicians these days: they don't believe in anything, don't get emotional about anything, even when they're under direct attack. They believe they can emerge intact with the right word-shifting formula.

'Come on,' he said, patronising me. 'I congratulated you on the Coode Island story. You were right. I was wrong.'

'You congratulated me after the fucking thing blew,' I said. 'You did fuck all before, and you did nothing after. The chemicals are still there. Imagine if that ship had gone up five minutes before it did. There'd be nobody left alive in the city and these suburbs.'

He leaned back in the chair. 'So what are you telling me about this stuff for?' he said. 'I don't buy the crap about getting this information around to my colleagues.' He smiled at me. 'Hey, you're scared. The great Jack Speerman is scared shitless.'

I smiled at him. 'Too many people dying,' I said.

'Yeah.' He fell back in his chair, rubbed his lips with his fingers. 'I'll make some inquiries,' he said. 'But you've got to get me the evidence. The public servants will only hand me the stuff they want me to know.'

'I will,' I said.

'Before you go,' he said. He took the newspaper from his desk and dropped it open in front of me. 'Gas,' he said. 'They're saying the woman wasn't murdered; that it was gas. You're up against the police force as well. They have a very bad person there—you remember Bluett, he did all sorts of jobs for the painters and dockers—and you and I know how hard it is to get at someone like that. They've been doing favours for years, and when something like this comes along they pull those favours in.' He scanned the paper quickly. 'The dock worker isn't even mentioned. No one knows about him. You're the one I heard it from.' He looked at me, questioningly.

'I saw him dead.'

Nick stood up. It was his method of dismissing me. The set of his shoulders had altered. I wasn't sure whether he was taking up a burden, or dropping it. You can never tell with a politician. They've altered body language to suit themselves.

After seeing Nick Harris, I drove to the Royal Melbourne Hospital. From the foyer, I rang the public relations section of the Victoria Police. Cops are so burdened with the politics and the corruption rife in their force that the only cops who are enthusiastic about solving anything are new recruits, and they don't have the experience. One of the most enthusiastic and experienced men was an old friend of mine, Frank Connolly. They had switched him to public relations where he couldn't solve anything and wouldn't be any trouble. I got along well with him.

'Fuck,' he said. 'I haven't heard from you for a while.'

'Yeah, you old prick,' I said, knowing that to enter Frank's life, you had to enter his language. I asked him for the names of the survivors of the explosion.

He reeled them off. I didn't take them down. 'Any without relatives?' I asked.

'What do you want that for?'

'I need to talk to him about the cargo they had.'

'So?'

'I need to be a relative, you know how it is.'

His tone changed when he finally answered me. There was respect. He knew I still wanted to do some of the things we used to talk about in the old days—set traps for the crooked and corrupt. 'Craig Bickerford,' he said. 'We haven't been able to notify anyone. He's in intensive care. Bad burns.'

There's no problem getting into intensive care if you can successfully pose as a relative. I pressed the inquiry button on the outside of the locked door, told the questioning voice I was Bickerford and had come to see my cousin. The door clicked and it gave when I tried it. They like relatives visiting patients bad enough to be bedded down in intensive care. It builds patient morale.

I kept my eyes to the front as I walked to reception. There were always alarming things going on in the wards each side of the corridor. And it upset me that the patients always looked like mounds sinking into the earth, no matter how many drips they had connecting them to the world above ground.

The nurse on reception pointed me to a curtained cubicle and I entered it. It was a room filled with the most elaborate, shining gear.

Bickerford's face was bandaged over his eyes, and the hole in the bandages for his nose and mouth seemed to be smeared with gell, as if the dressings might rub away the flesh. Several tubes entered his nostrils, the thicker one contained a fluid with the colour and consistency of light cream. Four drips were connected to his arms and several tubes emerged from his lower body to disposal containers. The drip needles were firmly taped to his wrist so they wouldn't twist out when he moved. He didn't look as if he'd be doing much moving for a while.

'Hi, Craig,' I said. 'It's Jack.' I guessed he was so out of it he wouldn't know—or care—who anyone was for a while.

A nurse entered behind me. A large handsome woman. 'We're still cooling the burns,' she said. 'He has dressings that are absorbing the heat. It was lucky he was in cold water for so long. I'm afraid he can't talk at the moment. He can hear you, though.'

'Can he write?' I asked. I wasn't sure whether the bandaged body was awake. I pulled out a note pad and a biro. 'Is it alright if I try?' I asked the nurse.

'He wasn't writing yesterday,' she said, seeming worried that they had overlooked that test so far today.

'You'd be busy after the staff cutbacks,' I said, excusing her. It was becoming increasingly clear the government wanted to turn medical care into something out of a Third World country. Last week they had announced a new policy of having day theatre surgeries at the hospital, the patient not even spending a night under observation. Cost per patient was the priority, whether they lived or died. Hospital administrators would have made great clerks of the Third Reich. Where does that leave the minister for health, and the premier?

I put the notebook under his left hand, the right was bandaged and looked swollen. I placed the biro between thumb and forefinger. He gripped it. 'I just want to ask you some questions,' I said. I turned to the nurse. 'His lawyers want to know a few things. It might be best if you weren't here.' She backed out and allowed the curtain to fall.

'What sort of cargo were you carrying?' I asked.

In large letters growing larger, he printed 'NEW FUEL'. With those words I knew he knew something. If he had thought it wasn't the fault of the fuel, he would have printed just 'FUEL'. But adding the 'NEW' meant there were connotations that had to be tracked down. New anything worries most people because it hasn't been tested. It makes everyone uneasy. 'NEW FUEL' held tremendous significance to this burnt man. He was trying hard. Watching his hand work, I was worried the needles would work their way out of the veins at the back of his hand.

'Is that what exploded?' I asked. 'The new fuel?'

He printed 'PHOS' and ran off the page. I placed his hand back on the notebook. 'PHOR', he wrote, and then 'US' on the sheet. After I turned the page, he wrote rather than printed, 'Saw it burning under water'.

'You're going to be okay,' I said to him.

'No,' he wrote.

'Whose fault was it?' I asked.

'The fuel,' he wrote.

'Its destination?'

'SYRIA', he printed. As if he was resting his case, he let go of the biro and his hand fell off the notebook. It was a clear sign that he had had enough.

'If I can find anything I can do for you, mate, I will,' I said. I looked down at him. He had escaped fire and water and was going to pay dearly. No one should have to put up with such torture. I felt my eyes watering and turned away.

Syria, I thought. Why the hell was that country buying fuel from us? They had oil over their border.

I moved out of the room. The nurse fell in beside me. 'How bad is he?' I asked.

'If he survives the third and fourth day, he has a chance,' she said. 'We want your name and address,' she said.

'I'll be back,' I said, moving past her and heading for the door. It was unlocked for those going out. It was great to get away from the seriously damaged. I thought of the fight Craig had in front of him over the next few days. He had given me a break, but it was only a small one.

I headed for the coffee shop down on the first floor, careful that no one followed me into the elevator. Over a hot chocolate, I mulled over this new information. Syria? Why were we trading chemicals with Syria? Why had the fax indicated Indonesia? This was a hazardous course. Syria was the centre of much of the terrorism that was created in the Middle East and beyond. This was beginning to look like a case of chemical weapons being manufactured in Melbourne's western suburbs. This was a political powder keg.

From the hospital I walked down to the public library. It was a great day apart from the wide swathe of smoke overhead. Passersby constantly examined it, trying to gauge, as I was, if it was about to descend on the city. I went through the side entrance to the library. Immediately my world was peaceful and remote. The books were at my disposal, here only to massage minds with ideas. I wondered how much they would charge me to holiday here.

I pulled out the *Oxford Companion to Politics of the World*. Syria. The country had a geopolitical importance out of all proportion to its relatively small population and economic resources, I read, because of its formidable military power and its support of terrorism throughout the world. It bordered Israel, Lebanon (where the chemicals would have been unloaded), Turkey, Iraq and Jordan. A huge and deadly cocktail of nasty influences and motivations. The answer was obviously a question. Why wouldn't we trade with it? It would have considerable wealth to throw around. At present it was being harassed by Israel over a new peace agreement. They were each threatening to attack their respective populations in Jerusalem and the West Bank. What was new? Only that, for the first time, it appeared to be having an effect on Australia in a pretty direct sort of way. I left the library knowing that the machinations of Middle East politics had been brought to Australia by our government's willingness to sell arms to anyone.

The day was still beautiful if you looked to the north. To the south, the cloud hung like some child's nightmare of the future.

Later in the day, I picked up the photographs I'd taken at Newport. They showed the acts in graphic detail. It may not have been proof that they were unloading chemicals into the sea through the power station, but it was enough to have them explain what they were unloading there and why.

Eight

I was constantly surprised by Willa's beauty. I had expected it to be of the fading sort, which in itself can be very attractive. But it was as if I was seeing her for the first time. I had an image of her that I carried with me, but then, seeing her again, I hadn't counted on the animation and the sheer personality.

I walked through the restaurant where we had arranged to meet. It was Italian casual in Carlton and the food was excellent and the price reasonable. At the table with her was Peter Bresler. He didn't see me at first because he was busy talking to Willa, trying to convince her of something, something of considerable significance to him. She was shaking her head and the hair flowed around her face. She saw me and smiled, a wisp of hair across her face. It was very welcoming. Her face was alive, directed, beautiful. I'd never expected a woman to look at me like that.

Bresler looked up as I reached the table. Immediately he was accusing. 'You're dragging her into a lot of trouble,' he said. I could feel his dislike. The bastard's jealous, I thought.

'Yes,' I said.

He was amazed. 'You don't deny it?' He turned to Willa, holding his hands out, palms forward: ipso facto.

'Yes, there is trouble,' I said, 'but she was in it before I came along.'

There was nothing about him I liked. There was no meeting on any level, not even the fact that we were males. He played too many superficial games. This was the second time I had met him and I watched as he visibly ran through attitudes and roles he might apply to me. The first was the big stare. Grave—where's your responsibility to this woman? 'You're claiming you can help her?' he said as a question.

I smiled, dismissively. He changed tack. This time he was the smooth, competent type. This time *he* was dismissing *me*.

There was nothing natural about him at all. I could see that Willa was bewildered by his response. She had obviously brought him along this time to clear any misunderstandings that had occurred last time we met. But there were no misunderstandings. We disliked each other.

'Where do you come into this, Bresler?' I asked.

'I'm a friend,' he said, and his proud tone claimed more than that.

'Are you a friend she listens to?'

'No, she makes up her own mind about things.'

'Okay, but I have some serious stuff to talk about here, so why don't you fuck off?'

'Listen, you bastard,' he began, 'I could have you taken care of very easily.' He grabbed my thigh close to my knee and squeezed. It was supposed to be painful and debilitating.

'If you want to play with my leg,' I said, 'I suggest you change sex. Or I'll change it for you.'

He backhanded me across the bridge of the nose and I just looked at him. His ring had caught my cheek, and blood ran down my face. Willa was shocked. She looked at him as if he was some creature that had finally broken through the crust of the earth. 'Peter,' she said. 'What the hell is going on?'

'I can't stand you being fooled by this idiot.'

'She's not being fooled by me,' I said.

'Shut up,' he said, imagining that because he had hit me and I hadn't retaliated, he now had dominant status. I reached under the table and squeezed his thigh. It hurt him. He jumped up, threw an arm around my neck and pulled the back of it against the high back of the chair. I almost laughed. I twisted easily, my shoulder pushing my neck away from the back of the chair, and punched him in the side of the ribs with a twisting right that flattened him. He fell to the ground.

Willa stopped me from following him down and doing some permanent damage to his structure. The restaurant manager ran up and asked me to leave. Willa put a stop to that. 'No,' she said. 'That'll be the end of it.' Wealth and status over perceived injustice. Willa smiled at the manager. 'There'll be no more trouble,' she said.

'He'll have to go,' he said, standing up for his rights.

His glance at me was contemptuous. He wasn't going to back down just because one of his regular socialites wanted him to.

Willa told him sweetly that if I had to go she would have to go and she wouldn't be back, ever. The conversation was conducted in vehement undertones. He rested one hand on the table as he stooped down to hear her. He closed his eyes, made a decision. 'Okay, fine,' he said. 'I thought it was becoming dangerous for you.' He smiled and moved away.

I sat down and Willa patted Bresler's seat for him to sit down. When we were settled, Willa handed me a list of chemicals and explained that Bresler had copied them from the burning ship's manifest.

I looked down it.

Methyl ethyl ketone, butanol, toluene, acrylonitrile, benzine.

I looked up at Bresler for an explanation of how he had come by it. 'It looks dangerous,' he said to me, smiling at Willa, 'but the shipping company said it was all okay.' He turned to me. 'They're chemicals that are used for making plastic and foam for foodstuffs. Obviously harmless.'

'Can you get the actual manifest?' I asked. 'There's not much we can do with this.'

Bresler looked at Willa. 'Willa only wanted to know the chemicals. It was a hell of a job getting that. I told them we only wanted to reassure people about the lack of danger from the smoke and gas.'

'Who's them?' I asked.

'Friends,' he said.

'And why would they think you could help to reassure the population?'

'You're asking me to tell you what I do.'

I nodded. He was evasive. 'I bring influential people together,' he said.

'Public relations?'

He laughed dismissively. 'Something like that.'

'Right,' I said. I folded away the chemical names and placed it in my pocket.

'Hey,' he said, 'I want that back.'

'You can get another,' I said. 'You could probably get the manifest.'

'Willa?' he appealed. She looked at me, a question furrowing her brow.

'We'll check these chemicals out,' I said. 'But there's no proof that these were the chemicals on board.'

'I went to a great deal of trouble . . .'

'Hardly.'

'Willa,' he said, in a pathetic effort to save face. 'He's going to get you into some real trouble.'

'At least I warn her first,' I said.

He nodded at Willa and left.

'Where the fuck did you find him?'

'He did get the list of chemicals,' she said.

'Not the right one, though. You remember I covered the Coode Island fire? These chemicals are from that fire.' I pulled the list from my pocket. 'Acrylonitrile,' I said. 'When it burns it becomes a cyanide gas. Luckily the smoke from that fire was blown high over the city; the cyanide dispersed.'

'Why couldn't the ship be carrying those chemicals?'

'It was the explosion that killed the crew,' I said. 'No one else is dropping dead, and cyanide is instant. I could be wrong, but I don't think so.' I glanced down the list, stopped at benzine. 'Benzine may be aboard. It gives off a smell like burning petrol. Benzine is a carcinogen. It can cause cancer with the smallest exposure to it— especially if an individual is allergic to it, or susceptible in other ways, like a flagging immune system.' She began to look at me with some respect. 'Don't be impressed,' I said. 'When I covered Coode Island, I took a crash course on chemicals.'

I brushed my fingers across her hand. She smiled at me. I smiled back, seeing how the folds of her clothes fell against her body.

We left the restaurant after I had eaten and she had had a coffee and nibbled at a sweet. We agreed that we should hide while we collected and collated information. My farm, an hour and a half from the city, seemed a good proposition.

I also had the feeling that she wanted to be with me as much as I wanted to be with her. Walking across the road, I put my arm around her waist, and she dropped her head on my shoulder for an instant. It was remarkable how such small things can change the colour of the world. I had to use considerable willpower to bring myself back to reality. No matter how we felt about each other, there were other people who didn't like us.

Back at my mansion, I left Willa in the car with the Ruger in her lap. She was reluctant to handle it until I told her there was a bullet in the breech, the safety catch was off, and if she didn't point it away from herself she would be the one to be shot.

I climbed up the plumbing on the outside of the greengrocer's, walked across the roof and stepped across a one and a half metre void to the bathroom window. If there was anyone waiting for us, or if the place was booby-trapped, I would be coming up on it all from behind, where it was visible. I slipped through the window, landing on my hands and rolling onto the floor. I knew immediately the place was empty. I walked down the stairs, removed the timber across the door and waved Willa in.

She continued the conversation we had been having in the car: it worried her that we had details of chemicals but had no real source for them. She wanted to confront Bresler, I could see, show him she no longer trusted him. 'I don't see why he would deliberately mislead me,' she complained, referring to Bresler.

'There are plenty of reasons. He may have just wanted a list, any list, to impress you.'

I packed a bag, and pushed the Browning automatic shotgun into a golfbag and surrounded it with golf clubs. Willa was in the kitchen taking food from the cupboards and the fridge. 'There's plenty of stuff down there,' I called.

I was surprised by the closeness of her. She was beside me. Her whisper was hard, full of fright. 'Someone is here.'

'Walking along the hall?' I asked.

'Yes.'

'What was she wearing?'

'For Christsake,' she said. '*He's* wearing a tweed coat.'

'It's alright,' I said.

'You know him?'

'Did you see his face?'

'No,' she said. 'What the hell are you talking about?' she added.

I walked out into the hall. She stayed where she was.

'No one here,' I said, turning back.

'He was heading for the stairs.'

'It's okay,' I said. 'It was Laurie.'

'Who the fuck is Laurie?'

'Who *was* he?' I said.

'What?'

'Did he have a three-quarter length coat with raglan sleeves?'

'Yes.'

'A coat from a different era, right?'

'Yes.'

'Look, I don't believe in ghosts. either,' I said. 'I mean, it was a funeral home.'

Willa looked bewildered. 'That's fine,' she said. 'I don't mind ghosts. I mean, what can they do?'

'They're certainly no help,' I said.

In my office, I ran off the list of chemicals I had been given when I covered the Coode Island fire. Identical chemicals and in the same order as Bresler's list.

We hit the freeway to Geelong. It was the sort of drive the convertible loved. It was built to float down freeways. Travelling with Willa took me back to the days the road had been a two-lane rough top and I had run it many times to Geelong thirsting for sex, the anticipation building to a great high. Barely a car on the road late at night. Then later I had covered the Lara bushfires, just after the road had first become a freeway, and found the bodies of two families, their naked bodies white in the black ash. The mothers had remained with their children and the men had run for it and been caught hanging on the barbs of the paddock fence. Strange associations. I couldn't help feeling the road in each of its identities had made me what I was now.

Turning off the freeway north of Geelong on a short cut into the Western District, I saw we were being followed.

Beyond the first turn-off to the backroads, I killed the lights and pulled into timber near some cattle loading yards. Our pursuer flashed past, driving a white Ford with a lowered suspension. It meant he had something extra in power. I pulled out after him. We had about thirty kilometres before we lost bitumen and I would be swamped in his dust.

Our pursuer panicked about five minutes later, having lost my tail lights. He gunned up, almost doubling his speed. He'd kill himself when he hit the hole where the bitumen ran out. There was no warning sign there because only locals travelled the road. At his speed, he would have no time to slow, and there'd be disaster if he went for the anchors. He was doing an easy one hundred and sixty.

Willa glanced at me occasionally. She hated driving at speed without lights, but I knew the road. I'd driven it drunk, with no memory of the trip at all.

By now the pursuer in front of us would feel isolated. If he was sensible, he would turn back. His speed over country roads showed he wasn't a country boy. He would begin to wonder about the loneliness of the place and where we'd disappeared to. Slowly it would dawn on him. I stopped the car, stood on a fence post and watched him through the glasses. If he didn't turn around, he had about fifteen kilometres to live.

Willa came across and stood beneath me. I looked down at the top of her head. It was a smooth swathe of hair. Clearly she hadn't been running her hands through it in any anxious fashion.

'You're liking this,' she said, without looking up.

'Who else would do it?' I asked. 'Somebody who didn't like it?'

'You're a bit sick, you know,' she said.

'You're kidding,' I said.

'I can understand it, understand the excitement.' She turned and looked up at me, smiled as if it was a joke.

The night was cool, but there was no wind. It was so clear I knew it would rain before morning. Five kilometres away the tail lights expanded and fuzzed. He was slowing, stopping. The car was motionless for a few minutes and then it U-turned and headed back.

He passed our backroad entrance again at speed. He knew he'd lost us. I jumped down from the post and asked Willa to drive, without touching the brakes. They light up like beacons at night in the flatlands. When we hit the timber country and camouflage, she hit the lights and we travelled down single-lane bitumen roads to the farm.

Nine

My Staffordshire bull terrier showed up in the lights as we wound our way up the last section of the drive to the house. He ran along beside the car. The porch light was on and it looked peaceful and pleasant. The terrier's name was Sacco and he was allowed the run of the place after he had saved me from a crazed bullock.

After the fires a few years back, a neighbour's bullock, singed by the flames and full of rage, came loping down my drive towards the house. I took a stock whip out to meet him. On the first crack, he went for me. I ran for the garage and didn't look like making it until Sacco flew at him, grabbing the side of his jaw and hanging on. The bullock changed direction, jumping two fences, snapping the top wires, and shaking Sacco as easily as waving a handkerchief.

Sacco hung on and brought the beast to a standstill, bellowing. He let go and trotted out of the paddock. I shot the bullock where it stood under a peppercorn tree, bled it, hung it, and had a travelling butcher who avoided the meat inspectors come and cut it up for me. It was tough meat, though, filled with adrenalin. Sacco had never shown aggressiveness before the incident, nor after. He could just tell when real danger was about.

With Sacco doing the obligatory bull terrier bounce around my legs, I threw on the stable lights and saw the horses were quiet. Nothing odd about the evening on the farm.

'I love the lake,' Willa said, as I returned to the front of the house. She stood with her hands on her hips and her legs apart, silhouetted against the moonlight on the lake's surface.

Willa was intrigued by this hideaway. That's how she thought of it. She didn't know it was my headquarters for a planned assault on the thoroughbred breeding industry. The horses I bred here would storm the racetracks of the country. Every bloody horse owner thinks he can beat the system. I knew that. Like any gambler, I was just putting my bets on with a breeding program and was hoping for the luck I knew was necessary.

The house was two soldier-settlers' homes joined together, with large verandahs added. I had bought the place midway through a bad drought. The thick volcanic black soil was five metres deep, and beneath that were streams of underground water that were easy to tap. Several light windmills were dotted around the paddocks, feeding water to the stock troughs. I had planted stands of native trees and, down the side of the stallion paddock, a dozen walnut trees.

It was the lake, though, that had the capacity to turn the scene from that of a pleasant little farm into something entirely beautiful. Apart from the changing light and weather it reflected, it was alive with waterbirds. As we stood there, half a dozen swans came over the house to avoid the electricity pylons in the next property, and their clear, plaintive calls gave the scene a sweet music.

Inside the house I checked the firearms, placing them within easy reach. Willa went and showered. I gave her one of those thick white towels you only seem to be able to buy in America. She wasn't talking, and I took her lead. She was the employer. Whatever she decided, I knew we were stuck with this one. It wasn't a case of taking your bat and ball and going home. They would come after us.

I went down to look at Shy Bride. She was using the box thorn hedge to keep out of the wind. I led her up to the three acre paddock where she had a lucerne mix, away from the thorn that a struggling foal just might tumble into. I ran my hands over her legs, checking for any tender places. The huge belly moved all the time. She was close. The wax from the teats had loosened. She would probably foal in the next forty-eight hours. As I left her, she swung her neck hard against me like a swinging scythe and I nearly fell. A wicked sense of humour.

I cooked up pasta with a sauce that came from anything I had in the fridge—olives, capers, canned tomatoes, garlic, olive oil and anchovies—and grabbed up a good red wine from the cellar under the verandah. There was a ladder, but the cellar was so full I lay on the verandah and took hold of a bottle. Further in was my antique gun collection. From that low viewpoint, with my head close to the wooden floor, I noted something that was strange out near the shine of the lake, but I registered it as the odd angle from which I was looking and forgot about it.

Willa came to the kitchen fresh, clean-skinned, no make-up. Her face had lost none of its strength or beauty. She carried the wine under her arm to warm it as she moved around the kitchen. I could feel she was relaxed and I felt it might be a problem. She needed the edge back if we were to survive.

I didn't spare her. I told her about the dock worker and the burned survivor. 'And to top it all off, we have Syrians chasing us,' I said.

She was silent for a moment and I knew this was the danger period. Would she feel it was all too much—new elements entering the picture so quickly? I felt she wouldn't break down, but then I didn't know. When she spoke, it was with a complete acceptance of our problems. 'Where do the Syrians come into it?' she asked.

'My question,' I said.

'But here?' she said. 'They're involved in something in Australia, in Melbourne?' Her voice was sceptical.

'There are no hiding places,' I said. 'The Australian government has been selling arms to everyone for years. If you're marketing death, you bring the nasty customers. We won't even participate in banning landmines, because we're selling them all over the world.

'Crime is changing here. The police are well behind these criminal organisations because they don't know the languages. We have Vietnamese and Rumanian drug rings; Croatian and Serbian terrorists have trained here; Japanese cults have tested their gases for annihilating half of underground Japan; so why should we be surprised?'

I sipped the red wine. It was good. crushed raisins without the sweetness.

'I think we give everything we've got to the politicians and the police,' Willa stated. 'I'll pay to have them look at it seriously.'

'You'll have to pay more than Abidex and whoever else is in bed with them, and that's not going to stop our real problem.'

'Yes?'

'They want to get rid of us.'

'But if we've given the information to the authorities?'

'Somehow, I don't think that will stop them.' I looked out through the plum tree to the water. 'If they come for us we have to seriously defend ourselves. I mean, I think we have to be prepared to shoot.'

I could see Willa was cold on that idea.

I sipped the wine. 'Are you with me? I don't see you have much choice.'

'What do you tell yourself when you have doubts?' she asked.

'What about?'

'Doing these things? You've done it before, haven't you?'

'Yes,' I said. 'And I don't have any doubts about having to do it. Only about being able to do it.'

I forked the pasta and tried to discover if it was my defensiveness that was making me irritable. It was usually a sign I was hiding something from myself. Nothing in me rose to the bait.

Willa stood up and took her pasta to the table. 'What if everybody behaved like you?'

'Most do. People'll do anything to protect their own interests.'

My mind blanked for a moment, and then found the reason my previous cock-eyed view of the lake had seemed so odd. The boat down by the shore had been tied down keel-up. It was now upright, as if it had just been used.

'And after all this, presuming we're still around?' Willa demanded.

'We hand what we have to Greenpeace and watch them go to work.'

My mind left our conversation as I wondered about the boat. Linda may have used it for swimming a horse, but I knew she would tie it down again. The winds coming off the lake could tumble the boat across the paddock, panicking the horses and causing major damage.

I remembered I had told her the boat was full of redback spiders because it hadn't been used for months. It was the only cover for them in that paddock and they tended to congregate. I had meant to kill them, but hadn't got around to it. If anybody had inserted their fingers around the gunwales as they lifted it, they'd be feeling very sick right now. One bite meant they could get to the hospital for the antidote. Several bites meant they probably wouldn't get to their car.

I came back to the conversation with Willa. I was uneasy, though. Willa thought it was because she was verbally pinning me down. 'Why not hand all the information over now? We could publicise that, convince them that they're too late.'

'We don't have it all now, and we mightn't live long enough to get it if we're not serious about surviving.'

'Killing them is like joining their ranks,' she said.

I came back at her with a question. 'Is it justified for someone to break the law to ensure that one of the mainstays of democracy is continued?'

'What does all that mean? Kill someone?'

'I didn't mean that. But it could mean that?'

'What did you mean?'

'For instance, should protesters be charged because they have broken the law of trespass or public nuisance, or have defended themselves against police attack?'

'If the law says they can't do it, they would expect to be charged.'

'But one of the tenets of our law is the freedom to express themselves in a free press. If they don't break the law, they can't express themselves freely, because the press isn't interested. So to get to express themselves, they have to break the law.'

'I can't take you seriously.'

'Think about it.'

'Is this a way of justifying killing?'

'I just want you to think about it.'

After Willa bedded down for the night, alone—we were irritated with each other—I took a pump-action shotgun with seven shells in the magazine and slipped out the window of the study behind the bank of French lavender.

I squatted there for five minutes and then moved behind the cactus growing near the tank-stand. I waited there another five, looking across the lake that was still lit by the moon. The front paddock had a stand of trees off to the west, but it was too far away to watch for anyone approaching the house.

The ground of the adjacent paddock rose away from its border with the front paddock like a rising loaf of bread. The yearlings were there, running with several donkeys to quieten them. I could see them close to the box thorn where the fox cubs came out in the early morning.

The younger mares were in the next paddock again, their swollen bellies silhouetted against the mist rising from the strawberry clover covered ground. None of the horses were curious about anything but food. The donkeys, the first to notice things out of the ordinary, were browsing peacefully. I moved forward and Sacco appeared beside my legs, gazing up with his wide grinning mouth open and happy. What the hell was I worried about?

I walked straight down to the boat. The grass was still short, so nothing lay in wait for me there. The boat was on damp ground and I pulled the small Maglite torch from my pocket and approached openly. The ground showed me Sacco had been down here. He had dug up the ground around the boat.

It was what was in the boat that was interesting, though. The body lay face down, one arm propped over the bow. I casually felt for a pulse. He was fucked.

I shone my light on the back of his hair to check for spiders. Several moved down his neck, away from the light. I lifted his head by his nose and checked his face. I had no idea who he was, except that Sacco had kept him in the boat. He didn't appear to have a weapon, but he looked a bad'un. He stank of gun oil.

I looked down at Sacco. 'You happy little bugger. You're pleased with yourself, aren't you?' He wagged his whole rear end and dropped his bottom jaw in a gigantic grin. Obviously he had rounded up the poor bugger. My scenario had the stupid bastard run for the boat, imagining the low sides would save him from a dog bite. For some reason, Sacco had picked on him. It wasn't in his nature to play with people so savagely.

'What happens if he's an innocent bystander?' I asked Sacco. 'You'll be for the high jump.' That seemed to increase his happiness. He jumped around in front of me, turning circles, chasing his tail.

He would have run around the man barking, growling, keeping him there to be found, and then the little red-backed bastards had crept up the legs of his strides, or the sleeves of his shirt, irritated by the man's banging on the metal hull, and sunk their fangs in.

I found the tracks where Sacco had followed the man to the boat and I back-tracked. They crossed into my neighbour's property and over to the huge rolled bales of hay in the corner of the paddock. There was a dark four-wheel drive there. The guns were in cases in the station wagon section. The shotguns were actually short-barrelled riot guns. There were several semi-automatic military weapons I hadn't seen before. This man had been a mule. He carried all the guns to and away from the target area. If the real killers were pulled over by cops, they would be clean.

Presumably Sacco had surprised him and snarled him away from the vehicle, not allowing him to grab for the guns. A bull terrier has a growl that sounds as if his throat is already filled with blood. Defy it and he'll be more than midway through a limb before the person next to you thinks about chocking him off.

I took all but one of the gun cases from the car and threw them into the box thorn, really high, so they couldn't be seen if anyone walked past. In the case I kept was a 9 mm Feather rifle with a long 25-round magazine. It was light, around two and a half kilos. It wasn't accurate over about seventy metres, but that was all I needed.

I went over to the drain outlet I had blocked for a few weeks so that four hundred hectares of salty ground would be washed out. The water was about two metres deep. It was good friable soil and I knew clover would grow there. I pulled away the rocks from the steel plate that covered the cement drain outlet, tugged the plate clear and watched the water pour down into the lake over dry white earth.

By morning the boat would be rocking gently and no cop would bother to look underwater for evidence. As far as they were concerned, he would be a trespassing duck hunter who had thought to use a boat he'd annexed. I returned

to the box thorn and retrieved a Japanese twelve
bore and a belt of No. 6 shells. I placed it in the
boat after blurring the bloke's prints over it.

It was disturbing that they had caught up with
me so quickly. I looked down at Sacco. This was
the second time he had saved my life. I thought
I just might dedicate the remainder of my life to
the breed.

At the house, I gave him some stale bread with
molasses. I thought payment might ensure my
safety.

For the rest of the night I watched for any
vehicles approaching the farm. I wondered if they
had left the area already, not being able to find
the weapons or their carrier. The weapons didn't
identify the type of assassin. For a moment I
reflected that this was overkill. We were only two
investigators. Then I realised that the burning ship
was the answer. The crew had died. Murdered?
Ann Hough was dead. It might even mean a good
portion of the arms industry was endangered, and
if anyone was endangering those vast profits, it
was us.

Morning was pink in the east. Clouds that
looked like toy cut-outs hovered over the farm
without changing shape. They were grey and
tinged with pink. I walked over to the foaling
paddock. Shy Bride was still hanging on. She
was locked in a trance. Occasionally she changed
the weight from one back leg to another to
accommodate the shifting foal.

I took coffee and bantam eggs fried in olive oil into Willa. Naturally she was pissed off with what she imagined the day had in store for her.

'You mean we just stay here.' She took a desultory stab at an egg yolk. 'I can't. I'll be expecting something to happen.'

'Yeah,' I said. 'It's already happened.'

'What?' She spilled her coffee as she put it down on the small cupboard beside the bed.

'Have a look outside.' I pointed down to the lake. The boat was riding about fifty metres off shore in the pink water dawn. I was testing her again. 'There's a body in the boat,' I said.

I had anticipated this would be the turning point in our relationship. I expected her to walk briskly to the phone and ring the cops. It wasn't such a problem, because there was nothing to link me to the death. I walked out of the room.

If she passed this one, she was in very deeply. I knew very rich women have what is often mistaken for character, but it's only a capacity to remove themselves from awkward or humiliating situations and, having confidence in that ability, never having to confront the more destructive realities of life. Was Willa about to remove herself?

'The boat looks pretty down there,' she said. She hadn't panicked. 'Did you kill him?' The question had a tone of unconcern. I shouldn't have doubted her.

'No. The spiders did.'

'I tell you one thing,' she said, 'I don't have to put up with your humour.'

I grinned at her. 'No one ever does.'

I left her to finish her breakfast and walked through the study and out the back door to the drive. Dust coming around the bend over the rise. It was approaching fast. I walked into the garage, tipped the two hundred litre drum of fuel on its side, ready to roll it out on the drive, and stood near the Feather 9 mm, which was balanced above me on the rolled roll-a-door.

A police car approached slowly up the dirt drive and came to a halt just outside the garage.

'You've come at the right time,' I said to the cop as he stepped from his car, looking tough in his riding breeches and leather boots. 'Some drunk is sleeping it off in my boat.' He wasn't interested in sleeping drunks.

'You're Jack Speerman?' he asked. His offsider opened the passenger door and stepped out. From his attitude, he seemed to have his hand on a gun. I looked away from him. If I become too focused I can't help making people uncomfortable. If Victorian cops feel uncomfortable, they're a hair's breadth away from pulling the trigger. That's just how they are in this state. It's a shoot-your-problems police culture.

'Yes,' I said.

'You've got illegal chemicals on your property,' he said.

'Probably,' I said. 'So have half the farmers in the state.'

'Where is it?'

'Who told you about it?'

'You asked for tests from a Werribee vet. He sent them to the Victorian Labs and we're here to investigate.' These cops were strangely cooperative. The talkative one had a pleasant face despite the leather boots.

'So what were the chemicals?' I asked. He looked across at his partner, hoping for some input. He was out of luck there.

'You don't know?'

'No, I just took them to the vet, what's'is name, at Werribee to have them tested.'

'Yes, he said you were concerned.'

'So, what was the stuff?'

'One was a mixture of kero and petroleum jelly and phosphorus, and the other was a mix of agricultural chemicals.' He nodded over to the stables. 'Over there, are they?'

'Yeah,' I said. There was an unlabelled bag of calcium I had been using as a food additive, and a twenty litre drum of metho I used as an antiseptic whenever I needed to give shots to ill horses or electrolyte drips to those about to race or travel.

Linda chose this time to arrive to muck out and ride. She waved to me and then started in on the talkative cop. 'Saw you with Cheryl,' she said. 'Getting it off, are you?'

He managed a slightly embarrassed grin. Linda stopped to talk as she pulled on work gloves. 'Cheryl's terrific,' she said to him with considerable significance, as if Cheryl wasn't a woman with whom to trifle.

'I'll get the stuff,' I said. 'Be a load off my mind, getting rid of it.' I walked into the feed-room, made sure the metho lid was tight, and upended the calcium into a flax bag and placed that again in a dark plastic garbage bag.

I walked out carrying both. Linda was surprised.

'What's this?' she asked.

I winked at the cop and looked at Linda. 'Drugs,' I said. 'It's a wonder you didn't spot them there.' Linda was quick. She knew not to pursue the matter. 'Put them in the boot?' I said. The passenger cop popped the boot and I stowed them up against the hump of the petrol tank.

'Thanks,' he said. He was a small dark bloke with broad shoulders. He didn't have leather boots, though, and he felt that. His hair was crowding his eyebrows and his teeth must have bothered him because he spoke with unmoving lips.

Linda said she had to get to work.

The cops said they'd be going. 'You don't feel like checking that drunk down there, do you?' I asked.

'Not our business. Not even drunk in a public place. Sorry.' No imaginative development, no sense of mystery. Mustn't have read as a kid. I smiled and walked away up to the house. The car moved off. Linda went to the stalls and led the horses out to the day yards where she would saddle them.

Inside, Willa was sitting with her bag on the table beside her. She looked fresh and the lipstick was bold and inviting.

'Our friend was right about the chemicals from Abidex,' I said. 'Basically it's kero and a jelly so it will stick and burn. This is a new one, though. It has phosphorus in it. That means it will burn underwater or inside a wound. Phosphorus burns at room temperature. If it gets into the blood-stream it can burn when it reaches oxygen in the lungs or the fatty deposits around the organs.

'You know all this?'

'After the Coode Island thing, I stored infor-mation on chemicals. On the Internet there is a monograph on phosphorus in literary fiction. Dickens once reported on a case of a man who spontaneously combusted. Wilkie Collins sug-gested to him there was a chemical that could burn in blood. I just followed it up.'

'God, you always had strange interests.'

'Nothing compared to the obsessives on the Internet.'

'So, what did the police say?'

'They just came to pick up the offending mate-rial. They wouldn't take my body,' I said, pointing through the window to the boat.

'What do we do with it?'

'I'm afraid Linda has to find it. We'll be working horses down there later.'

Willa looked down at the lake. Her hair was
pushed back off her strong brow and she looked
formidable. She began sieving through the circumstances in which we now found ourselves. I
could tell from her questions she was undergoing
a search of where her values now lay, and how
and why they had been altered.

'I don't understand why Ann's husband's death
would mean that she had to die?' she said. 'I know
it's easily explained by just saying that's how these
people are, they want to shut down any possibility of their losing profits and deals. But I don't
understand the nature of people like that.' She
glanced at me.

'We have to take care of the thing in the boat,'
I said, not having the energy to follow or help
her with personal philosophising. 'And then we
move from here. It's not safe.'

I pointed to the horses being saddled. 'You
ride, don't you?'

She nodded. 'Not something I'm contemplating
right at this moment.'

I persuaded her to look at the horses. Linda
had already mucked out and saddled the four
horses. Sacco had captured a patch of morning
sun and was lying down on his barrel side, his
legs stuck out in the style of a dead sheep. I

looked at him just as he opened his great mouth in a smile and sighed.

The horses Willa and I would ride were only up to slow work over three or four kilometres. They'd be taken along like that until they were fit enough for four hundred metre hit-outs.

Linda's friend Josie turned up once the horses were saddled. She lived in an old shearer's hut close to Linda's place and in the early mornings she kept binoculars on the stables. When she saw the horses saddled, she rode her motorbike over. She was an extra dairy hand and newsagent employee, and occasionally typed up copy at the local paper. Her one indulgence was a mobile phone so that her variety of employers could get her immediately. People lived like this in country towns. Part-time work was all there was, and if you missed a call, there were a dozen others who wanted it.

As two horses were usually ridden together, I thought it was an opportunity to have the two-year-olds Apple and Art Shy gain some experience of moving with a crowd.

Willa and I being oversized compared to Linda and Josie, we got the four-year-old geldings. Josie said our arrangement was that she would get money for riding two horses each morning, so I said she would be paid this morning for two rides.

She often reminded me she was trying to live independently and might have to register for the dole to get her teeth fixed. It would mean trips to Melbourne to the dental hospital. At the moment she was counting on the two-year-olds showing good manners on the track so that she would pick up extra riding, even a full-time stable job.

Willa got to ride Crumble, a liver chestnut about sixteen hands, with a nice sense of the ridiculous. If you couldn't ride, he made you feel you never would, moving beneath you all the time as if he had no idea what he was going to do next. His one season in work, he had won two on bush tracks and been placed in his only run at Sandown. If he knew you could ride, he strode along, solid beneath you. Willa could ride.

I swung onto a horse that had been something of a disappointment. Sea Flight had blinding speed over four hundred metres but ran out of puff very quickly if the jockey couldn't hold him down, conserving energy. He had a good bold eye and wasn't going to fret over his losses. He knew who he was. He had probably won every paddock gallop he had ever had with his friends and relatives, over short distances.

The plan was to ride with the two-year-olds in the centre for a while and then change positions, and at the end of the ride have them boxed in again in an unpressured way.

I ran my hands over the shins of the two-year-olds, checking for soreness. Neither of them flinched. You can count on every young horse getting sore as their training intensifies. The young bone of their shins develops surface cracks where surface ligaments pull at the young bone, inflaming it. Once their shins are tender, I take them out of work straight away, before they lose confidence. Some trainers fire the shins before they put them out, or bandage them and run them on shots of cortisone. The country race clubs can't afford expensive tests for drugs.

We walked the horses down to the front paddock. Linda was talkative. 'I bet you came back up here so the toxic fumes wouldn't get you,' she said to me, winking at Willa.

'Have you heard anything this morning?' I asked her.

'The ship's still burning,' she said.

Sea Flight moved beautifully. He responded to leg aids and I manoeuvred him into position to unchain the gate and then open outwards. The other three rode through. Willa was sitting easily, the horse under perfect control. I remembered she had ridden to hounds or played polo in earlier days—I could never remember which. Advertising executives had flooded both sports with their presence, they being the only people who could afford to maintain the necessary number of horses to ride several times a week. It had seemed wrong somehow, but, of course, it wasn't. It kept interest in horses alive.

Art Shy was a taller horse than the rest. He was a daisy cutter, though, his hoofs skimming the tops of the short grass.

Linda pointed down to the boat. 'There's somebody lying in the boat,' she said.

'Yeah,' I said. 'I mentioned it to your copper friends. They weren't interested.' I rode down to the lake and into the water. Sea Flight didn't hesitate. His long ears were pricked and he moved his head up and down while he concentrated his gaze on the boat. He knew there was something strange there. The water was up to his knees.

'It's not good,' I called back to the group.

'Shit,' I heard Linda say.

The problem for me was that he had been moved. His legs had been twisted as if someone had tried to get access to his trouser pockets. There were several dozen redback spiders on his clothes and running around the gunwales. I looked around for crumpled corpses in the middle distance. Some of the spiders appeared to be panting, or at least raising and lowering themselves in significant aggression. Perhaps they sensed they were afloat in an alien environment. Perhaps some seagulls had picked off a few of their mates.

Linda rode up. Art Shy was dancing in the water. She was stopping him from staring at the moving surface because if he became too fascinated with it, he would begin to think the earth was moving under him and finally rear and fall over.

'Jesus,' Linda said, moving around the boat. Art Shy wasn't watching the boat, he was trying to get a good focus on the water. 'You told me about the spiders. I didn't believe there were so many.'

I scanned the property in search of a body. It may have been that the glands hadn't replenished the amounts of poison expended on the first victim. But if he'd been bitten several times, he'd be feeling sick.

'We'll leave him until we finish the ride,' I said. 'It's not as if I haven't reported it already.'

'Yes,' Linda said. 'He's a dead scone anyway.' A quaint expression I thought, born fifty years ago in some country kitchen. It hadn't caught on, despite the satisfying way it trivialised the event.

'What is it?' Willa said, establishing her innocence as Linda and I emerged from the water.

'An accident. The man's dead. He was obviously going to borrow my boat. The spiders,' I said pointing back. 'Linda, I think I'd better report it now. I'll catch you up.'

'Should we do anything?' Josie asked. 'Pull the boat up.'

'Leave it to the experts,' I said.

I went back up to the house, watching the three women trotting the horses around the lake. The horses were moving well, the two-year-olds nicely up on the bit.

I left Sea Flight feeding on the lawn around the house, the reins linked through a stirrup. He had a terrific temperament. Most horses would be charging up and down, wanting to join the others.

My call was diverted to the sergeant, who was still eating breakfast at home.

'Are you sure it was spiders?' he asked.

'You blokes are the experts,' I said.

'Yeah, well just pull the boat in. If the wind gets up, we'll be chasing it all over the lake.'

I told him I'd pull it up near the gate and for him to watch the redbacks. He wasn't a gung-ho cop. He wanted to know the best spray for spiders.

Before I left the kitchen, I faxed the Werribee vet for the detailed results of the tests. My note was straight. I told him the police had been and removed the chemicals but I would like to know what they actually were. He wouldn't be in his office yet, but there is nothing like a fax for getting prompt answers from those with bureaucratic bents.

In the lake, I just pushed the boat with my foot and it speared into shore. I hooked a lead rope to the ring in the bow and pulled it part way out of the water. The redbacks ran across the bloke's jacket and one stayed glued to his throat. 'You got yours, didn't you, mate,' I said aloud. 'And I didn't even have to try.'

I began Sea Flight with some slow pace work. He didn't seem to notice the difference in weight between Josie and me. She had a light work saddle, but I was riding in an English hunting saddle. He kept his back legs under him, a beautifully conformed action.

The horses ahead were now working around the edge of the strawberry clover paddock on soft ground. The two-year-olds were moved back and forth around Crumble at about three-quarter pace, enough to send some earth up behind them. The older horse knew he wasn't racing but I could see him shift a gear before Willa caught him and settled him down. I hadn't known she was such an expert in the saddle. From where I was, it looked as if he had slipped the bit, even manoeuvred his tongue over it.

When I headed into the twenty hectare clover paddock, Sea Flight wanted to make up ground, but he was prepared to do it in a workmanlike manner, settling down under a firm grip and blowing with every stride. Some experts claim the thousand metre horses didn't breathe from the moment they sprang from the starting gate to the moment they passed the post. It was easy to believe. I could run, myself, without breathing for a minute and my expertise wasn't running.

By the time I approached the stables, Linda and Josie had finished washing down, and the brass scrapers, catching the morning sun, were swishing litres of water from the heavier coats of the two-year-olds.

When we were ready for coffee, the police car swept through the front gate, along with a closed van. We all walked down the drive to meet with them. A few shots were taken and then the sergeant called Homicide to discover whether or not he should spray the boat. Would it destroy evidence? Certainly would, he was told. But unless there were suspicious circumstances, it didn't matter.

I hadn't seen the sergeant before but he was white-haired and had the heaviness of a sportsman that liked too many beers and polly waffles. The skin beneath his eyes had fallen away a little from the actual eyeballs, and the area there was filled with unshed tears. 'The only thing suspicious is that there are so many redbacks in one place,' he said to his Homicide contact.

He looked at me while he listened. 'I didn't believe it either,' I said. 'But there are so many silky cocoons about under the seats and gunwales it's obviously a breeding ground.' I pointed to the gap beneath the gunwales. I wasn't sure the cocoons belonged to the redbacks. Could be the white-tailed kind. I had been bitten by one several years back, and I'd had little reaction—I thought it was because I had dosed myself with vitamins.

'Yeah, okay,' he said to Homicide without commenting on my statement.

I decided I was being too eager and I had no need to be on this one. I reversed tactics. 'It's bloody suspicious, alright,' I said.

The bloke from the funeral parlour was certain he wasn't going to move the body until the fucking spiders had been wasted.

'They take a lot of killing,' I told him.

'I hate fucking spiders,' the sergeant said to me. 'Could you look for his wallet?'

'Hey, it's bad enough it's on my property and in my boat. I'm not going to put prints on his wallet or his zip or whatever.'

'Yeah, I see what you mean,' he said.

'He'll start to stink when the sun gets up,' the funeral attendant said. 'Hit the buggers with spray and we'll get him out of here.' In country towns, everyone gives coppers advice. 'I mean, shit,' he continued. 'No one's gunna go to the trouble of collecting all those fucking spiders when they could have shot him up close with his gun and left it as suicide.'

'You reckon?' the sergeant said.

'I'm bloody sure of it.'

The sergeant deferred. He didn't have the same experience of bodies and the circumstances in which they met their demise.

'Yeah, well I've got work to do.'

The sergeant didn't like me losing interest. 'You sure you haven't seen this bloke before?'

'Positive,' I said. I glanced over at the hay rolls in the neighbour's place. The vehicle wasn't visible, so I couldn't point it out to him. 'He must have come from somewhere,' I said. 'Or somebody dropped him off and they'll be coming back. Maybe he's staying at one of the neighbours. I'll give them a ring when I go up to the house.'

'No,' the sergeant said, 'I'll do that.' Visiting the affluent in the district was probably his idea of a good time.

Our group moved off.

'It's so bizarre,' Linda said. 'I mean, I've seen half a dozen redbacks in the wood heap and under the pump cover, but that.'

'The boat is twenty times the size of a pump cover, and it's the only protection in the paddock.'

'What's it doing there?' Willa asked. 'With a paddock full of horses.'

'It was tied down. The horses didn't mind it. In fact they woke me up sometimes with their drumming.'

'What do you mean?' Willa said.

'They'd all stand around it and bang their front feet down on it.'

'Would have driven the spiders away.'

'Yeah, well they got bored with the drumming a long time ago.'

At the house, Linda and Josie broke away to the stables and Willa and I went inside. Sacco followed us up to the kitchen door and flopped on the earth against the bank of lavender. There was nothing on the fax, so I called the vet.

He was hesitant. 'As soon as I have time,' he said, 'I'll fax it to you.'

'You had time enough yesterday to fax it to the police. I'd like it through now.'

'Yes, yes, I'll do it.'

Half an hour later it wasn't through, so I rang again.

'Has anyone in your family died?' I asked.

'No,' he said.

'Do you have an emergency operation under way?'

'No. What are you talking about?'

'Send me the fax as soon as I hang up or I will personally drive down and collect it myself. Do you fucking understand that?' I hung up.

A few moments later the fax came through. It was interesting. The phosphorus mix was expected. The second chemical breakdown wasn't. The form was letterheaded the Victorian Labs and it said that there was a mix of 2,4-D and 2,4,5-T. Each was an agricultural chemical. For some reason, it reminded me of something nasty I had read about. But I couldn't place it. I knew 2,4,5-T had become something of a cause célèbre. Four babies with distorted limbs had been born in one street that had been sprayed heavily for blackberries in a country town. It had been the incident that had alerted me to the dangers of agricultural chemicals.

Willa filled a glass of water and poured it into the fern that was hanging over the kitchen bench. She filled the glass again and drank it. Turning to me, she said, 'Do we have enough evidence to satisfy the media?' I didn't say anything. 'It isn't enough, is it?'

'I don't know. I want more. We have some chemicals identified, some being poured illegally into the bay. It's a small story.'

'You mean small compared with the story you think is there?'

'They wouldn't kill anyone for that. I smelled burning kerosene from the ship,' I said. 'It's unmistakable. Like jet fuel.'

Willa leaned her elbows on the bench and rested her head in her hands. Her hair fell down, covering her face. She remained that way for some time.

Abruptly, she threw her hair back and stood up. 'We have to face what we have here. It's an international game, and there is considerable interest in killing the story by killing us. Am I right? Is that what you've been telling me?'

Linda came crashing through the back door. 'The old mare is down,' she yelled. 'It's on its way.' Her face was excited in the way of a child anticipating the best of things. I took the field glasses and walked out the back door, keeping the walnut trees between the mare and myself. But I saw she was beyond bothering about how close we were, she was in deep labour. She was lying on the ground, and she was in trouble. All the effort of a horse is concentrated on the first few seconds of the birth spasm, and if the foal's not out after that, you can bet she needs help. Putting the glasses on her, I saw the problem: the foal's front feet had been caught behind the anus, and the straining flesh there was a shiny mound. I raced down to the paddock, vaulted over the fences between and then slowed to a walk. 'Hey, come on,' I said softly. I wanted her to know I was approaching so she wouldn't suddenly take fright and try to rise. 'That's right,' I continued. 'It's almost out, just don't rush any more, okay, not till I get there.' She raised her nostrils to the sky, turning her head so she could see me coming. I knew I had her trust. For the last few months she had been in the habit of getting cast by lying with her legs uphill and I had had to roll her, using her front legs as a fulcrum. I knelt behind her now and the thin tissue the foal was encased in as it slipped from the womb was blown out a small way, in the style of a child blowing gum. I pushed my hands in and found the front feet, the fetlocks stiff, jammed hard there. I tried to push the legs back for leverage, because the joints were bent the wrong way, but the foal was stuck there. I simply pushed the joints from beneath, hard, and they bent, and then I grabbed the slipping hoofs and pulled them out through the vagina. The mare heaved and the foal in its white sliding skin, seemed to spill all over me. I broke the bag and the nostrils quivered, drawing a little air, then sucking, and then exhaling with a spray of moisture.

I was aware of Willa and Linda behind me. The foal was a deep liver chestnut, and already it was beginning to scrabble with its front legs. Shy

Bride was exhausted, the sweat had sprung in half moons beneath her eyes and her chest was heaving. Despite this, she wanted to stand. I touched the pulse on the inside of the knee. It was pounding. Up around a hundred, but irregular.

I looked at the foal in the spring grass, blood on its delicate hide, wondering at how beautiful she was, and how pathetic it would be without its mother. The next few days would be a long road if she died. An image of the small child in that classic photograph, running, crying on a Vietnam road burnt by napalm, flashed into my mind just as my thoughts turned to helping the foal to its feet. Linda threw a salt solution over the umbilical stump to stop infection.

It flashed at me again in the same instant that I decided to help the mare up first. It wasn't going to get that precious first milk if the mare wasn't encouraged. Willa and Linda lifted the foal clear of the mare. I pulled the mare's front feet straight out in front of her as she lifted her neck. I put my shoulder against her huge neck and we pushed up together, the way two children might as they squat back to back and, pushing against each other, rise easily, effortlessly. The mare shook herself and then whinnied to the foal. It thrashed about with its long legs but fell over.

What happened to that crying girl, the blisters from the napalm stiffening her body? You fucking bastards, I thought, meaning those that prey on war, the arms dealers.

The mare turned and sniffed at the foal as Willa and Linda stepped back. The mare took the skin along the spine and nibbled it hard. The foal rose against the pain, using this other pressure to steady itself.

We watched as the mare guided the foal down her side to the milk. The foal honed in on the shadows under the belly, instinctively knowing that was where the milk waited. The first few sucks were wide of the mark, but the mare swung her nose around onto his rump to reassure him, and then he found the supply.

The heart beat was down around fifty and regular, so Shy Bride seemed okay. Linda went for oats and Willa and I walked up to the house.

Josie said she'd never be placed in that bloody position. She wasn't impressed with the process. It seemed strange she hadn't seen a foaling. But then not many people do. Horses foal at night and it's only thoroughbred breeders and the like who make sure that the valuable offspring survives.

'You're crying,' Willa said to me. I felt my eyes brimming and shook my head.

'Is it the foal?' Willa asked.

'Yeah,' I said, thinking of the small girl burning on the road. People who could design weapons to maim children were beyond humanity. If they had been before me, I could have made them ask for mercy. It seemed my emotion only arrived when I was within the aura of the innocent who had been hugely damaged by brutality. I had no feeling for those who could look after themselves.

I put my arm around Willa. She looked up at me, brushed her fingers across my face. But I had emerged from my emotion with the knowledge of who and what we were dealing with.

'We seem to have stumbled onto an arms deal,' I said, looking up to the house, seeing it in my mind as a burning hulk, no refuge for a burning girl. 'What they're making at Evans's place', I said, 'is a combination of phosphorus and petroleum jelly. It's napalm.'

I don't think she believed me at first.

'We're about to sell one hundred millions dollars worth of small arms to Indonesia.'

'I don't believe it.'

'And we train their officers. Most of those go straight to an East Timor billet, continue the killing and oppression there.'

Ten

Suddenly it wasn't just the stud and the Williamstown apartment that weren't safe. It was the world. Diplomats and arms dealers had access to networks that were unscrupulous and efficient. And Evans, our little chemical manufacturer, with his polluting ways, the boss of Abidex, became a very sinister bastard indeed.

I had misjudged the players. At the most, I had imagined a shady chemical company anxious to protect its alleged right to continue making money, one that didn't want to be sued out of existence and have the Environmental Protection Agency descend on it in a serious way, suspending its operations. Now I saw we were dealing with a dangerous business that had lobbied the Australian government so effectively, the country had invested six billion dollars of its own money in arms manufacturing, and lost most of it. I was relying on that information from another muckraker who had waded through the politics of defence and our new love of Asian dictatorships and had written about it in one of the country's august journals, the *Bulletin*.

A government like that could go along with the removal of an inhibiting embarrassment to its developing industries. That embarrassment just now was us. We were beginning to collect the information that made the politicians and bureaucrats look like fools.

The illegal arms trade personnel had a high murder rate during the Gulf War. Competition was fierce and covert. Apart from weapons designers being shot outside their apartments, the traders themselves, attending legitimate arms exhibitions, were often found hanged in the cupboards at their hotels or slumped over their room service meals. Killings like that were rarely solved, rarely even investigated until years later, and only then if the death had more significant repercussions down the track.

In this country, the focus of these greedy desperates was Willa and I.

I found Willa on the verandah. She was leaning against the rails, her long back and legs foreshortening the verandah support. I watched her for a moment but, aware of me, she turned.

'The only plus we have at the moment is the ship,' I said, giving her the good news. 'Let's hope it burns a few more days.'

Willa's hostility was immediate and complete. 'What are you talking about?' The question was from an interrogator angry a comment had been made that went totally outside the boundaries of the investigation. In this case, I had ignored the environment and the rights of the people of the city.

'I'm not being glib. They'll be running around covering up. They won't be so focused on us.'

Gradually she regained her composure. A slight tremor to the fingers the only indication her nervous system was still vibrating.

'The people they've thrown at us have been brute force operators. No subtlety, no finesse. Whoever found the body in the boat has run back to his employers to tell them it will need a bigger operation to get rid of us. Now they'll use a different animal.'

'Which means what?'

'It means the only time you see them is the moment they're about to kill you, if then.'

Willa threw up her hands. 'Oh, Christ,' she said. 'This is so bloody ridiculous. I just want to know when I can get on with life.'

'We'll have to disappear,' I said. 'Until we know what we're up against.'

'I'm packed,' Willa said.

I walked outside. I had an idea. Behind my property there was close to four hectares of box thorn. It had tracks woven through it, made by livestock looking for warmth on freezing nights. Linda called that she'd be mucking out the stables. I walked under the old plum tree and put the glasses on the box thorn. I saw immediately it was too dry, too easily torched. I turned the glasses to the south-west, where our dirt track joined the main road. It was the only way out. That wasn't a bad thing in most circumstances, because anyone coming to my property had to drive down past two other farmhouses and drive out the same way. It inhibited local theft and duck shooters who saw spontaneous opportunities. The people who finally arrived to kill us would, if necessary, kill everybody in the farmhouses along the road.

There were two cars, one north and one south of our road. Two parked cars on a road that wouldn't see more than a dozen cars and two milk tankers a day if you were lucky.

It would be risky to try anything before nightfall. Three kilometres away a crop-duster was spearing along low over a lucerne crop that had taken the fancy of a plague of crickets. He cut his run about three hundred metres from the house. The foaling mares moved uneasily.

I went inside to check my arsenal of contemporary weapons. We'd make a run for it.

I took a ladder and climbed up to the manhole. Willa stayed below to take the cache. An Anschutz .243 bolt action with a good German variable scope to the power of 12. With my own wildcat loads, it was accurate out to four hundred metres. A Holland and Holland side by side 12 gauge, an ancient and elegant gun for quail because I didn't want to load it with BB shot. The Browning 12 gauge automatic with extended magazine was a definite headhunting machine, but not much use over sixty metres.

But there was nothing to stop many people with powerful automatic weapons.

The Barrett .50 I left. It fired an armour-piercing shell that would go through the intended target and then through the walls of the neighbouring farmhouses. Not a good look. It had helped me survive on the beaches of Queensland with a nasty variety of bird smugglers, but here it was out.

I gave Willa the .22 after removing the silencer. It was a case of the more noise, the more confusing. I also gave her the Holland and Holland loaded with No. 4 shot. It was a beautifully balanced weapon, and with the two wide-open cylinders for barrels, there would be a wide spray at a comparatively close range.

I heard Josie's motorcycle take off. I had been too concerned with Willa's and my safety to think of her. I rushed outside with the glasses. The way Josie rode the cycle, there was no chance of catching her. I watched her progress. Would they let her pass?

Seeing the approaching motorbike before Josie saw him, the bloke to the south stepped from the car and opened his hood. She hadn't reached the main road. I yelled to Linda, who was close to the stables, 'What's Josie's mobile number?'

Linda yelled it—018 65934. I rushed to the phone in the kitchen. Dialled it. Sweated on an answer. If she made the main road before she answered, she would stop her bike next to the bastard to answer it. Pure convenience when being country friendly. There were several beats of time and I said to Willa. 'Put the shotguns in the car.'

Josie answered.

'Come back,' I said, fast and hard.

'She's turning,' Willa yelled from the window. 'The other car is following her. They'll come down here.'

I headed for the convertible as Willa slipped the guns into the passenger well.

The adrenalin hit me. Heading down the drive, I unhooked the canvas top and let it fall back. Space to manoeuvre when shooting from a vehicle is vital. Any spot-lighter after their fifty rabbits a night knows that.

I rocketed down the drive, stopped, ran to open the front gate. As I accelerated through, the gate swung back in front of me. I slammed through it, the hinges pulling from the rotten post. The gate stayed with me, a new emblem attached to the grill. I didn't care how professional these bastards were, they didn't have their weaponry. Josie raced past me as I pulled away from the centre of the track.

With my foot on the accelerator, I heaved up and doubled my other leg back against the seat so I was sitting on my heel, my pelvis against the wheel, giving me only straight-on control. I felt the elation there is in knowing you have a chance at outlasting a bucking horse. I had the Browning

in both hands, so when the car came over the
rise I was ready. There was a rapidly diminishing
two hundred metres between us. He peeled off a
few shots as I let him have it. His windscreen
blew into a glass cloud. His car was airborne off
the shoulder of the road. It went through the
fence and rolled into the paddock of Charlie
O'Brien's dairy farm.

I went after the second car. As soon as I came
over the rise towards him he slammed his car in
reverse, tried a reverse turn, misjudged the loose
dirt on the road, stalled, and I clipped him down
his right side the moment he got the car moving.
He accelerated backwards into a pine tree on the
corner. My front gate was spinning in the air and
I had to accelerate to miss it. I U-turned on the
main road and headed back. I looked at the
wreck. The driver was moving, but he wasn't
healthy. We wouldn't see him again today. His
head was shifting on the crumpled sill of the
door, his tongue hanging out. I stopped the car
to watch him. Slowly his tongue retreated and he
began waking up. At that moment I was experi-
encing an emotion we hide from ourselves: blood
triumph. I retrieved the gate and propped it high
in the back seat.

On the way back, Charlie O'Brien was out on
the road, a shotgun in his hands. I slowed down
to meet him.

'What the fuck is going on?' he asked.

I was bouncing with the full dose of adrenalin, my jaw shivering as I answered him. 'Charlie, there are some people trying to kill me,' I said.

'You're jokin',' he laughed, nodding to the wreck. 'I wouldn't've reckoned that.'

'I rang the cops,' he said, 'and the ambulance. He won't be killing anyone.'

'Can you keep me out of it?' I asked. 'I mean they're about 800 metres from my place. No need to bring me in. It's just a traffic accident really.'

Charlie laughed. He was keen to fool authority, like most farmers who had always been swept around by the whims of bureaucrats. 'What is it?' he asked. 'You pull off some sort of racing coup?' He hoped I had. It's the tough battlers who like to see the neighbours score a bit of success. It rubs off on them.

'Yeah,' I said. 'And the fucking bastards can't take it.'

'Hey,' he laughed. 'Can't take their own fuckin' medicine.'

Back at my front entrance, I propped the gate up and bound it to the post with yards of baling twine. It would last the use it would get over the next few weeks. At the house, it was obvious they weren't sure who would be appearing. Linda emerged from the stables, the Anschutz in her hand, Josie from the strip of box thorn close to the foaling paddock. I'd left the bank of thorn for cover from the prevailing winds from the south-west. Willa had stayed in the house with the

Holland and Holland. My glance swept the house and surrounds. I saw the foal was up and drinking. The mare was contented, so the milk was running.

At the house, Willa threw in the suitcases and Linda and Josie came up.

'We've got some respite,' I said.

Linda was angry. 'What the hell is going on?' Josie stood back a bit. She didn't want to know about it and was anxious to leave.

We turned when we heard the noise of the hoofs. The stallion, Realgar, came beating along the lane from the back paddock with a bunch of mares. Somehow he had made it over two fences to get to them during the night. Or someone making a reconnoitre from the north had left gates open.

He was a seventeen-hand horse and he was rearing and pawing the air, letting go a long stray kick occasionally at the feedboxes. He had caught the action, probably smelt the adrenalin on the breeze, and wanted to find the source. Triumph was coursing through his veins as he whirled around the mares. He was doing something better than racing; he wanted to make sure he would keep doing it.

I grabbed two bales of fresh scented lucerne hay and took them to the mares. I cut the baling twine and hurled biscuits of the stuff all along the lane. They settled down to this novelty, eating immediately. Finally the stallion consented to sniff the stuff. I looked him over. His legs, his side, up under the flanks. He was undamaged. He picked up a biscuit and stood magnificently, his head high, his nostrils wide and snorting and his muscles quivering like a war horse scenting battle.

He whirled suddenly and galloped back down the lane, the lucerne biscuit held high. The mares continued eating, so he came prancing back in an extended trot, the hoofs stretching well beyond his nose. A beautiful shoulder and a free-flowing action.

I left the horses reluctantly. They weren't going to help our present condition, but watching them kept the hollow sourness from my mind. The four of us went into the house and planned our action.

'I'm no part of any of this,' Linda said. 'Neither is Josie. I don't even want to know what it's about.' And she became more demanding. 'But are we going to be safe working around the farm?'

'They're only after us,' I said. 'But I don't think either of you should be around.'

Linda was standing with the palm of her hand on her hip, her slim body at an aggressive angle. Josie had her arms folded and was kicking at the gravel with her toe. She was ready to burst forth but she wouldn't until she knew the whole story. These were two women who knew the score.

'These people are following Willa and I because we're about to expose their business for what it is.'

Linda ignored this initial explanation. 'The two-year-olds are close to a race,' She said. I looked at her. She was certainly single-minded.

'I don't think it'll be safe here for a week or two,' I said.

'I'd like to take them across to Banfold's,' she said. 'I've got empty stables on the place there whenever I want them. The old bloke said it would do him good having horses in the stables again. Josie and I could work them there.'

'I suppose I can ask Charlie to feed up,' I said. I was counting on farmers being always ready to help out neighbours. That was as long as there was no feuding over water rights or access roads. 'Keep an eye on the foal. He can cover my place with binoculars from his kitchen. He'll know if there is anybody snooping about. And after today whoever's after us will need to recruit more people. Take them time.'

Willa got up to put on coffee. 'We can disappear in Melbourne,' she said. 'We're too obvious here. It's inviting trouble.'

Linda came down to the stables with me. She was unconcerned about everything that had happened this morning. She focused on what she knew and what she wanted. She wanted to race the two-year-olds soon. 'They'll be fit in a week or two, and they haven't shown a sign of shin soreness.'

I thought then that she was obsessive and a shade insensitive to the dangers we were in. But then the good trainers are obsessive. As long as the love of gambling doesn't have them manipulating their owners' horses for dreams of huge amounts of money.

'I don't want to know about this business of yours. I mean my . . . ' and she laughed charmingly, 'my life will still go on, even if yours doesn't. I'd like to take the horses over this evening.' She looked up at me sharply, a level gaze met mine. Her obvious determination gave me faith in her. 'We only need to come to some arrangement.'

'Okay,' I said. She showed an expertise around horses that impressed me. She had trained everything from show-jumpers to polo ponies and had always wanted to get her hands on some good thoroughbreds to train. She had obviously fallen on her feet with me.

'I've got my owner-trainer's licence,' she said. The smile was wide and triumphant.

'When?' I asked.

She looked at me. 'You don't remember the reference you gave me?' I did remember, but I had also thought she'd be up against it, not too many women were allowed licences by the Victorian Racing Club. 'Banfold gave me one, too,' she said. That explained it. Banfold had been one of the most revered racing men in the state.

'You have plenty of bloody initiative,' I said, grinning at her. She pulled lease papers from her pocket. 'When you took on this job, I thought you'd be away for a while,' she said. 'I meant to ask you to sign them before.' She shrugged. 'I mean, it seems you're not going to be able to put your mind to things.'

This would mean I'd only receive a third of the winnings instead of all of it. That's the regular arrangement when leasing horses. The owner doesn't pay the trainer and so his equity dwindles to one-third. It seems an unfair system until you realise how risky it is to train a horse. Very few horses win. Of the twenty thousand odd born in Australia each year, only about five per cent of those get to win one race, and of those wins, the vast majority are on bush tracks.

Linda had a more ambitious system, though— for an owner-trainer, that is. 'You pay me to train,' she said, 'and I take thirty per cent of the winnings.' It was a terrific deal for her. She had money for the best food and chemicals for the horses, and she could make more than thirty per cent if she bet on her horse when she knew it was a sure thing. She could also keep the odds high by not telling me when she was setting it to win. She had the instinct of a winner. The big trainers who found they had a champion on the way simply demanded an owner's share. She knew she had me at a time of trouble and that my priority at the moment was my life.

I took the leases over to the boot of the convertible and signed them on the metal.

'It needs to be witnessed,' she said.

'Have Willa do it.'

'When you come up, right?'

'Yeah.'

She ran out of the garage giving cries of delight. I followed her. She turned and gave me an ambiguous look as she walked up the path. Her body would have that tiny perfection, I thought, tiny waist, curving hips, slender legs. I hadn't seen her in anything but jeans.

'You'll need to give them some work through the barriers,' I called after her.

I had kept control of my lusts at the farm. I knew myself well enough to know I would never put the hard word on Linda or Josie. But I never lied to myself. They would be sweet women.

Inside, I rang Max Abrahams. He was a student of Middle Eastern politics. A former lecturer in the subject, he was now something of a guru for the small magazines and the occasional radio program. One of the good things about being a muckraking journalist is that you have access to the best information. We hear or read an individual who appears to have that extra edge on the other specialists in his subject, and from then on we go to him for guidance and information. Max was one of the best.

'Hey, comrade,' he said. He thought I was a pinko lefty and it amused him to address me in

that style. I'm actually a conservative. In a way.
I want the planet to remain as is, none of the
very dramatic changes that have appeared on
the horizon. I regard as radical those capitalists
who, despite the evidence, feel the world can
support their greed without depletions of the
environment. They, on the other hand, think it's
radicals who want to deprive them of their right
to ravage the earth. And it was becoming increasingly obvious to me that some of their breed were
trying to kill Willa and me. Indeed, anyone who
threatened their little scams.

Max was out of favour with his academic colleagues because he applied his knowledge and
experience of human weaknesses to his interpre-
tations of Middle Eastern events. He was envied
and hated because his long range forecasts were
more often right than wrong, and because he had
the temerity to attempt a forecast. He loved
Freud and knew that the unconscious darkness
was behind the motivations of the Muslim leaders—all leaders, in fact, although those in the
West had heard of Freud and tempered their lusts
accordingly.

After a suitable amount of banter, I said, 'Tell
me what's happening to Israel this week.'

'Big news,' he answered.

'Isn't it always?'

'Israel is trying to finesse an agreement on the
Golan Heights. It also wants the part of Jerusalem
that is going to really upset Syria.'

'So what's changed?'

'It means most of the peace agreement is about to be suspended.'

'Max, tell me who would be involved in the terrorism that might result from that.'

'Looking at the Syrians, it would be the Hamas, I suppose—at least their armed wing, the Qassam Brigades. They're the ones into suicide bombing. They've been trying to disrupt any links that might be forming between Israel and the PLO. Why do you want to know?'

'It seems our burning ship had chemicals bound for Syria.'

'Have to go in through one of Lebanon's ports. Wouldn't be hard, though. What sort of chemicals?'

'I'm getting them tested.'

'I'd like to know.'

'Do you think it's odd they would be buying chemical weapons from us?'

Max was silent for a moment. It was a new one on him. 'It pulls you up, put like that. But there's no reason at all why they wouldn't. Syria bought them from South Africa, the French. Why not buy from us? It's only another week's shipping time, and it's probably safer.

'It's incredible that our pollies didn't ever get the message on chemicals. Stupid pricks. Civilised countries have their chemicals thirty miles from their population centres,' he said referring to the burning ship.

'They're going to pay this time,' I said.

I told Max I'd get back to him and hung up. Willa had been listening. 'Volatile stuff,' I commented.

'I don't believe it,' she said. Here we are supplying the worst with the worst.'

I couldn't get much out of Willa for the rest of the day. Linda took the two-year-olds over to Banfold's place. Apple didn't like the idea of the float and I didn't feel like hounding him in, so I put him in the round yard, backed the float up, lowered the ramp and put a bucket of oats in the float. I watched him from the verandah with Linda. He thumped on the ramp a few times, and then went up to eat. We went down then and I tied him in. Art Shy had been in and out of the float already and he was eager to get in. He liked any sort of novelty.

Linda left, saying she'd be back for feed time, and I watched the float moving against the horizon beyond the lake as it headed south to Banfold's.

'This is getting too much for me,' Willa said when I entered the house.

I watched her as she shifted around the living-room. She examined the polished wood floor, the lake through the window, the horses milling in the lucerne paddock. 'Tell me about it,' I said.

'It's all reaching so far. I thought it was going to be a case of exposing a powerful chemical company, not international arms dealing. How do we expect to resolve it?'

'A little bit at a time,' I said. 'We fix our end. The things that affect us here.'

She settled down after that, but then she walked around the phone a few times as if she wanted to ring someone. 'You can ring anyone you like,' I said. 'Specially if they can help us now.'

Linda was back several hours later. 'The horses were fine,' she said. 'Old Banfold is spoiling them already. Giving them sugar.'

'Not too much of that,' I said.

She laughed. 'He wants me to sweat the horses,' she said. 'He has no idea about modern training methods. He said I should put four rugs on them and trot them around. Get the excess fluid out of them.'

Linda thought she would stay over for the night. Josie said she had relatives she'd stay with in town for a few days.

I was asleep before nine o'clock. The two women were still up.

Around one a.m. I woke to someone moving around the bedroom. I thought it was Willa. It was Linda. She was still dressed.

'I couldn't sleep,' she said.

'Mmm.'

'I've been watching the late news.'

'Oh yeah.'

'What's going on?' she asked. 'You have a part in this?'

'What did they say is going on?'

'That the ship is burning again.' She walked around the bed and looked at an unsigned Streeton on the wall. A boy fishing in a deep well.

'I didn't know it had stopped.'

'They thought it had. Now they've run out of foam again.'

'Well, they've never prepared for emergencies in this state.'

'They say it's alright, though.'

'What's alright?'

'It's not polluting anything.' She had finally wandered to the bed and was just standing there looking down at me.

'A ship burning for a few days has to be polluting something,' I said.

'There are some dead birds, but they say that was expected. It won't be too many.'

There was an expectant air about her. 'You don't have to, you know,' I said.

'I know,' she said.

I ran my hand around the back of her leg. She unbuckled her jeans and stepped out of them. 'Would this upset anything between you and Willa?'

'Not really.'

She knelt down and kissed me. The feeling that swept over me was that everything was possible and everything I might do was alright. I knew enough to know it never is, but the circumstances were quietly outrageous and they excited me.

'Stand up,' I said as I swung my legs out of bed. Her skin was like glossy paper. 'Very nice,' I said involuntarily, and kissed her stomach. 'Oh God,' she said. I turned her round as she stepped from her clothes. Her body was strong and supple, her legs wide.

Her breasts were surprisingly soft. I thought they would be as hard as her body. I picked her up and placed her on the bed. She whispered, 'Fuck me, please, fuck me.' I wondered if her voice could be heard throughout the house. Her slim legs gripped me hard, urging me.

As she was leaving the room, she whispered, 'Remember, I did this after you gave me the horses.' Moments later I was asleep again.

Willa was in my bed when I woke. 'You are a bastard,' she said. 'You fucked her, didn't you?'

'Yes,' I said.

'You really are filth,' she said. It seemed that whatever filth I represented, she wasn't repelled by it. We caressed each other as if she hadn't accused me of a thing. Later she moved quickly, her moistness hot and bottomless. Her shaking breasts were smooth and vulnerable. Very few are chosen for the sexual big time. I was beginning to think maybe I was one of them.

Later she said, 'Do you fuck her all the time?' It was said cavalierly, but that denied the interest she showed.

'No,' I said, 'it was the first time.'

Eleven

I woke in an empty bed. I was tempted to contemplate the previous night's performances but
that would have led in only one direction. I
needed to get up. I was feeling fresh, as if life
was a novelty. The morning had a sharpness to it,
given an edge by danger and sex.

I walked around the kitchen in the dark preparing breakfast. By chance, I had been allowed
to live a life. Millions of shots from my parents'
loins hadn't. I dwelt on that thought for a while.
It gave me some happiness.

From the windows I would see the shadows of
anyone moving outside. The Browning automatic
was beside me at the stove. If anyone burst in, I
wouldn't be the only one to die. I knocked on
the window and Sacco appeared in the courtyard,
emerging from the garage where he was bedded
down. If anyone had been out there he would
have alerted us.

I wasn't worried about being silhouetted as I
moved around the kitchen. The glow from the hot
plate as I cooked the new 'lean' eggs and crisped
the bacon was diffused by the pan.

The coffee was marvellous. I wanted a bottomless cup. I began to feel the false confidence that

comes with feelings of immortality. It happens rarely and I immediately suspect it, but that didn't mean I couldn't enjoy some of it, no matter that it might have overtones of the psychotic. I took trays of eggs and hot buttered toast and coffee into Willa and Linda. Willa rose on one elbow, looking at me strangely, as if she hadn't seen me before. Was she one of those woman who need to be wooed afresh each day? Or did she wonder if she suspected she had been been taken advantage of? 'Thanks,' she said, sitting up, 'leave it on the chair.'

'Has to be eaten hot,' I said.

'Is everything alright?' she asked, turning in the bed.

'Don't know,' I said. 'It feels alright.'

'Have you checked?'

'No,' I said.

'That's strange', she said, 'that you feel it's alright. Whenever I feel like that, I'm wrong.'

'Yeah,' I said.

'Yeah, what?' she asked as I walked back to the kitchen.

In the other bedroom, Linda was dragging on her jeans. When she saw the tray, she said, 'I'll eat in the kitchen.'

I slipped her plate into the warming drawer, poured some more coffee and turned on the television.

The burning ship had the media confused. The screen showed shots of it as it rested in the sand off St Kilda beach, but the reporters weren't following the obvious leads. There were no serious questions about how it had happened. The journalists simply reported that the causes were being left to official investigation. None of the networks carried even a hint of the depth of the conspiracy surrounding the burning ship.

Linda walked into the kitchen. She grinned at me as she sat down and crossed her legs. 'Have a good night?' she asked. There was a promise of more.

'Relatively speaking,' I said. I felt like touching her, stroking the glossy skin.

'I'm going over to Banfold's. Do Art Shy and Apple first. I'm meeting Josie over there.'

'Don't stop for anyone on the road,' I said. 'I'll come down to the gate with you. Open it for you.' I pointed to the shotgun, as a reminder of everything.

'Do you think so?' she said, meaning is it necessary?

'I'm just careful.'

Outside the air was still, with a crispness that felt like frost. The gun was warm in my hand, having absorbed some warmth from the stove. The barrel was slightly slicked with oil. Sacco joined us before we left the front garden. He knew when anything moved close to the house and he was totally unworried. If there had been strange scents drifting in the air, he'd have stopped every few metres, one front leg lifted and his nose high in the air. If he couldn't identify a smell, he would have looked anxiously around, switching to hunting by sight.

While Linda took the two training pads from the tackroom, I looked down towards the water. Nothing stirred anywhere. The light spilling from the room attracted some of the mares in the lucerne paddock and they came up to look. Linda was in the habit of handing out a few handfuls of oats in the early morning, so they expected something whenever she was around.

I sat in the back of her old ute as we headed down towards the gate. I tried to look beyond the pool of the headlights on the black dirt of the track. Sacco ran beside the vehicle. I jumped out and opened the gate, walked around while she drove through, closed it, and walked down to the lake's edge. Sacco put up a large quoll, but it moved like lightning. I only identified him as the native cat when I saw a flash of the large white spots on his side. I called Sacco back. He was trembling with suppressed hunting lust. I walked around the small boulders that had been placed at the lake's edge to stop wave erosion during the winter rains.

I walked slowly, Sacco darting back and forth, taking all the water smells past his nasal discriminators at terrific speed. I watched Linda's lights find the main road, and soon she had disappeared over the dawn horizon towards the town.

I walked up the lane made to separate the stallion and the mares coming into season in the spring. The ground was firm there and the grass thick. I stayed down at the mares' drink trough for a while, listening to the farm. It was around six a.m., the first pink fingers moving across the sky.

I heard a motor cough. It came across the water of the lake in the still air. It was some kilometres away on the main road. It caught the second time, and I heard its muffled sound as it moved onto the road. I knew the sound of every neighbour's vehicle. All the farmers around here had V8s and diesels. This was a strange motor. There were no lights, but the engine sound was heading north. The house had been watched all night.

I walked to the stables and climbed into the rafters. From under one of the eaves I took a paper-wrapped parcel. The paper was oil-stained. I stripped it away and unwrapped the cloth. There was one of the ugliest handguns ever made. The Glock 40. Despite the looks, it was beautifully balanced, and was one of the toughest and most efficient handguns around. It had accounted for some deaths on a previous job in Far North Queensland and its slug signature was no doubt recorded, but I wanted to use it again. Seventeen shots in the magazine, very little recoil, and superb accuracy for a handgun. I loaded it and slipped it through my belt under my loose shirt.

Willa was watching the television when I came into the house. She was in a robe and her legs flashed as she uncrossed them and stood up. 'I don't believe how incompetent they are,' she said, outraged the early morning programs had no new information.

'Who's interested?' I said. 'No one wants telling detail unless it affects them directly. They just want the story.'

'Thanks for breakfast,' she said, quickly. 'You mean the myth as moulded by network news.'

'The media can't do anything more,' I said. 'No way in hell. No chemical tests have been done, and they're frightened of libelling the chemical owners, the shipping owners, or anyone else.'

'I don't like it here. There's no real sense of what's going on. We're too far away.'

'You mean you think you can find out when you're closer to the city; where it's at, baby,' I teased in sixties West Coast vernacular.

'Something like that,' she said.

'Our mate Evans is about thirty kilometres from here. He's got a property. I think we should pay him a visit.'

'How do you know he's there?' She rubbed the palm of one hand, her red nails an elegant contrast against her white skin. She leaned back against the kitchen bench, one knee revealed.

'I don't, but my guess is he'll be down for the weekend. That's why people like him have country properties.'

I guessed Evans would tire of the anxiety that comes when a person responsible for some criminal act knows he is close to exposure. First, he's ready for them. He knows he's okay, and he'll bluster through. Then he changes his mind and decides to have his company spokespeople deal with it. Then, after a few restless nights, he feels he's worked hard over the three months since his last holiday and he should have another brief period of relaxation. This would bring him to his racehorse stud on the plains of the Western District, about a half hour's drive from where we were.

The best time to track him was after dinner. The big houses of any district, surrounded as they are by thousands of hectares of land, are usually well lit up at night, blinds undrawn, because there are no close neighbours to spy upon them. Little do their occupants know.

During the day I made sure the mills were working and that the brood mares had access to the lucerne paddock. When we did leave, I wanted to feel the farm would be capable of running itself for a few days. Shy Bride's foal was strong on its feet now and occasionally tried to reach the oats I placed on the ground. The foal looked at its mother, not comprehending why she couldn't nibble close to the ground like her. She staggered a bit, her legs splayed, and then, showing impatience, pushed at her mother with her head. Eventually the foal settled down in the lucerne paddock where she could nibble the flowering heads.

On the late news there was a short grab of a fireman on the job. He was assailed by reporters as he stepped off a tug, and his edgy weariness was apparent. His hero mask was down. He had forgotten that all comments to the press had to come from senior spokespeople. 'It's a weird fire,' he said. 'It keeps burning under foam. It's even burning under the surface.'

Willa gazed at the burning ship as a helicopter circled it to the west. 'What I want to know', she said, 'is how it caught fire in the first place.'

'Chemicals mixing,' I said. 'It happens all the time.'

'It would have to be negligence, criminal negligence.'

'Perhaps someone didn't know the real cargo. Would they tell the crew they were carrying different chemicals than those recorded on the manifest?' I swung back and forth in the chair. The lake down the slope behind me was shivering in the light from the moon.

We took to the trail bike about eleven p.m., dragging it under the fence into a neighbour's paddock and exiting from there to the north. We stuck to the backroads and luckily the bike's exhaust wasn't one of those straight-out affairs fancied by scramblers and mud hounds. We could actually hear each other if we yelled hard enough.

We made a complete circle of the Evans stud. It was pretty much bare of timber. Through the glasses, the homestead could be seen to have a lush garden surrounded by high gums.

The best observation point was to the east of the house on a hill, about one hundred and twenty metres high and topped by a rocky outcrop. We laid the bike down in a small gully and began the climb. I took the Glock and Willa the Ruger. She slipped it under her belt like an old hand. It was amazing the way she had adapted to the excitements. It was as if she had always had a thirst for questionable action.

Even though we were fit, the steepness pulled at unused muscles. About a thirty metres from the rocks I heard voices. Staring at the silhouetted rock, I also made out half a dozen curious cattle who had ambled up to see what was going on. They were about fifteen metres from the top. They were unaware of us.

'What now?' Willa asked.

'We wait for a while,' I whispered.

'They'll find us,' she said.

'They're not looking for us.'

I heard the clink of a shovel on rock. One of the bullocks moved back.

'Christ,' Willa whispered. 'What's going on?'

'Stay here,' I said. 'I'm going for a look.'

'What about the cows?'

'They're harmless,' I said.

I moved forward on my belly. Closer, I heard
the yap of a dog, and someone cuffed it. They
didn't want to be heard, either. I reached a large
basalt outcrop, as bulky and well formed as a
work by the English sculptor who made smaller
rocks out of larger rocks.

It was a bizarre sight. We had stumbled on two
poachers. They had half a dozen Jack Russell
terriers on leads and they were sending them
down fox burrows. They had several foxes
skinned, the glistening bodies looking no larger
than those of hares. The Jack Russells were not
interested in anything but the kill.

A new dog was selected for a burrow. The exits
were netted, the nets loose so that a retreating
fox would lose himself in the folds. The dog flew
down the burrow. There were muffled snarls and
yapping and then sounds of a dog gagged by fur.
Within moments the fox hit a net. It didn't make
a sound. It was promptly dispatched with a base-
ball bat. Nothing was to hole the skin. A couple
of pea rifles were up against a rock, but they were
only along to give a feeling of security or to shoot
a reluctant fox in the ear.

The two men were overcome with their luck
or their daring. They went about their work
chuckling, their quick movements showing suppressed glee.

I looked down at the homestead. It was dark,
but there was a light in a window at the east wing
of the place. Nothing that looked like a welcom-

ing for the owner. Wealthy individuals like Evans wouldn't arrive anywhere without creating their own noisy light show. They always had to feel they had *arrived*.

'What the fuck are you doing here?' The two fox hunters were behind me, their guns pointing down around my knees. They were casual with them. They could always deny having me at gunpoint.

'Same as you,' I said.

'Bullshit,' the shorter dumpy one said.

'Looks like he's from the house,' the taller one said.

I showed the Glock. 'What's this look like? Look like I'm from the house?' I turned and looked down at the house to remind them of what I was doing, also giving them a chance to move on me if they wanted.

'So, what's it about?' the short one said. They moved in the night, knew the sort of work undertaken at such a time.

'The new owner,' I said. 'Evans. He ripped me off. I'm bleeding.'

The newly skinned fox twitched a little too much and the tall bloke whacked it with a bat. 'Bloody cruel that,' the short bloke said, looking away from me. 'That fuckin' dork,' he added, spitting, nodding down to the house. 'Everyone's rippin' him off here. Stud master's servin' his mates' mares. Manager's even knockin' off his hay, sellin' local.'

I grinned at them. 'You blokes work f'r'im?'

'Nah, 'eard his flash mates a'gunna fox 'unt t'morra. Gettin' in first, like.'

'Down is he?'

'First thing t'morra. Like, 'e's gunna stock-take.' He started to laugh.

The tall bloke walked back to where the dogs were tied. 'Teaser ain't been down. We got fuckin' work to do.'

'You put him down,' Shorty said, 'I'll salt the hides, pack'em down.'

I started walking down the hill, 'Yeah, see ya, you guys.'

'Yeah, right,' Shorty said.

The cattle shifted away uncomfortably into the darker than dark. In the still air I heard the tall bloke say, 'He's got a gun, so he's one of those undercover fuckin' copper pricks. Evans'll go like fuckin' Bondy.'

Willa emerged beside me and we headed down to the bike on the track.

'Easy, wasn't it?' Willa said. 'I thought I was going to have to rescue you.' I laughed and kissed her. I had never felt like I'd had a partner.

'We'll come back for the fox hunt tomorrow,' I said.

'Don't we have to be invited?'

'The locals always are. We'll fit in. They love audiences anyway.'

Around the front of the property on the metal road there was a dark gleam of a car about four hundred metres off the gate to the homestead. 'We're not the only ones watching here,' I said, and then I felt the ticking of fear deep inside me. A black Mercedes. It was us they were watching? But who? The black Merc would not only be spotted around here, it would be remembered. There was a wild card in this bloody pack. I didn't like it. I liked predictability in the opposition; that's where I gained the edge.

We headed back to the farm. It was a beautiful night, the wind brisk and exhilarating on our faces. In the moonlight the country was visible to the horizon. At Charlie O'Brien's, I slid the bike to a stop. The light was on in his kitchen and he was at the door in a second. 'Charlie,' I said, 'anyone been down the road?'

'Not a fuckin' soul since you went out,' he said. 'Been nothin' around tonight,' and he meant within seven or eight kilometres, because that's how sound carries on a night like this. When his eyes grew accustomed to the light, he saw Willa. 'Sorry about the language,' he said, nodding to her in what I could only call deference. I would never have suspected he had it in him.

'Don't worry,' Willa said. 'I'd use the same language to describe the people we're concerned about it.'

We tooled slowly along the track to the house, a few water birds rushing across the water to avoid the noise. 'You were right,' Willa whispered to me as I cut the motor. 'We're not going to be attacked here. It's a safe place.' She stepped off the bike and took my hand. She moved in against me. The movement was forward, her body pliant as if she might melt against me. It was a new sensation. Extreme acceptance. Mine. She led me down to the treeline. She moved back against the trunk of a gum, unbuttoning her shirt. In the moonlight, her skin was as smooth and cool as marble. I moved my lips over her, opening her jeans, a terrible, carnal lust taking me.

I took the jeans to her ankles, licking her knees, feeling the heat of her skin. I pulled her shoes off and she stood on her jeans. For a moment I thought, Jesus, I'm too awkward for her, and then I saw her smooth white bottom against the trunk of the tree, and nothing mattered anymore.

Twelve

In the morning we waited by a small creek that crossed the road to Evans's place for about half an hour, watching the expensive cars and horse trailers arriving. The weather was unseasonably hot. As we waited, we heard on the radio that the three survivors had died. They hadn't made it through the crucial third and fourth days. It was after that length of time the body dysfunctioned badly, creating the vast swellings that closed off the organs from efficient bodily administrations. Drugs could only do so much. I saw the bandaged head again, pathetic in its vulnerability. Behind it, the mind so eager for life. I had felt his need to live.

Watching the cars pass down the road, Willa recognised faces as the cars slowed for the turn, said she knew too many people to go along with me. I felt she'd be disguised if she let her hair swing down and applied make-up. 'Your hair is so thick, you can hide in it. Nobody's going to look at you on the pillion of a trail bike.' I had taken the Ruger from her. If Evans made any move against us, I wanted to be able to finish him, discreetly. I'd given her the Glock. She wiped the oil off it with tissue and made a space for it in her rather large purse, dangling from her wrist.

An hour later we trailed in behind a few locals in their utes. The buffalo lawn at the front of the house was the scene of general confusion. Saddled horses were milling, and several scarlet coats mixed with the black coats of the rest of the jodhpured crew. Stirrup cup was being ladled out to inspire the timid jumpers. I caught the sexuality of the meet. It was in the movements, the animal scent, and the flirting from behind tight, novel costumes. There were also some very fit horses here, the last rib just showing through their coats, their bellies lean but not tucked up.

A handsome woman with a 'jolly good' sort of voice walked to the photographer quite close to us. 'It's marvellous having the press here. Usually it's all so one-sided. Foxes are such a nuisance, you know.' She smiled. 'Even if it is the foreign press, we do appreciate it.' The photographer spoke to her in French and then changed to a halting English. 'It is pleasure to be here. Very, aaah, very exciting.'

Willa said, 'He speaks French with a Parisian accent.' It was handy having a companion with a rounded education. I looked at the photographer's companion. He had a good suede leather coat. He was tall and very alert. He was aware of us although he was watching the steps of the homestead. 'Can you speak to them?' I asked Willa.

She walked over, smiled and began a conversation in rapid French. The two men were uneasy at first, but then the taller one became voluble.

I sat on the seat of the bike, watching the scene in front of me. Evans hadn't fronted yet, but a horse was brought to the stairs for him to mount. A beautiful-looking beast. It was big, with good bone. Probably a warm blood crossed with a thoroughbred——ride like a rocking armchair.

A truck lumbered up the drive filled with noisy, excited fox hounds as Willa returned. 'They're covering this for *Le Monde*.'

'What?' I didn't believe it. I watched them walk back to their car——a black Merc.

'They're covering this hunt as one of the English idiosyncrasies that have hung over from Australia's colonial days. They're doing a story on the few families who have owned the land from the time of white settlement.'

'It's bloody strange,' I said.

'You could be paranoid on this one,' she said.

'*Le Monde* has no photographs in its pages,' I said. 'Not of the features kind.'

Willa laughed. 'So they're a couple of con men.' As she spoke, she pointed out the Master of the Hounds.

He was wearing a red coat, posing for the *Le Monde* photographer by pursing his lips to one of the fox hounds, through the side of the cage on the tray of the truck. He'd been a Test cricketer of some renown who had also been the first entrepreneur to benefit from the mini-skirt craze that hit Australia in the sixties.

Now he was an athletic fifty-year-old who still wanted his body to give him sensations that are usually lost by most people in their fading youth. I'd spoken to a friend who had profiled him for the *Australian* colour magazine. To still have the desire was impressive. But the fox hound he was offering to kiss was not impressed. It growled and snapped at him in a shocking manner. 'Fuck you,' Dave Birdley screamed back at the dog in the same pitch. The hound's face was eager for a challenge. He would have liked the Master of the Hounds to be the fox. Birdley raised a crop at the animal and it didn't back off, growling deeply with only a shiver of his dewlaps. A marvellous photo opportunity for *Le Monde*.

Finally Evans appeared on the high verandah and took the steps down to mount his horse. He was a thick little person. You may have thought of him as chubby except he moved without any awkwardness. He was fair-haired with an olive skin. His broad cheeks seemed to force themselves out from beneath his hunting cap. If he removed the hunting cap, the rest of his head might just expand to balance the cheeks.

I asked one of the bystanders where the hunt was headed. He pointed to a far treeline along the southern end of the property, and then west. Finally he pointed somewhere behind the house, and finished up on the hills behind the place,

where we had been the night before. He said they
would be in the field for approximately three
hours. Spectators, like us, were not to get in the
way of the hunt, but could observe from strategic
points around the course.

'What if the fox doesn't run the course
proper?' I asked.

'Then', he smiled, 'a deviation is required. It
will be up to the Master of the Hunt.' He nodded
towards Evans.

At that moment, the hounds were loosed from
the truck. They were in action in an instant, and
several huntsmen gave the dogs some discipline
by unhooking their stirrup leathers, reversing
them, and giving several reprobate hounds a bit
of carry on.

The horn sounded, a bit like a strangled bugle,
and the riders began moving off, the hounds at
the heels of the Master of the Hounds. The riders
trotted along behind the Master of the Hunt in
their various degrees of seniority. Some very
small children who were being led by their parents brought up the rear.

The spectators had to head for their various
posts well away from where the action was. They
had in fact been given positions that would cover
the foxes' escape routes along low, unseen
ground. We followed along.

'Keep an eye on the *Le Monde* pair,' I said to
Willa. 'I want to know what they're up to.'

Several kilometres away, down one of the dirt roads, we pulled off with the others and settled down to watch. I saw the face of one of my companions of the night before give me a wink from the driver's side window of a battered old ute.

I left the bike to speak to him. Willa was about to come over, but hesitated and then walked back to sit on the bike. There were people with whom she simply didn't wish to speak. That's why people like me know a great deal more about how things happen than people like her. It was why people like Willa hire people like me.

'Are there any foxes left?' I said nodding out to the paddock where the hunters were strung out over several hundred metres as they waited for their hounds to begin their baying run.

'Doubt it, mate,' he said. 'Might put somethin' up along the old creek.'

I raised the glasses to watch the lead riders. Two of them were in top hats. 'I gave the glasses to Shorty. 'What are the top hats all about,' I said.

'Coupla Jew boy mates of Evans's,' Shorty said. I had forgotten the casual racism of the country. Lately I had only mixed with people who knew how to hide it.

'Yeah?' I said.

'Yeah, they reckon they charge 'em three times the real rate t' join.'

'So what happens if a fox takes off into the next-door property?'

'It won't.'

'How come?'

'We give Jocko a fox carcase this mornin'. He dragged it north along the creek, right. They'll git goin' when they 'it the creek.'

'Jocko a member of the hunt club?'

'Yeah.'

'See ya round, then.' I walked back to Willa.

'We'll front Evans when he gets back to the house,' I said.

'What are we going to say?'

'My guess is he's behind all the shit that's coming down. So we'll tell him to call off the dogs. He'll see we can get to him much more easily than he can to us.'

Being an observer was revealing. I witnessed the foolhardy courage of some of the hunters. In a well-organised fashion that I felt would have been frowned on by the English hunt clubs, jumps had been arranged along the course. Barbed wire fences had their strands bound together with rolls of hessian, so the horses wouldn't be injured. Several hunters showed their horses bare wire and then turned to take the fences in full flight, the barbs uncovered.

Along the timber of a dry creek the hounds picked up the scent and began baying. The hunting horn sounded out and the chase was on. It was something of a catastrophe. Riders were pitched off almost immediately. Horses baulked at fallen tree trunks, their riders travelling in marvellous, arcing high dives to drum hard earth.

The spectators also broke formation. They wanted to be in on the kill as well. Willa and I had the best conveyance to do this. I headed up the hill we had explored last night. Willa was laughing, her arms firmly around my waist and her mouth close to my ear. 'No wonder it's so popular,' she yelled. 'Everyone is laughing at everyone else.'

'Except the fox,' I yelled back. A tiny fox had broken cover and was hairing up the hill towards the burrows that had been raided last night. He was four hundred metres in front of the pack of hounds and they didn't look like they would gain on him. Evans broke away from the other huntspeople. It looked as if he wanted to run the creature down and kill it all by himself. I thought of the burning girl on the shattered road, the soldiers immobile, not knowing what had been done in their name.

We were approaching the hill at right angles from Evans. I throttled back so the fox wouldn't have to contend with another sound approaching. The fox didn't hesitate. He flew into the rocky corridors at the very peak of the hill and fled down the other side, out of sight of Evans and the hounds. I laughed aloud. It had won, today.

The fox's scent would also be lost to dogs around the dens. Aaah, what a subtle little fox. It risked death to escape cleanly. He could have

holed up in an untouched den, but he obviously
knew they weren't safe from dogs. Evans, presuming the creature would only hide in a den,
pulled his horse up at the rocky outcrop. He
dropped his reins and ran into the rocks with,
shit, I couldn't believe it, a handgun. He was
obviously the Ruler of the Hunt.

The Master of the Hounds—the cricketer—
arrived next, followed by three or four huntsmen,
and they left their horses and ran into the rocky
outcrop. The others were still three or four minutes behind. The horses stood unattended, their
flanks shivering, blowing loudly, their noses flared
and pink. We left the motorbike on the opposite
side of the rocky outcrop. Behind us the *Le Monde*
team was heading up the hill, the photographer
leaning out the window of the Merc now with a
video camera.

The cricketer also had a handgun and they
were all totally exhilarated by the chase, jumping
around on the rocks, laughing, looking for the
entrances to the den. 'We need that bloody little
dog of yours, Jocko,' Evans said. 'Put him down
the burrow.' The top hats of the two Jewish riders
appeared over the rock, silhouetted against the
sky. The cricketer yelled, 'Hey, look what we've
got here,' and mockingly aimed his handgun at
the hats.

'Jesus, Dave,' Evans said. 'Don't do that.' Dave
winked and lowered his weapon. The two top hats
rode into the amphitheatre of rock.

Evans saw me then. 'Who the fuck are you?'
Then his eyes flickered as he refocused on Willa
behind me. His manner changed abruptly. I
turned around. Willa had flicked out her hair and
taken off her sunglasses. She ignored Evans, walking around the burrows just as the hounds
arrived. The poor fat dogs were exhausted. They
made some pretence of excitement at the
entrances to the comprehensive den network, but
one or two lay down immediately on arrival.

The sound of a shot was painful, the explosion
out of all proportion to the calibre because we
were enclosed by rock. One of the top-hatted
blokes toppled from his horse. I looked at the
cricketer, but he showed me empty palms.

Willa was the first to the victim. I saw his hat
lying with a ragged brim. He had been shot in
the side of his head. His dead arm began to shake.
His horse skittered sideways, a leg disappearing
down a burrow and snapping. The horse began to
flounder. Jocko walked to its head and, the
moment it stilled, put a bullet in the centre of
its forehead about five centimetres above the
eyes. It flopped on its side, its huge sigh sounded
like relief.

Evans said abruptly, 'Okay, who shot him?' He
wanted this over quickly.

Jocko swung open his revolver. 'Only one shot
from here.'

The cricketer pulled out his weapon and laid
it on the rock in front of him. Two other riders

pulled out their weapons and proffered them. The remaining top hat was incredulous, but he was pulling himself together remarkably. He looked down at his former companion, looked around at the weaponry and decided to leave the scene. Throwing a keen glance at all of us, he walked out of the amphitheatre, leaving his horse.

Evans called for a phone from one of the cars and rang the police. 'Keep everyone out,' he said. In fact, no other huntspeople or spectators had entered. He walked over to me.

'Who are you?' he repeated.

'Jack Speerman,' I said.

His eyes changed. From a slight but querulous bewilderment, they began to turn nasty. 'Just who do you think you are, coming up here?' he whispered vehemently.

'I'm somebody you've been trying to kill,' I said in a normal pitch. 'I don't fuckin' appreciate it, mate.' I grabbed him by the front of his belt so he couldn't leave. 'You send your arseholes after me again', I said, 'and I'll come for you.' I longed to be able to drop him here. If he'd still had his gun in his hand, it may have been possible: self-defence. I let go of his belt. He let me see the careless possibilities in his eyes. 'Stay around. We'll take care of you,' he said.

'Is this you?' he said loudly, pointing to the body, meaning did you do this?

'No,' I said. 'I thought it was one of your anti-Semitic mates.' He walked away, asking everyone to wait for the police on the lawn of the homestead.

Willa walked up to me. 'I don't suppose you managed to do this?' she asked. She was only half-joking.

'It came from the rocks behind us,' I said. I retraced the way we had come in, walked around the sloping rocks, and saw an easy way up. I didn't want to leave fingerprints on the shiny rock, so I placed only my knuckles on the rock as I went up. No matter I was going up after the killing, someone would eventually want to link my prints to it. Willa came up behind me.

We looked down on the murder scene. From six metres up it was filmic. The dead horse had centre stage, and for photographic purposes, the murdered man could easily have been a fallen rider. Evans was stopping people leaving the entrance to the amphitheatre. A few he had missed were walking away. The furthest away were the *Le Monde* team, moving fast, really, but chatting away as though they had no real connection with what had happened behind them. I watched the photographer take a shot of a horse cantering heavily past him to the top of the hill. Suddenly, I wanted to run after them and bring them back. I handed the racing glasses to Willa and asked her to watch them.

I backed away from the edge of the rock. A video camera had fallen into a crevice. I tried to retrieve it, but my arm was nowhere near long enough. I debated whether I should use a looped rein from a bridle to get it. I decided I didn't want anyone else to know it was there. We'd be back for it later. If they had shot film, it would at least reveal the killers' interests, the individuals they were covering.

Thirteen

The police car arrived, spraying grass and dirt as they negotiated the steep rise. The two cops thought they had the case pretty much solved the moment they arrived. With all the weaponry displayed on the rocks, they imagined it was only going to be a simple case of forensic work and a ballistics expert. They didn't look any further than the area enclosed by rock. They gave the dress circle a miss. The video camera was safe.

Watching the cops, I knew there would be a lot missed. They didn't even clear riders away from the murder scene. Willa nudged my arm and handed me the glasses. I saw the vehicle with the French-speaking pair wind its way down a back-road away from the house to the highway. The police car had passed by them on the way in.

I decided I didn't want to lose them. Reporters leaving a wide-open murder scene was just too unbelievable. What a splash for *Le Monde*. We made our way down the rocks and walked to the bike. We were sitting on it at the time the addresses were collected, so Willa's presence went unrecorded.

With the bike out of gear and the engine off, I headed the bike down towards the homestead.

We could have gone for the gate to the road, but it would have looked as if we were running. This way we went unnoticed.

I didn't have much faith in the cops solving this one. The Homicide Squad were two hours away. The local police don't call them in immediately because there is very little apparent homicide in the country. From my reporting days, I knew that genuine homicides are often listed as suicides. Many of the domestic murders were recorded as accidental deaths. If they found a dairy farmer's wife hanging from a milking machine, it was suicide, no matter that it would have taken an agile monkey to tie the rope, the woman was sixteen stone and there was a manual winch in the generator room.

One woman on a property with a frontage to my small lake was found with a bullet hole in the back of the head, and the local sergeant declared there were no suspicious circumstances. However, despite the history of neglect of rural, domestic murder, the local cops would have to call this one homicide. It was too sensational. Even the cops could see the headline: 'Society Fox Hunter Shot At Kill.'

The murder would be a severe embarrassment to Evans. If he was unlucky he would be linked to this killing and Hough's death in the same story. He would have to stay at his stud tonight. The investigation would demand it. It seemed to me he would be vulnerable.

We could still see the dust from the black Mercedes as we reached the homestead. We haired off down the dirt road to the main highway in pursuit. It was a straight run, and the potholes left after the first winter rain had been filled.

Willa held tight. She was amused by the proceedings. I felt her breasts as she laughed. A kilometre or two from the town, we spotted their car. It was travelling well below the speed limit. They took the road to Mt Leura, a hill that overlooked the volcanic cone behind the town. The cone was the plug of a volcano left after the sides have been eroded. Only two cones left in the world, and a local gravel contractor had begun to demolish this one until the town fathers had been alerted to its tourist value.

'I know this place,' Willa yelled. 'We'll have them trapped at the top.' We zigzagged up the eastern face of the mount that was visited annually by hill-climbing enthusiasts. Occasionally competitors skidded into space from the narrow roadway as they raced against the clock. Did they have the need for the same near-death experiences that rejuvenated me?

I glimpsed the vast lake system to the north. It was weird that you could drive through this country without seeing water, when a good third of the view from sixty metres up was spreading lakes. The volume of water was increasing each year and eating up farmland.

We roared into the carpark at the top. The *Le Monde* team were out of the Merc and snapping shots south to the coast. Very cool professionals. If they were held, their film would show them as legitimate. They barely looked at us, which gave me an advantage. I slowed at the opposite side of the carpark and sedately motored up behind them, hanging the silenced Ruger down where they could view its formidable shape.

'Up against the fucking car.' I said.

The taller one in the suede jacket was fidgety, anxious to move. Everything he did was very obvious because he was silhouetted against the sky. He dived for his camera bag. I put a shot through it. 'Spare camera fucked,' I said. If there was a camera in that bag it was loaded with brass shells.

'Tell them,' I said to Willa. The short one looked at her, so I knew he understood us. He had that thickness which usually means strength, but his hands were slim and soft.

'Vous are under arrest,' she said, smiling at me. They didn't seem to appreciate our Australian racist humour. I wondered how I would go in France.

I smiled at them. I took gaffer tape from their bag and Willa told them to cross their wrists. The suede jacket said, 'Non gendarme.'

'You're dead right,' I said. 'We just want information. We couldn't care less you shot the fox hunter.' Willa translated. They appeared to relax.

'Non nuclear testie,' I said, out of bastardry.
These military assassins were always in favour of
bigger weapons. They looked blank. Out of their
line of sight, I smiled at Willa. '*Rainbow Warrior*,'
I added.

Willa said something in French, although it
didn't include any mention of the *Rainbow Warrior*. Her words renewed tension. I looked at
Willa for a translation. 'I told them you would
shoot them if they didn't tell us. So, just stop
your childish fooling around. They couldn't care
less about the Pacific tests.'

'Don't get too far ahead of me,' I said. I looked
around at the pine trees backing onto the carpark.
I thought of shooting one of them to make the
other talk, but that sort of nastiness should be
carried out in secluded areas. And for all I knew,
they were coming from the same place we
were—they wanted revenge.

'They'll talk,' she said. 'I know Frenchmen.'

The suede bloke spoke again to Willa. 'He
asked who you wanted to kill,' she said. 'Was it
the same person they killed?'

'Non,' I said to them.

We sat them in the back seat of their car, both
back doors open, with Willa and I leaning in
either side so we looked like tourists if anyone
else came up to the viewing park. We asked them
what their story was, and slowly, with some
prompting, it emerged. I hit one of them once
across the knee with the gun and he looked at

me as if I was somewhat uncivilised, but it seemed to do the trick.

The dead man's name was Hasek, which I guessed was Polish. It meant nothing to me. He appeared to have no connection with the chemical company or the shipping company.

It was the suede individual who did all the talking. His name was Marc Paris, a pseudonym if ever I heard one, and he told us Hasek was an Israeli arms supplier and that they had been hired to kill him. They were freelance, they said. And they didn't know who their employer was. There was no way of checking any of their information.

Willa ran questions like a professional. I could see they liked her. They trusted her. They understood her sort of woman. She told me later that Frenchmen looked at a girl and could see the beauty she would be, looked at the older woman and saw the beauty she had been. They worshipped beauty.

I had no idea what to do with them. They were one of those other conspiracies that pass you in the night, only we had bumped into this one. They weren't going to tell us more unless we tortured them, and I was rapidly losing taste for that sort of interrogation. I also felt we were exposed on this hill top, only one way up and down.

We left them there with their hands tied. I was reluctant but Willa argued they were no danger to us. Only to Greenpeace, I thought.

We called into Charlie's dairy farm on the way back to the farm. His property ran between the road and the lake, a narrow strip to the main road, and no one could pass down our track without him seeing. The motor from his dairy was ticking over in the style of the motor from *The Texas Chainsaw Massacre*, and he came out as we rode up to the dairy yards. 'Not a thing down the track all day,' he said. 'I gave a call to m'niece at the hospital, nurse there, you know. She reckons those two blokes you had the altercation with 'll be in there a week or two.' There was a hint of a smile on his thin lips.

Back at the farm, Sacco welcomed us. I rang around the Melbourne media, alerting them to the shooting at the fox hunt. It would make good colourful copy, and why not have the media do some of the work for us? Evans was due for some pressure. Not that it would be any more than a superficial job. Reporters suspect any story that doesn't come through a public relations source or has no media history. It was considered risky to break a story, as no one knew the extent of the interests and influences of Australia's three media proprietors.

Coming into the kitchen, Willa sat across the table from me. She crossed her legs and smiled at me as one swinging foot gently bumped my leg. Her look of direct challenge became something else when I leaned across and ran my fingers inside her shirt. The swell of her skin beneath my fingers was delicious. Her back arched slightly and there was a fineness to her movements that was part of inducing a sexual trance, a wantonness in her limbs that was as strong as mine.

Beneath the rough farm clothes was silky underwear. The jeans slipped to the ground and she easily stepped away from them, legs glossy with light. I reached out to touch her and she knocked my hand aside. She pushed her pants down and they were draped over her thighs. I waited for her to include me in her lovemaking.

Her waist was very narrow but the curves of her hips were generous. 'You're going to fuck me, aren't you?' she said, as a statement with a hint of a question. She allowed one thigh to slip across the other.

When she smiled a small bubble of moisture ran across her lips. She licked at the sensation she felt. She ran one hand behind her as she turned away from me, and I watched as she stroked her smooth buttocks.

'You want me to fuck you now, don't you?' I said.

'Yes,' she said smiling, 'I want you to fuck me. I want you to put it in.'

She began shivering with anticipation, her delicate knees shaking. I put my arm around her and pulled her towards me. I moved her forwards over the table and gave her a gentle smack. She opened her legs. She squirmed against me as the rhythm became rougher. 'You can do anything,' she said, kissing me with lips that were soft with lust.

She gasped when I joined her. 'You like dirty fucks,' I said.

'All fucks are dirty,' she said. Her body became so small as she pushed against me, beginning strongly, only to fall away to a gentle quivering. 'Oh, Christ,' she said. 'I'm coming.' I couldn't speak.

We left the farm again on nightfall. On horseback. We rode the two geldings and led an older horse. They loved the novelty of a night ride, prancing sideways, snorting the cool night air from the lake. This was to be a guerilla operation, confront Evans at his place, and use surpise to get to the bottom of this mess.

Heading towards Evans's property, we were hidden from night travellers on the road by our distance from them, and the phalaris grass as high as the horses' withers. The bike couldn't be used. The slightest sound around the property tonight and we'd be pursued. We had about a twelve kilometre ride because I had wire cutters and we took short cuts through neighbouring farms. When we got close to the Evans place, we emerged onto the road again. I didn't want to be given away by walking across the paddocks and having curious cattle follow us.

I watched Willa in the moonlight, her body undulating with the movement of the horse, her shirt buttoned low. I couldn't help thinking of her wanton seductiveness. Her jacket was open to the coolness. Her skin looked as smooth as polished stone, a creaminess to it that I wanted to touch now. She grinned across at me. It was conspiratorial and I felt a rush of affection. I couldn't remember the feeling, but the sensation was familiar.

'You know why I'm along, don't you?' she said.

'I think we have the same motive.'

'No, tonight, I mean,' she said. 'It's to see you don't go overboard. Put everyone in a situation we can't go back on.'

It was the old question once put to me by a philosophy tutor. 'How much force should you use to protect yourself and your family from a threat of violence?' Willa had merely disguised it.

'Willa,' I said. 'We're about to get ourselves in so deep we're the only ones we can depend on to get us out. Evans wants to kill us, be sure of that, and we're going to stop the fucker one way or another.'

Willa felt the breath of my rage. 'I don't think violence is the answer,' she said, coldly.

'You'd better go back now,' I said. 'He's scared me shitless and wants us dead. This little trip is to save our lives.'

'We don't have the information we need,' she tried.

'When I've finished with him, we will.' We rode on in silence.

Out on the road, as we neared the Evans place, my horse began to amble. There is no more pleasant motion. It is pacing, except the speed is slower than a trot. Ahead of us, we saw lights in a number of paddocks around the property.

We came up on a roadside dam that was half full. Some stray sheep watched us approach in apparent equanimity, but they broke to run as they lost their nerve.

The paddock where we had witnessed the killing was unlocked. I dismounted and I walked my horse through after Willa and closed the gate. We were about fifteen hundred metres from the homestead road. Over the gelding's wither I looked towards the hill. Dark clouds occasionally obliterated the moon, producing total darkness, but I didn't sense any movement up there at all.

The police would have finished hours ago. In the quick light the moon threw between cloud banks I didn't see any cattle on the hill. Checking for them, I found them hunched down for the night in the low ground to the north, chewing their cud. Tonight nothing interesting was happening, so far. As we rode up on the shoulder of the hill, I saw the house. It was pretty much ablaze with light.

On the dark side of the hill, away from the moonlight, we headed directly upwards. At the rocky outcrop, I tied my horse up by attaching a small rock to the reins and pushing it quietly into a jammed position in a crevice. If we had to flee, it would be quicker than untying hobbles. I tied Willa's horse to the stirrup of mine with a quick knot that would only require a quick tug to free it.

The amphitheatre was still cordoned off with yellow tape. Further around I pulled myself up and moved onto the dress circle. I was sure there was no one about, but sounds carry beautifully at night.

Above the dark void of rock that held the video camera I took the corks from the four-hooked fishing spinner I had brought along and then lowered it to where the camera showed a lighter colour against the dark. It was down almost two metres and I trawled the spinner back and forth over the object until the hooks found a natural hold. The camera was then retrieved easily.

It was one of those marvellous pieces of technology that replay through the viewfinder——and only a newsperson who has had to wait for film processing at the labs would understand my appreciation——so I rewound and played it with Willa, as we sat crossed-legged, staring into the tiny, detailed picture.

I saw then why the top-hatted bloke had been killed. It had been a mistake. The little screen flickered, but the definition of the tiny picture was very clear. At the moment the video picture was jolted, the head of the top-hatted rider had momentarily blocked Evans's head.

We played it again. The cameraman had been lying against the marksman and the jolt from the shot had moved the camera. The killers had been after Evans. But why the tape? Wasn't that just evidence of the murder they had committed? If they had been caught with it in their possession, it would have taken them through the courts to a twelve- to fifteen-year gaol sentence. Willa and I slid down the rock with our find.

Maybe the killers were expected to prove they had made the hit. If they were working for Australians there would have been no problem. Their employer would have picked up the paper the following day and seen the story and been satisfied. But maybe their employer was from a country where the media was government controlled and known to be so corrupt that no reader believed it. The film would need to be produced as proof.

So, who the hell was trying to kill Evans? Were they the same people trying to kill Willa and me? Was Evans the one trying to kill us? Had I been wrong about that? My imagination needed to supply a scenario that fitted the facts, and quickly. I was about to confront Evans, and yet here was evidence that he himself was a target.

'What do we do?' Willa said. 'It could be the same people after us.'

'You heard him today,' I said. 'He wants us.'

I wasn't going to allow the evidence of the video tape to influence me. I had a gut feeling, and I knew you either used that feeling or you died.

'We're risking a lot, doing this,' she said.

'If we walk away, Evans has the advantage. We'll never get this close to him again.'

The house was laid out in a U-shape below us. The internal angle of the U was a huge courtyard, but it was facing back towards the hill, towards us. The bottom of the U was the front of the house. We decided to approach at the front, the back was too much like the funnel of a trap.

We tied our horses beneath a blue gum on the edge of the huge garden. As I was examining the front windows for access, I looked around for Willa and was shocked to see her twenty metres away, moving towards the stairs at the front of the verandah. She was too far away to call, and by the time I waited for her to recognise her position, she was on the verandah and knocking on the door. I slipped the Glock from my waistband. Shit, I thought, what the hell's she up to?

She knocked on the huge old door and pulled the bell. I stopped moving forward when lights flooded the verandah. The door opened and the housekeeper said, 'Yes, can I help you?'

Willa swept past her, saying she had come to see Robert, she hoped he was about, it was a very urgent matter. The door closed behind her. The verandah lights were turned off.

I knew what she was doing. Using her style and status to bluff her way to the seat of the problem and make him see the error of his ways. It was a variation of the strategy employed by warrior aristocrats of the Middle Ages. They would dine together to solve the problems between themselves, while their knights and infantry continued to slaughter each other on the battlefield.

I stepped up onto the verandah, hoping I would be able to follow Willa's progress through the house. To date, Evans hadn't shown the hypocritical and pragmatic make-up of an industrial aristocrat. He wouldn't be impressed by Willa's gambit. He would hesitate, perhaps, but that was all.

A light from a window at a corner of the building flooded the verandah. I moved towards it, finding the boards newly laid and solid beneath my feet. Evans must have spent hundreds of thousands bringing the old place up to scratch. The curtains on the windows were lace, so I could see through.

From my angle, I could see Willa sitting in one of those high-backed, antique chairs designed to cope with layers of petticoats. Evans was sparing no expense to return this house to its former glory. Moving out of the pool of light, I crossed to the other side of the window. Evans was behind a leather-topped, oak desk of magnificent proportions. On each of the side walls were leather-bound stud books. He had an indulgent smile on his face. He was talking, but I couldn't hear a word and I couldn't lip-read. At this point, though, they both seemed relaxed, as if it were a social occasion.

I went around the corner of the house and began trying the windows. The third gave a little, and without a squeak. It was so smooth, I knew the windows had been sashed and weighted in the refurbishing. I stepped into the room. It appeared to be a large sitting-room. One that had been expensively furnished and was rarely used. I could smell the new leather and the fresh carpet. I slid from there into the hall. I eased a shell into the breech of the Glock. It made a noise, but not one that could be heard in a house with bluestone walls about thirty centimetres thick and doors closing flush with thick carpet.

I opened the door next to the study and eased through. The door into the adjoining room was open and I could hear their voices.

'You have an interesting way of doing business,' Evans was saying, 'but I have nothing to hide, nothing I would need to kill anyone for. I've been quite open on this, that cargo was bound for Djakarta. Quite legitimate. The government's factories have supplied more than two hundred million dollars worth of arms to Indonesia. Who in the hell cares where they end up? I couldn't give a shit whether my stuff is used in East Timor or not.' The last sentence revealed him. His tone was harder, nasty. He knew he wasn't fooling anyone, and didn't care. We were in trouble. He was just curious about us. He wanted to know more about Willa before he let the trap fall and he walked away.

Why was Evans still talking about Indonesia when the surviving crewman had said the ship was bound for Syria? I glanced through the door. I saw the wall of racing pictures. Shots of his horses reaching the barrier first. Horses paid for by villagers in Third World countries, screaming as they stood over their babies' bodies smoking on the ground. I balanced the Glock and moved forward to peer through the door to the left. Evans was leaning forward, his hands on the desk flat down, as though he had put all his cards on the table. On his lap was a machine pistol.

You certainly got us in here, Willa, I told her silently.

'So,' Willa was saying, 'you didn't kill my niece?' Oh, Christ, my mind whispered to itself, she's in deeper than I thought. He's just practising being nice because he doesn't believe she's accused him. All businessmen depend on pleasant demeanours, no matter the insults, using the logic that the accusation might just go away. But I knew he wouldn't just walk away from that one.

'I know about it, of course,' he said. 'Her death was most unfortunate.'

'If I had killed your niece,' he said, 'what would you do about it? You've come here alone to insult me, and think you can just walk away.' The tone was breaking into anger. He took the pistol in one hand and stood up, keeping the weapon below the table line. 'What right have you to do that? You threaten me and think that's the fucking end of it.' His voice took on a sheen of dedicated nastiness. He had been along this road before.

Willa was very calm. 'No,' she said. 'I came to call a truce, remember. My being here, in front of you, proves we can get to you far more easily than your people can get to us.'

'Yes, but you're here alone, in my house, miles from anywhere. We dump your vehicle in a lake and nobody has any idea where you went when you left here. You came here alright, and then you left. You were upset. You said I'd killed your niece and you wanted revenge. Sound familiar? Sound like the sort of story heard a thousand times in coroners' courts?' He slapped the table hard, the gesture taking him into the beginning of rage. 'Yeah, well, fuck you. And your fucking mate is dead meat. I have someone for him he won't believe. We're watching for him. There's something nasty waiting for him. He's only got to raise his head and he's a goner.'

I was through the door with the Glock at arm's length in front of me. I looked into his eyes, letting him know I wanted to kill him. Let him reach for the pistol. I was smiling at him. He desperately wanted to raise the weapon. His eyes grew bolder, almost reached the peak that signals action, but then his mind began to function. He relaxed.

I should have taken the weapon then. But there is a debilitating need in me to walk the edge. I love the edge. I wanted him to give me an excuse to kill him.

'You piece of slag,' I said, moving to his desk, picking up his correspondence spike and driving it through his hand. He screamed, jumping forward, the pistol thumping to the floor. Behind me Willa whispered, 'Oh, Christ.' I backhanded him with my free hand. 'You have everyone else do your killing,' I said. 'I do my own.' I stepped onto his desk, put my foot on his wrist close to where the spike protruded and pulled the spike out. He screamed. He slumped forward onto the desk, nursing his hand.

'I'd like to show you the girl you killed,' I said, glancing at Willa. She had cringed back against the wall, breathing hard. I knew she didn't understand the brutality raging in me.

'Are you listening, you prick,' I said, whacking him across the head with the heel of my hand. 'If you don't fucking listen, if you don't answer, I'm going to kill you.' I punched him lightly in the side of the neck to get his attention. He held the wrist of his injured hand as if it might stop the pain. He was focused on his pain and not on me. I put the barrel of the Glock on his eye. 'Listen, you fuck, why do you think you can get away with killing people, killing us?' He looked at me like a prisoner whose guard had overstepped the mark and would be the subject of his report. It had obviously been a long time since he was at anyone's mercy. Fuck him.

'It's easy,' he said.

'Not for you it's not,' I said. I whacked him across the neck with the Glock.

'Someone's here,' Willa said, and it was almost an apology. I dived from the desk over Evans. A bullet slammed into the wall behind me as I rolled, firing at the legs I could see through the well of the desk. It was a knee shot and a piece of bone hit the wall. As he fell in front of me I had the weapon on his eyes a metre and a half away, reaching for him with the muzzle. His eyes were deeply recessed, no fear. He raised the gun and I shot him. I rose beneath Evans's chair. A mistake. As he fell, he grabbed at the machine pistol. He had time. I shot at a second bloke coming through the door, his shirt tugged over his fat stomach spreading with blood, and then I scrambled over the desk, waiting for the bullets from the machine pistol. Evans wasn't functioning well. His right hand must have hurt even to squeeze the trigger, let alone point and aim. The bullets splintered the racing pictures.

Willa was through the door in front of me. If I took time to turn, I would lose the split second I had on him. I rolled for the door as the bullets smashed the door frame. I fired once over my shoulder and was through the door and running. It was then I was caught on the side of the head. There was no pain, just a whack as though I had

been hit by a pillow that sent me reeling. I saw
a bloke in a leather jacket holding Willa by one
wrist. He'd forgotten he needed her close to stop
me firing. I shot him. I twisted again and saw
Evans had gone. I wondered why? If he'd had any
guts, we'd all be dead. Bullets hit the door he
had fled through. Willa was firing with the .22.

I scrambled to my feet, felt the dizziness reach
for me, and shrugged it away.

We ran into the hallway and headed for the
room to the north where I had the window open.
Opening the door to the room, I saw figures on
the verandah. We raced further north along the
hall and burst through into a kitchen with hanging
saucepans and frypans and huge wooden benches.
Out we went though the back door and onto
cobbled bluestone in an area grand enough to be
called a cloister. Around the eastern corner we
had to jump onto the verandah. We rolled across
it and dropped a metre or so to the dirt. I pointed
to the foliage behind the tennis court. It was away
from the horses, but there was no cover towards
them. We crouched low and reached the bush.
Lights were snapped on and suddenly the garden
looked like a military compound. 'Their horses
are down here,' someone yelled.

'It's okay,' I said to Willa, but it wasn't what I
felt. Willa vomited. 'I've had enough,' she said.
'No one lives like this.' She refused to look at
me, regarded me as a piece of horror. We headed
around the back of the homestead, through a

silent pine plantation, and then across behind the big barns to observe the stables. She was with me, but only just. I had crossed her boundaries of suitable behaviour. She had been in the middle of it, so close to death, and still she managed to remove herself from it, judge me. How did she manage it?

The haystacks had a marvellous odour. They smelt like spring. No mould in these bales. I felt I just wanted to lie in them for a while until the activity subsided. But by morning the whole place would be searched.

'There's someone in the stables,' Willa whispered. To get to them we would have to run across thirty-five metres of open ground. It was a shadowy space, but you make a noise when you run, and already they were alerted. I turned to talk to Willa, but she'd gone. Oh fuck. I waited for her. A few minutes later I saw where she'd gone. The haystack nearest the house was alight. She was back beside me in an instant. 'That'll pull them out,' she said. I wasn't sure either of us was going to continue living with independent actions like that. I suppose she thought planning would avoid bloodshed.

'And light us up,' I said.

'Not if we come in from the other side.'

It meant a four hundred metre run around behind what looked like a disused shearing shed and some heavy timber cattle yards. We started on our way.

When we came up behind the double doors of the stables we saw Willa's ruse had worked. The double doors of the stable were wide open. A fire tender was being pulled across to the haystack with an old Ferguson tractor.

We found a jumping saddle and a bridle in the office. They were beside a chair where they were being worked with saddle soap. Two cups of coffee were on the table. But that was all. One horse only. A huge warmblood. Where the hell were the others? Their boxes were mucked out and fresh straw laid. For some reason they must have been out in day yards.

I liked Willa's escape vehicle. Near to seventeen hands. He wouldn't be fast, but he'd be reliable and he'd jump. I saddled him up quickly. 'On your way,' I said. 'Head for the gate in the hill paddock. Close it when you go through. We don't want them to know which direction we're travelling.'

'They know your farm,' she said from her great height.

'They'll be wary of that, they haven't had much luck there so far. They'll want to stop us before we get there. If you need to go around the lake, come at it from the other direction.'

'I'll wait,' she said.

'You won't. One of us has got to get away.'

There were ten horses out the back in the day yards, lit by the fire. I took a chance and walked behind the horse yards looking for a kind eye. I wanted a big, almond-shaped eye, soft but alert. The first few had piggie eyes, the next was a big horse with narrowness between the eyes. The second last yard had a horse that looked at me with pure intelligence. This was what I was after.

I took a piece of soft rope and fashioned a war bridle. It was quick. A rope up behind the ears, down the cheeks of the horse and a loop right-angled to that, lying against the gristle between the bone of the face and the beginning of the nostrils. It wasn't great at speed if the horse wasn't trained to it, but a jerk on it could bewilder a first-time wearer long enough for you to leave his back or have him avoid an obstacle at a slow canter.

I led him out of the stable and down by the cattle yards. Willa was there waiting for me. I was angry and pleased, all at once. I wanted her safe and I wanted her with me. We moved off slowly. I knew we'd be fine for a while. Those fighting the fire wouldn't be able to see any distance in the surrounding dark.

As we descended the eastern slope of the hill, a spotlight lit our scene. It was one of those moments when your belly crawls and your ears lie flat back against your skull, the adrenalin courses and you're so fast everything appears in slow motion. I turned the horse so a shot over his ears wouldn't panic him, and killed the light with two shots. I guessed I had a dozen left. My horse lurched under me, taking off at instant speed. He coped with my weight and I coped with his speed. I stayed on.

Behind us the beams of headlights cut the dark.

The vehicle was gaining fast. He certainly was not going to slow for the horse, let alone the gate. He was going to take us both. I felt the horse balance himself, his driving legs strong beneath him as he surged. He knew a chase when it was on. Ahead, Willa's horse was slow but determined. I hung back so he could take the gate without feeling pushed.

I let my horse's head go as soon as the warmblood's heels disappeared over the gate. I was fine going up, but the change of direction as he reached down for the ground on the other side of the fence unsettled me. I pulled too hard on the reins so when we landed he was not certain. My balance was tight. We crossed the road, slowing.

Behind me the gate crashed open and the vehicle charged again. Willa was nowhere in sight. I straightened the gelding, knowing we would have to take the barbed wire. Suddenly a pure confidence ran through me. The horse felt it, as they feel all changes in their environment, and easily took the wire glinting in the lights of the vehicle.

The vehicle came through the fence, the zinging wires sounding out above the motor. I took to some rough ground over which the horse travelled easily, but the vehicle had to slow to a crawl. While I was still in their field of light, I headed south, and then doubled back, heading north-east to the far fence.

The gelding was blowing hard, so I slipped from his back and ran at his shoulder. When I was blowing, I jumped on his back again. I turned and watched the lights. They hadn't found Willa, and they were way out of line with the direction I had taken.

Willa was back at the farm. She was totally exhilarated that we had made it back. She met me as I rubbed the horse down with dry grass. 'I don't believe I did that,' she said. I slipped my arm over her shoulders and hugged her. 'I feel so young,' she said. 'I should have been doing this all my life.'

'It might have been a short one,' I said. I held back. I'd been angry about her fronting Evans, putting our lives at risk. It didn't seem so important now.

I put the horse in the day yard without water. He was still hot and I didn't want him down with colic. I tossed a cotton rug on him just to keep the chill out once he was cool. He had lasted well, his jumping ability astounding. He was one of those broad brutes just under sixteen hands. He had carried me easily. Willa hosed her horse down, and threw a hessian rug on him.

'We get out of here now,' I said. 'Evans has about twenty people over there.'

We packed the convertible and headed away. As we turned off the gravel road onto the bitumen, and there was no longer a possibility we would be trapped in the cul-de-sac, I asked Willa why she had walked so boldly up to the front of the house.

'I didn't want us to get involved in the dark side of all this,' she said. 'You know, personally involved.'

'Killing, you mean?' I looked across at her.

'Yes,' she said, her face hard, her eyes uncertain.

Close to Geelong, I turned on the radio. The fox-hunting death was midway down the news bulletin. It had been an accident, the police decided. Guns were carried by huntsmen to put down injured horses and hounds. After a horse had broken a leg on the hunt, a gun had misfired and put down a perfectly healthy middle-aged businessman. There would be no investigative journalists chasing up that story today, though, no matter how colourful the circumstances. The burning ship had a sensational new lease of life. World opinion had condemned the Victorian government for having chemical wharfs so close to the city. Not that the present government cared, the reporter commented. World opinion was to be disregarded.

In the suburbs above the Geelong cement works I pulled into a quiet street and we curled up on the seats and slept.

Fourteen

We spent the rest of the day at various locations around Werribee South. The river was beautiful. Old clinker-built fishing boats and later nineteen fifties models with short masts were anchored in the quiet water that was pushing through to the sea over a sand bar. It was a pity that overflow from the sewerage pools made it into the river during flood time.

We didn't go too far down the roads leading over the river—we didn't want to make anybody nervous. Market gardens and drugs can cohabit with considerable synergism.

It was a good place to contemplate exactly where the hell we were in this bloodbath. We worked Willa's mobile heavily. We were attempting to discover exactly who wanted to get at Evans—apart from ourselves. According to financial journalists and Willa's influential—and consequently more knowledgeable—friends, there were many people who would like to throttle him. But that's all we had. The image of someone throttling another is almost a comical one; if someone says they'd like to throttle someone, the bet is they'll do nothing at all.

The picture of Evans that emerged was of a bright opportunist who had cornered a market others were reluctant to enter. There could be no argument about the chemicals involved not being bad for the environment. The Australian Medical Association, a conservative body, was even now campaigning for the chemical industry in Melbourne's western suburbs to be controlled with strict legislation. Frightful cancers were on the increase. It was only a matter of time before public prosecutions descended on those still manufacturing them.

No one knew where Evans came from, and no one knew that he was deeply immersed in the arms trade. He was new money, she'd been told, having built a fading chemical business that made kitchen cleaners, glassware sparklers and drain unblockers that were mainly acid and occasionally killed children when left around the house. He had upped the ante when he had begun manufacturing agricultural chemicals under licence from a German firm.

From the convertible, overlooking the river, Willa rang an old university friend, Germaine Mercieca, now a respected scientist who was investigating the damage done by the leaks into the Pacific from the Johnson Atoll war chemicals storage base. She was now back in Washington, where she was delivering a report to the military authorities. Willa talked about the explosion on the bay. Her voice was measured and friendly.

These two people liked and respected each other. After giving Germaine the story of the burning ship, she sat back and listened. I could hear Germaine's voice. It was warm and humorous.

I wrote 2,4-D and 2,4,5-T on a piece of paper and Willa told her these were two of the chemicals on board. Germaine's voice changed to an iron certainty, one of great concern.

Willa wrote on my note, turned and handed it to me. She had written Agent Orange.

She hung up. 'The combination of the two is Agent Orange,' she said. 'It contains the deadliest substance on earth. It creates a dioxin so deadly that if half a cupful was poured into New York's water supply it would kill everyone in the city.'

'So how many cupfuls are now in the bay?' I asked.

'That's one of the problems. It's unstable, and no one knows exactly what will happen if it's mixed with salt water. If it's mixed with fresh water and left contained, it gradually strengthens the dioxin. You remember that town in Italy where some of this dioxin escaped into the air, they had to take away topsoil over quite a few square kilometres. It took them several years. The residents were evacuated.'

'It was developed from clothing dyes in the twenties, and later it was tested on the Jews in the death camps during the Second World War. She said it's all documented. I.G. Farben was one of the companies involved.'

Willa was tapping the pencil on her teeth. 'I think I own shares in one of the subsidiary companies.'

Oh, Christ, I thought, how does Australia, so totally bloody isolated, inherit all this horror? I must have been thinking aloud.

'Because we don't investigate,' Willa said. We just accept whatever we're told. She knows this because she found that at the exact moment that our prime minister was telling us that that plan to burn the gases on the Johnson Atoll was fine, because the technology was safe, the American scientists had closed the facility down. It had become critical and was already leaking. That was in 1990. All documented.'

By nightfall the skies over Melbourne were clear of gas—according to the news. A good wind was blowing from the north and any little pockets of gas would land on the ocean surface, harmless to humans. Hearing that, I felt a small joy, as if I had been believing that the fire would scar this portion of the world forever, and now we were saved. We had chances again. It was an emotion that didn't entirely run with logic, but it demonstrated the strain of optimism that emerges when news contains hope: it postpones having to do anything to right the wrongs that are happening. It also stops you thinking about the marine creatures and their environment.

According to Germaine, there was no scientific protocol for the analysis of fluoro-dioxins,

because that group of chemicals were so deadly.
If the gases landed on the ocean surface, they
would immediately enter the food chain, our
food chain. It was no wonder, she had said to
Willa, that cancer had now reached epidemic
proportions.

Willa propped her legs against the dash con-
sole, as if they needed support. This information
seemed more devastating to her than our present
situation was.

'I know this is horrible,' I said. 'But we have
more immediate problems.'

'Someone has to do something about it,' she
said.

'Yeah, well I suppose a chemical report, you
know the sort of thing, whose making what,
where they're all stored. But I don't hold out
much hope. Remember Rachel Carson's book,
The Silent Spring? That was the first alert to all
this, and then the chemical companies poured
money into propaganda and people's concern just
dissipated.'

Willa got out of the car and walked to the
small cliff overlooking the sea. She folded her
arms. I knew she was right, we should be concerned, but right then I just didn't feel it. I
stepped out of the car and walked towards her.
She turned to me. 'Germaine said there's enough
chemicals and explosives stored in the western
suburbs to destroy half the city. If that goes up,
that would begin the chain reactions in the west,

because all the flammable stuff, the tank farms and chemical plants are so close together.'

I knew all this, knew it had to be taken one step at a time. But she was looking for an instant campaign, something she could pour all her emotion into. 'Okay, do something about it later,' I said. 'Forget it for now. We have to survive.' She looked at me briefly and walked back to the car. I looked back towards the river. The gold fairy lights over the small pier gave images of hope in the calm water of the anchorage.

It was evening. Willa had made many more phone calls, using all the contacts she could think of. Now we were sitting there above the river entrance, sipping a red—from plastic cups—that had been rolling about in the boot for several weeks, each of us checking our notebooks for anything that the other might need to know. Willa said she hadn't ever realised the animosity that could surround those businessmen who were outside the magic circle of operators who had been schooled at Scotch College and Melbourne Grammar.

Willa became moody. As I looked at her, I saw she was unaware that she was biting one finger. She was locked away in her mind and nothing I said at the moment could move her. I reached across and touched her arm. 'What's wrong?' I asked her.

'I've been very stupid,' she said after much cajoling.

'What are you talking about? We've been doing what we can, not what we would have liked. But none of it's stupid. Not in the long run.'

'Personally,' she said.

'I don't think that's been stupid either,' I said. I knew a woman who has seen the dirty violence of a friend can never forget or forgive it, but we were alive.

'It's not us,' she said.

I waited.

'I have something to tell you,' she said. 'You're not going to like it.'

'Hey,' I said. 'I haven't liked much today.'

'I should have mentioned it before.'

I sipped the red. 'Go on.'

'It's Peter,' she said. 'His name kept coming up today in connection with Evans.'

'What do you mean?'

'Look, I was aware he was powerful, into stuff I didn't know about—that was part of the attraction. But now, I suspect he's an arms dealer.'

That swung me. I had wondered she'd tolerated him, let alone been close to him. But now I sensed that it was the incredible attraction of opposites at play. Often it has no relation to anything logical at all. It may have an appeal to a secret need to know the worst of people, and this may or may not be hidden from the individual themselves. Or it may be a matter of great sex.

I remembered a beautiful artist of great wisdom and style who fucked the brains out of a former premier of the state, purely to discover whether her theories about male power were valid. Apparently they were. But on finding out, she didn't cease the fucking.

But I couldn't equate Willa and an arms dealer. I looked across at her. We were silent for a time.

I placed an arm around her and pulled her towards me. 'You'd take it from anyone,' I said.

'I like it from you,' she said, as if she were a young woman repeating a lesson. At first she was unresponsive, but slowly she began to perform. I could feel it getting to her again. She began kissing me, my neck, my shoulders, my nipples, until she was attached to me like a leech, moaning, asking for more. She was opening up the darkness of her mind to me. I entered it to learn and play, although I hung back occasionally to feel the power between us and to keep her craving alive.

Moments after it was over, she pulled on her clothes and we were back to business. Her different attitudes were dazzling. For an instant I wondered how she had been with Bresler. I knew my instinct about him had been right. With his possible involvement, certain pieces of the puzzle were falling into place.

'We need to investigate Bresler,' I said.

She looked at me as if I could save her in some way. It was a tell-me-how look.

'We need to go back to the funeral parlour,' I said. 'We might be able to use Bresler.'

'I don't see how,' she said.

I had driven the car only a kilometre before pulling up above a small beach. I was hot again.

'Why are we stopping?'

I walked her down to the sand. I stood behind her and pulled her hair back from her face. There was not a movement from her, I stroked her neck and shoulders. 'The only way we're going to get anywhere with this', I said, 'is to trap them and kill them.'

'Isn't that what we're trying . . . ?' Her voice failed her.

'We've really been running. We'll have to stay in one place and wait for them.'

'I don't see that at all,' she said. I slid my fingers slowly over her breasts.

'Interesting way you give bad news,' she panted.

'Never fails,' I said.

'I don't want to stay here,' she said.

'At my place,' I said. 'It has a certain ambience for the sort of activity we're planning.'

'Jesus,' she said, as I unbuckled her jeans. 'Not in the sand,' she said.

'Take them off,' I said.

She did.

I eased her down onto her hands and knees. She was still warm, and she seemed smoother. I held her breasts inside her shirt as she rested them on the sand. She put her hand between her legs to cushion me. I understood Bresler's anger. Willa was very addictive.

Fifteen

The Williamstown Festival was rocking the suburb as we drove in. Nelson Place was barricaded off to traffic and the music from the band rotunda was a powerful joy in the heat of the evening. The relief from the bay fire must have added to the excitement. One day's grace and all caution could be neglected.

Archie Roach's bittersweet voice was loud over the elms of the park. His lament for lost lives and lost lands had a poignancy for everyone now. Blacks had been treated like shit for centuries was his message, but now whites were treating each other with the same unscrupulousness.

Willa and I walked beneath glorious elms festooned with tiny lights through the crowd towards the eating places behind the old two-storey customs house. Its white facade stood out in the darkness like a monolith. The music was setting down a beat to the night. We walked where we could be seen, under the lights festooning the trees. Occasionally I saw a group gathered near the waterfront looking across the bay to the beached ship.

From a small barge about two hundred metres off the pier, sky rockets zoomed off into the night, lacing the sky with gorgeously coloured patterns. Youngsters drifted through the crowd, high on speed or ecstasy, brilliant smiles on their faces. Children were necklaced with phosphorous solutions in tubes of plastic.

The import of what the city had experienced in the last few days was only just filtering through. All it would have taken was a wind change and we would have had our Bhopal, whole sections of the city's population dead or dying.

At the roundabout, a juggler was performing three metres up on a high bike seat. One wheel only. He was perched without handlebars and he was juggling a cane-cutting blade, a small chainsaw, running, and an apple. He was cool, moving the bike beneath him easily. And he was talking to the kids, asking for donations for this performance to be placed in his cap some ten metres away.

'Come on, kids. And if your parents won't give you two gold coins to place in the cap, they don't really like you.' He paused. 'They adopted you and are planning to give you back to your real parents.' There was a nastiness beneath the patter. It was still funny, though.

A big crowd was gathering, riveted by his daring. He could have abused them without humour and they would still have loved him for his outrageous performance. The chain on the saw was certainly turning. It wasn't as if he just had the motor running.

Everyone's eyes appeared to be fixed on the juggler. I looked around to check if there was anyone looking our way. Our would-be assassins would have someone watching. That was how it worked. This area close to my place would be covered. My healthy paranoia had often saved me.

'Now,' the juggler was saying, 'I'm going to eat this apple while I'm throwing around these lethal little instruments. I'm going to pass the apple under my leg and then e-a-t the apple.' I turned back to look at him. He was staring down at me as he smashed the apple into his mouth and flicked the remains back into his juggling regime. Then he smashed the apple several times against the side of his face, as if he were missing his mouth. I was stunned because as he performed he was looking directly at me, not needing even to take a second thought about what he was doing. I nudged Willa and gestured as he watched me. There was a flicker of a smile around his mouth.

Looking directly at him, I gave him the finger. Without missing a beat with the chattering chainsaw, he gave me the finger back, so sly it wouldn't have been detectable to the audience. I turned to leave.

'That guy in the blue shirt, yeah, you,' he said to me. 'You're leaving without donating. I know where you live.' The crowd snickered at this threat.

We pushed a way through the crowd. 'I'll see you soon,' he yelled out, as we headed past the coffee shops on Nelson Place and on to the funeral parlour.

The door to the apartment hadn't been touched. There was no split paint. If anyone was in there, it could only be a major locksmith, and that group of craftsmen abhorred violence. They were the proverbial in by the back door sort of blokes, and didn't like face-to-face confrontation. Of course, a locksmith may have let someone in.

It seemed okay, but I asked Willa to go back around the corner for protection. I grabbed a shrub from the pavement garden, taking with it a clod of earth, stepped back six metres, and threw it against the door. I dodged behind a parked car. There was no explosion. A few people looked at me strangely, but Williamstown residents have looked after their own business for years. It was the suburb the Painters and Dockers Union had lived and played in. A criminal organisation, it kept crime pretty much out of the suburb because they would have been shitting in their own nest.

I opened the door and ran my finger gently around it to locate any triggering thread. There was none. The plant was pretty much intact, so I replaced it, and Willa and I walked into the hallway.

All the windows along the upstairs of the pub across the road were shut. No one would shoot through heavy glass if they wanted an accurate shot. The mirror windows of the bar on the ground floor showed a view of me working steadily. It was as if I had glimpsed someone else at my door. Inside I retrieved the guns from the bag I'd been carrying, deadlocked and bolted the door and retreated up the stairs. If we heard the door go, we had five seconds to position ourselves before anyone would reach the top of the stairs.

From there we checked the rooms. Willa held the .22 with the silencer off, letting it hang at her side like an alien object. I carried a Browning automatic shotgun with three extra cartridges poking from between the fingers of my left hand. Another half dozen were in each of the front pockets of my jeans. The doors to the balcony were bolted, although the only way for anyone to enter would be from the top of a truck pulled in close to the kerb. The long kitchen windows looked over a steep abyss. I dropped the paper blinds down over the glass and turned on the lights. I wanted them to know we were here, right at home. The bathroom window was vulnerable, so I drilled and bolted it.

The windows of the bedrooms and study were bolted. The glass was ancient, so it was three times as thick as the modern stuff and very strong. Once I had thrown a rock at one to retrieve my keys that I'd left inside and it had bounced off.

That left the roof. I walked up the stairs and saw that the bolts were still shot home. I felt a presence to my right and whirled around. Mona was walking down the stairs in her beige suit. Ghost or not, I yelled at her. 'Hey,' I yelled. 'Turn round.' I wanted to see the worst. She kept walking. I plunged down the stairs after her. The hallway was empty. Willa looked out from the kitchen. She was holding the Ruger in front of her. I waved to indicate it was alright. 'It was her,' I said. 'I didn't see her face.'

'Terrific,' Willa said. She came down the hallway. 'I don't think I can stay here,' she said. 'I'm about ready to scream.' There was a tremor to her hand as she touched me. It was clear to me now that I only saw the beige figure when death was in the offing, not sex. It prompted a trickle of dread that threatened to pool in my mind. I put a hold on it, but not before I began to feel its paralysing effect. I didn't want the feeling to take hold of Willa, too. I had to banish it. The process is almost a mystical one, almost a parallel with meditation, except it is used while in the midst of action. It's an act of will imposed while marshalling your strengths. A stunt man told me about it after I had observed that the worse a situation got for him, the cooler he appeared to be.

I took Willa into the study and sat her down in a comfortable chair. I took both her hands and told her to concentrate on breathing regularly.

'Just think about drawing the next breath, cleanly and without effort,' I said. Once this was happening, I began to talk to her. 'This doesn't last forever,' I said. 'You think it will, but nothing ever does. We have a good chance here. We're going to hold out against these people; finally it will all go away. Let your nerve back, let it take over. It's cool and not easily phased. Bring it back, claim it.' I kept the suggestions moving for a minute or so and then told her to close her eyes. I loosened her clothing, and told her to think of the places she best liked to be.

I left her in a mild state of meditation, went to the phone in the hall and called Roly. He'd been terrific with his Evans information—now I wanted the rumours on Bresler. Roly was tense and it came out in his request for money. 'This is how I make a living,' he said. 'People pay me for information.'

'I've never given you any.'

'You weren't making a living from it then,' he said.

'But you were.'

He didn't answer me, but I heard him bending to his computer, breathing a little deeper, focused on what he was gathering. 'I don't recall the name, but I do have something on him. Yeah, Peter Bresler, here we are . . . Yeah, he's one of those people who make money by introducing money to money, money to ideas, or money to any opportunity really.'

'Specialise in any particular area?'

'Not that I've got.'

'Arms?'

'Everybody was trying to get into that for a while. But the Asian countries didn't want to buy from us. They went to Germany, England, the US. Arms were fashionable for a while. But I've got nothing on him along those lines.'

'Roly, if I make anything off this deal. I'll peel you off an appropriate amount, but I'd like you to keep working on him.'

'Yeah, sure,' he said as he hung up.

Most people ridicule the sixth sense, dismiss it, and generally behave as if it doesn't exist. I'm alive because I listen to it when it warns me. I know when other people have it. We look at each other and know.

I glanced out the hall doorway leading to the balcony and the image I saw in the mirror windows of the pub made my bowel heat. I squashed the feeling. I needed to survive. Down on the deserted street was the chainsaw juggler, walking as if his bike was a one-handed wheelbarrow. He turned into the courtyard entrance beneath the apartment.

I realised how perfect an assassin he was. He could see anyone in the crowd. He was so obvious he would be disregarded as a suspect. He had the perfect excuse to travel. I'm heading to Rome, Madrid, London, New York for the festival. A sniper's rifle would easily be concealed in his bike. I made a mental check to see how many people were killed during the various festivals around the world.

I raced for the windows on the stairs in time to see him step onto the tap of the gully trap, onto the side of the garbage skip, and then easily hoist himself into the seat. He pedalled under the overhang of the old rooftop tennis court and around the corner. I stuck my head in the study to rouse Willa. She would move slowly for a few moments she was so relaxed, so I said quietly, 'Bring your gun to the roof.'

The juggler was five metres high. Another metre if he stood on the seat. I was sure he could do that easily enough. I raced for the roof.

In my mind, I saw him pedal to the high back wall of the next-door house, step onto it, lift the bike over, pedal to the house, step onto the roof, climb to the peak, rest the bike on the chimney and the wall of the tennis court—the netting was no longer there—and walk across.

I reached the roof door and just stared at it for a moment. I was loath to unbolt it. I pushed myself. I had to meet this bastard when he was least expecting it.

The door bolts slammed back. I had no control over how hard I levered them. I dashed around the corner of the tower, under the cement canopy where the tennis players sheltered from the rain in the 1920s, and stopped suddenly when I saw him on the chimney. He would have been thirty

metres away. The size of the shot would tell at
that distance, and I had no idea what was in the
breech. If it was BB, I could open a hole in him.
If it was six, I wouldn't kill him. If I stepped out
now, he was fast enough to drop behind the
chimney and, with his agility, I was at a disadvan-
tage. I'd wait till he was walking across on his
bike. He'd have to concentrate on that. Wait.

He didn't use his bike. He leapt across the gap
and balanced on the wall. The tennis court with
its concrete seats appealed to his sense of theatre.
He looked around as if an audience was only held
back from applause by breathlessness.

He stepped from the wall, pistol in one hand,
and executed a marvellous double somersault in
the air. I caught him before he hit the ground.
The shot blew him backwards like a wild duck
dropped mid-wingbeat over a rice paddy. Something peculiar happened then. I wasn't sure
whether it was the force of the blast, or whether
I had seen an extra twist of the body, but he
disappeared over the wall, which took him down
between the wall of the building and the house
next door.

I rushed for the wall, another shot in the
breech. Then the torch, but the torch beam
showed nothing. There were not even footprints
in the loose earth at the bottom. To the left, his
bike was beside the gully trap at the corner of
the house.

Willa was beside me, peering. His weapon lay back on the tennis court so I didn't feel too much trepidation during the few minutes' search. But then I grew uneasy. There was no sign of blood. The only explanation was that I had hit him in the chest and he had been wearing body armour. Performing in the style he had, it could only be the new light plastic that interlocked like fish scales. The blast would have hurt him, maybe even broken ribs. But he was gone now.

I didn't want to leave the roof. It was like giving away territory that wouldn't be regained.

Willa was anxious as we walked back across the court. 'The noise,' she said. 'People would have heard that.'

'They'll tell themselves it was a car,' I said.

'You're kidding.'

'They might even check the street, see nothing, and not even report it. I've done it myself.'

Sixteen

With the shotgun in my hands, I used my forearms to take the weight as I twisted over the edge of the rooftop, dropped to the wide awning and then lowered myself onto the balcony below. The street was deserted. Above me I could see Willa's eyes watching over the wall.

The acrobat had to be in retreat. At the very least, he would have several ribs broken. Edging my head out over the balcony to look down I could see that the front door of the apartment was still closed. There was no one in the house. Our spinning acrobat had not been a diversion. He had been the main assault. I turned and looked up at Willa above me, silhouetted against the night sky, and smiled up at her. I hoped she sensed my relief.

Before I could make it back up over the ledge a Mercedes pulled alongside the pub, taking two carparks in the deserted street. I thought of the Frenchmen's Mercedes, but this was a dark blue in the street lights.

The main streets of Williamstown were always deserted by midnight, the suburb providing no short cut to anywhere else. The revellers from the eateries on Nelson Place were leaving on the bay road. Looking down at the Merc, I felt very lonely. If we were to disappear, there would be no witnesses.

I moved back across the balcony, placed the shotgun on top of the wall, and sprang over.

Willa was standing back from the wall, looking over at a very acute angle. 'It's Evans,' she said. 'I saw the car at the fox hunt.'

'He wouldn't use his own car,' I said.

'No,' she said. 'He's here to talk. He has to be.'

I wasn't sure he *had* to do anything, but we moved quickly off the roof, closed the huge door, bolted it and headed down the stairs to the hall.

'You have a false sense of security,' I accused.

The phone was ringing and I was reluctant to answer it. I didn't want to have to contend with anything else. Willa looked at me, picked up the receiver of the fax, her head at an angle, hair swaying down, and offered me the phone. I shook my head.

'Evans?' she demanded in a voice that was the one used on a recalcitrant across a church hall at boarding school. The head prefect at work, terrorising. She looked at me, nodded; she had been right.

'He wants to talk to you?' she said, handing the receiver over. My hands fumbled with hers and she placed the receiver firmly in my grip.

'Yeah,' I said.

'Deal,' he said.

I laughed. 'You're fucking joking?'

'I want to know who's trying to kill me,' he said.

'Me for a start,' I said.

'I don't want this conversation overheard,' he said. I moved uneasily. He wanted to come into our fort.

'This is a big turn around,' I said. 'Try the public phone next to the post office.' I flicked the phone onto conference so Willa could hear it.

'And have someone shoot me?'

'They can do it just as easily where you are.'

'I want to come in.'

I was unbalanced. I felt so much anger towards him, and yet I was inclined to open the door. My reasoning was that he just might tell us exactly who was after him, complete some of the puzzle. On the other hand, he might well be looking for a refuge. Perhaps he had as much need to disappear as we did.

'I need to talk.'

His voice was earnest, with a hint of petulance, but I was exhausted, no longer capable of determining whether his voice carried sincerity. I looked at Willa, feeling a clown as I raised my eyebrows. She nodded, yes.

'You'll have to come in by yourself,' I said. If there's anybody else, we don't open the door.'

'Yes, right,' he said. Flashing before me was an image of me killing him in the kitchen. I checked a laugh, close to hysteria. I checked the Glock, feeling it light and beautifully balanced as I shoved it down where it was hidden by the curve of the small of my back. I kept the Browning low.

Willa left to open the door and I walked out onto the balcony to watch him, the shotgun concealed below the balcony wall. The car door opened and he slipped out quickly. He was silhouetted against the orange light reflected from the hotel wall across the street. From my watching point above, he was foreshortened. I thought I heard him chuckle. But then he looked off to the side. His face became pure fright.

The acrobat capered to his side, a grotesque dance movement for the enjoyment of kids. He stepped behind him, a knife at his neck. He looked up at me and laughed. He even knew where I'd be. I raised the Browning as he pushed Evans out of sight below the awning. I jumped down the stairs for the hallway. Willa was leaning against the wall. She hadn't wanted to watch. I looked through the peephole, my vision slightly distorted. Evans was lying on the asphalt the blood spilling from a wound I couldn't see.

'I want to go away,' Willa said behind me. For an instant her voice sounded like that of a small child. 'He's totally mad, insane. Some bloody walking freak show.' Willa seesawed between reality and hope.

My hair prickled on my scalp and my ears had flattened involuntarily against my skull. I wanted to rush out in the street and confront the bastard with a shotgun, something I was sure he was prepared for.

'We'll get to the car,' I said.

'No,' she said in a small voice. 'I'm not leaving.'

The thought of moving promised relief. We had to do it.

'How?' she said. 'How do we get there?' I was missing a few beats. In my own mind I had already reached that haven. I shook my head like a punched-out boxer trying to bring back vision. I began to see a plan.

If he was on the ground, he had no view of the roof. He had guessed where I would be watching from. He would have no idea we would try and escape the building. Or was that already factored in? He must have guessed I had thought to use the place as a fort. Now I knew I couldn't maintain a seige here. There was not enough room to move. The building was a knockover for him.

'What do we do about Evans?' Willa asked. 'Don't we tell someone?'

'Leave him there. He's dead.'

She pushed herself away from the wall and walked with me to the kitchen. I pointed across the roof. 'We step from this building, walk to the end of the roof and drop to the ground. From there, we make our way back to the car.'

'He'll see us.' Her voice was dead. I knew exactly what she was feeling. The bastard created a feeling of dreadful inevitability. He was the stalking cat. His speed, agility and strength far outweighing that of his victims.

'He won't be here,' I said. 'When he gets here, we'll be gone.'

Our escape meant standing on the kitchen sink, opening the windows that twisted perpendicularly on central swivels, holding onto the heavy metal frames, and stretching across the void to the other roof. It meant a step of about a metre, but you had to push off energetically.

I stepped over first and held my hand out to Willa. She reached out her hand. Safely across the gap, I told her to crawl so there was no sharp metal sounds from the roof. I reached back and shut the window. I didn't want to leave signposts for the freak.

On our elbows, we moved across the space. There was an air conditioner pumping away in the centre of the roof and I headed around that. I looked back to encourage Willa—beyond her, I saw the acrobat, in the kitchen. My mind began to plead.

He was about twelve metres away. I thought of blasting him again, but I couldn't be certain of a head shot. That's how he had affected me. I was in range, I could put four shots into him, and I didn't want to pull the trigger. If I missed him with the first shot, he only had to duck below the window line and he could shoot at us. We had no cover at all, except the air conditioner. I was frightened to see him move so quickly, so oddly.

A nasty feeling of it all being over began to descend on me.

I stopped Willa with my hand.

'What is it?' Willa mouthed.

'Him,' I said. I could see her hand begin to tremble.

He opened the fridge and his smiling face was shown in profile. I wanted to go, but I had to see whether he left the kitchen to the left or the right. If he went to the left, to the roof, we were in trouble. He'd see us easily. Not only was the moon up but the metal roof was reflecting the light from the supermarket. We'd be silhouetted. If he went to the right, it meant we would be in danger on the ground. He shut the fridge door. I almost laughed then. Mona appeared in front of him in her beige suit. He didn't hesitate, he shot her several times. I wondered if he had seen her face. He ran from the kitchen, Mona still visible, and still standing. He went to the right as he moved from the kitchen. I jerked my finger at Willa, meaning run for the brick wall at the edge of the roof.

I looked back, and realised I had made a classic hunting mistake. We had acted as rabbits do when they hear a footstep—they run. He was back, looking first at Mona, who faded away in front of him, and then directly at us. I was sure I could see him smiling, despite his head being in silhouette. Or was the smile just an aura around him.

He ran from the room then. I knew we had about thirty seconds to drop from the roof, and run across the carpark before he made it to where we had left the roof. I jumped onto the roof of the all-night check-out chick's old Toyota. It buckled. Willa followed me, landing really lightly, and we hared across the space to where the gums grew next to the garbage skips. We backed into the shadow.

When he turned the corner of the wall we had jumped from, he went for the lit street. His movements were in a cavorting style and I remembered where I had seen it before. An old French film with an evil character who pranced down the street, kicking crutches away from the crippled, enjoying himself. The audience laughed with him. Our cavorting killer went into the light from the supermarket, and disappeared around the corner. My back shuddered from pure fright.

We ran like hell down the lane behind the Town Hall, around the front of the library, and across next to the kindergarten to the small park. Behind a bank of tall foliage we sprinted to the end of the park, and then down the street to Nelson Place. It was deserted at this time of night. We ran through the deep shadows of the elm trees that lined the street and the convertible looked welcoming, lonely by the police station.

I didn't want to be careful. I wanted to rush to it and move, move anywhere, quickly. Instead, I left Willa behind a tree and crawled under the car, looking for any telltale signs of interference. There were no wires running from the ignition, at least none that shouldn't be.

I stood up and slit the canvas and poked my head through to see if there was a telltale capsule of acid and explosive balanced there. It looked clear. I opened the door and stepped in.

Willa thumped into the seat beside me. 'We go,' she said, and it sounded like a primitive tribesperson trying a new language.

I was accelerating away when I saw the most dramatic challenge to a vehicle's speed I have ever seen. It was uncanny. The acrobat ran onto the road from the lawn of a block of apartments and ran towards us, front on. He leapt up, one foot on the bonnet, and I twisted the wheel hard. I looked back to see that he had landed off the side but was still on his feet. It was frightening. How did you get rid of a thing like that?

Willa shot at him, twisting awkwardly as she did. She may have been shivering with fright, but she wasn't going to be an easy victim. In the rear vision mirror, I could see him waving to her.

I tried to rid myself of this fear of apparent supernatural ability. Shit, I no longer believed in superman. I explained it to myself the only way I knew. A batsman faces a hard ball travelling at one hundred and forty kilometres an hour. His reflexes can't cope with that speed, and yet he does.

He doesn't have time to think about the stroke he'll play, a cover drive, or a late cut, or a leg glance, or any of the myriad of shots that he has in his repertoire, because he doesn't have time. He allows his subconscious to react in a way that it has over a dozen years of training and matches. The instant the ball leaves the bowler's hand there is a decision made on the ball's flight, and the stroke to make is factored in. This juggler bastard was the same. He had a life of training that gave him the ability to entertain, or kill.

I was so deeply immersed that Willa's voice made me jump. 'I have this terrible feeling', she said, 'that this is what you want, and you have me along because it interests you to have a witness.'

I knew what she meant. Excitement, danger, turned me into another person. I could transcend all the shit and failure in my life and have a chance of winning. It was the same feeling a mountain climber has the day after the climb. A time of total triumph, a rejuvenation of spirit. So, she was right, I did like it most of the time. It was just that this fucking freak frightened me, and I wasn't coping.

'I don't know,' I answered her. 'Sometimes, yeah, you're right.'

I had the feeling that any moment I was going to discover what I really cared about. My life? Ultimate excitement? As I headed north through the suburbs, I examined the contrasting feelings, but gave that away to rake through the circumstances of our predicament.

There was not a light to be seen in the rear vision mirror. No one was following us.

'Evans dead puts a hole in my logic,' I said. 'There has to be someone else directing it.'

Willa took one hand off the gun she had been holding so hard and touched my leg. 'The people who wanted him dead want us dead. That seems to be the important thing.'

'I'm not sure,' I said, placing my hand on hers. 'I think the fucking freak thing just kills for enjoyment.' She took her hand away.

'No,' she said. 'That's just the style.'

'What do you mean?'

She looked across at me, the palm of her hand rubbing the leather rest, as though the sensation would keep her mind on track. 'He is not demented,' she said. 'He might enjoy killing, but no one would hire him if he left messes behind him, if he killed outside his charter.'

I looked across at her. 'You've made it sound like a legitimate business.'

'Yes,' she said, 'I'm a bit slow. I'm beginning to realise it is for about half the world's population.'

'Well,' I said. 'I'm treating him like a fucking fruit-cake.'

We cruised around Willa's apartment block. The streets were quiet, the silhouette of the block hidden to some extent by tall trees. Her penthouse peeped out over the rest of the building like the upper deck of a warship. As the carpark had two entrances, I gunned the heap through at speed, swaying the lights from side to side as a probe. Nothing broke cover. Coming around again, I stopped, covered Willa as she made it to the foyer, and then followed her at a run.

The penthouse looked out over the river and the city on one side and into deep gum tree foliage on the other. We were only four storeys up, and the trees worried me. Still, there was a twenty metre gap between the sealed windows and the tips of the branches. A heavy possum would have fallen from the tips.

The huge living area had dark windows and exposed beams against the plaster of the ceiling. There was no sound here. A regular cocoon. The door was solid wood. Only a heavy rifle shot would penetrate it. Not that it was designed for such an attack. It was just that expensive apartments are expected to have such substance. There were two deadlocks on the door. I carried the Glock with me everywhere and I noticed Willa did the same with the Ruger. She had been badly frightened.

I could feel a change in her. A greater strength of mind. She made sure that everything we were doing had a base of common sense that she felt she could rely on. She had collected her mail and papers on the way up and now she spread the front page of today's paper on the kitchen bench, smoothing it. I read the first few paragraphs over her shoulder and scanned the subheads. They didn't have the chemicals analysed yet, according to the CSIRO and the Port of Melbourne Authority.

'It's all there,' I said, 'but the serious stuff.'

'Have you read this story through?' she said.

'Not all of it. It depresses me that they're so way off.'

'You didn't read the last paragraphs then?' she said, still fitting them together in the paper. I shook my head.

'It says here that Evans had recent contracts with Israel and Syria.'

'So, his deals weren't so secret,' I said.

'Perhaps they heard about each other.' She made each hand into an imitation handgun, pointed them at each other and said, 'Pop.' She was becoming aware of how close we all are to the dangerous things that countries do to each other. She gave a bitter laugh.

'It's time to use Bresler,' I said.

'How?' she asked.

'It's just possible he can get the manifest. If we have that, we have proof. That way we get Nick Harris revealing it in Parliament, its out in the open and we're safer.'

'Why do you think Peter can get it?'

'He had the details of the Coode Island fire . . . those chemicals. So he's close to someone who can supply those things. And he knew enough to make the list look authentic.'

Willa picked up her phone, dialled, and stood looking out over the city.

'Make it sound like you want to fuck him,' I said. 'We really need this.'

She looked at me coldly. Finally there was an answer. 'I have a problem, Peter,' she said. 'I know it's ridiculous, but just listen to me. Someone is trying to kill us. We need to know who was dealing with Evans, with this shipload of chemicals burning in the bay. We were trying to get it from Evans but he was killed tonight . . . I assure you, he is dead I saw it . . . Now I want everything, the actual manifest, all of it. Well, we can't get it any other way, and I happen to think it's very important that the public knows what the chemicals are that are smouldering away. You can get it?' She turned and looked at me, smiling. 'What about the Syrian–Israeli thing in today's paper?' He took some time answering that one. She made an appointment to meet him in the morning and hung up.

The lighting in the room was concealed and the globes were burning away on low. It was very pleasant not to be running. Willa tossed herself down on a leather sofa, her legs relaxed. She turned and stretched like a cat. She was pleased with herself.

'What did he say when you said people were trying to kill us?' I didn't trust Bresler to bring the manifest, but at least we'd have a chance to get him alone, find out what he knew.

'That it was ridiculous.'

'Did you convince him?'

'You heard me. I told him we saw Evans killed.'

'How did he react to that?'

'He was cagey, Practically anyone would want to kill Evans, he said. He saw straight away that anyone who wanted to keep the purchase quiet would want to kill us. If they thought we could expose it all, we were in deep trouble.'

'What about the Israeli–Syrian thing?'

'He doesn't know. Not sure whether to believe it. It's an unlikely scenario. He thinks it was told to the press to misinform. Put investigators off the track. Make it super hard.'

'Did he say "super hard"?'

'Yes?'

'Is he an Englishman?'

'He's lived in the UK.'

'How wealthy is he?'

Willa looked at me and raised her eyebrows. 'Jack, he has houses, cars and racehorses. He's powerful and influential. He has to be wealthy.'

During the next hour we speculated on all the possibilities. Evans had his napalm and Agent Orange on a ship that blew up in the bay. If someone wanted the stuff on a deadline, would he be blamed for that? I didn't think so, unless he had guaranteed a delivery date and that had been the essence of the contract. There had to be an out for a dealer in explosives. He would be insured. Dicey proposition for an insurance broker, and yet the big oil company didn't lose their insurance when a nuclear warship tied up at a Williamstown dock, fifty metres from where they stored their most vulnerable and flammable chemicals.

Had he blown the ship for insurance? No, that had to be ridiculous. The deaths of the crew would have weighed too heavily in such a calculation. Didn't seem feasible. You left yourself wide open to be discovered down the track.

Blowing the fucking thing in the home port was outrageous; killing the crew was inhuman; destroying the bay was setting yourself up for inquiries forever. Such a thing was unbelievable.

Willa agreed. 'No one would plan the death of a whole crew,' she said. 'Anyway, he would have enough money to be comfortable. He wouldn't have to do something like that.'

I didn't bother to answer her. It's always those who live on inherited wealth who state that X couldn't be crooked because he had enough money already. They don't understand that X had no money as a child and a youth, lived in poverty, and was very afraid that if he didn't keep making money, he would end up that way again.

So, for those with inherited wealth, there was a whole area of ignorance. It made them as vulnerable as a day-old foal. I thought of Shy Bride's long-legged filly, slipping and sliding for those first few minutes before a drink. Once they had made it once, though, I had never seen them fall again unless it was in a paddock of tall wet grass, and they were annoyed at themselves for being so careless. They might stamp their feet or give an oddly shaped bush a quick passing kick.

I looked at Willa. She had the fineness of a thoroughbred and she had grown up with a huge gap in her knowledge that had left her innocent. Until now that is.

'What are you looking at?' she asked.

'You,' I said.

'It's embarrassing.' And she did have the look of a child in a schoolyard having been propositioned for a date for the first time. How did she still have that childlike thing after such a remarkable amount of time? Perhaps because she was an innocent by nature. And yet she had obviously swapped Peter for me very easily. Had she known that excitement, going from one bed to another in a turmoil of lust and ecstasy? Could she go straight back to Peter if I was killed, no matter his profession? Could his lovemaking persuade her to betray me in the future, if there was a future? Even considering her a vessel of lust prompted a dirty sort of excitement.

And that pulled me up hard. The idle speculation around the motivations of lust had given me an answer.

'I think', I said slowly, still watching her length of thigh, 'that Evans sold the cargo to two different buyers, that he had to blow the ship so that neither of them would discover the deception.'

Seventeen

We stared at one another for a time. 'Using your imagination can lead you to the truth,' I said, smiling. She demurred, wouldn't argue about it. She stretched on the couch.

'Does your imagination tell you that with Evans dead, it just might be all over?' she asked.

'The freak?' I asked, remembering the bastard's last attempt.

'A revenge thing that made him chase us?'

'Revenge for what?'

'For you blowing him off the roof.'

'I don't think so,' I said.

'But it was only Evans we were exposing.'

'There is a greater evil,' I said. It sounded like I was some psychic at work. It wasn't all that profound, either, not even novel, but I felt it was apt for the current circumstances. I knew we had some respite, but it wouldn't be much.

She changed into a light summer dress that came mid-thigh, and she walked in it as if she were eighteen. There was a flounce to her step and her legs were lithe and capable. She poured me a whisky and crossed the room to give it to me. I held one ankle and she stayed beside me, sipping her own drink.

I ran my hand up between her knees. 'Let's get these off,' I said and ran her pants down her legs. She left me holding them, and curled up on the sofa.

I edged towards her but she moved away. She took off her bra, taking it from beneath her dress and running the shoulder straps over her elbows and hands. It was made from a shiny, silky textile. She threw it towards me.

'Take the dress off,' I said. For a moment she wasn't sure she wanted the play to continue, and then she stood up, walked towards me and turned to be unzipped. 'Do it, will you?' she said. The zip came down below the waist and I touched her back and then her hips. She put her arms to her side and I slid the dress down.

Facing me, she stood like an offering. An elegant, dynamic body that was submissive for a moment. I watched her face as we caught each other and her eyes never left mine. At first it seemed as if she were seeking support, and then she branched onto another line of existence, only to return, clinging to me, taking my movement to the centre of her body. Her skin was delicate and responsive to the slightest brush from my skin, and we both sucked and panted our way to a delirious pleasure.

I lay beside Willa, drifting in and out of those thoughts, finally dozing. The flitting dreams were those of a child. I felt again the enormous weight of being kept ignorant of the things that were happening around me. They had decided there were things I shouldn't know—while I suspected everything. But it was all continually denied. I was being denied. In my dream, I decided to take the first step towards discovery.

Awake a few moments later, I felt completely at one with all around me. I knew that if I acted, others would finally have to follow. The morning light followed me into the living-room.

I rang Linda, hoping to catch her before she left for the horses. She took a while to answer. 'How is it up there?' I asked, looking out over the early morning city, the sun just catching the tops of the buildings. They had the same look as a yacht far out on the ocean suddenly lit by the sun.

'Your neighbour, Charlie, right,' she said, 'he told me there were people looking for you. He told them you had shot through, that you owed money. He was doing the animals a favour looking after them. The foal is thriving, by the way. No sign of any joint ill. It's a good method of yours— that salt on the umbilical cord.' I thought back to the birth. I remembered Linda applying the salt. It stopped the infection that occurs on big studs. Infection through the umbilical infects the joints on foals. Massive doses of antibiotics follow later.

'I want those two-year-olds down here,' I said. 'Do you have any problems with that?'

She laughed. 'Why would I?'

'Okay, what I want you to do is ring around a few of those Caulfield trainers who've just got public licences. They'll be in that racing calender that arrived the other day. It's near the phone. They'll all have a couple of stables free. Talk to them.'

Willa came in as I put the phone down. 'What's going on?'

'We need to get close to Bresler,' I said.

'Why?'

'I'd say he was laundering money through racing. Money from illegal arms trading can't be declared. It's easy if you have track connections. And Evans has horses too. They would have known each other. People with good horses make a point of getting to know each other. It's a way for us to get closer to where they live their business.'

'I can look after Peter,' she said.

I looked at her hard. 'Good. If we get at him from two fronts, it's better.'

Over breakfast, I told her about how she'd changed. She denied it. 'I've always been hard,' she said. 'If you're hard on yourself, you can be hard on other people.'

'Well, you have a great style to cover it all,' I said, meaning that she moved through her life with a confident concern for people.

At nine-thirty I rang the state laboratories and asked for David Belden, the scientist's name on the chemical report faxed to me by the Werribee vet.

He picked up the phone and I asked him if he remembered the report. 'Certainly do,' he said. There was humour in his voice. I wondered why.

'You appear to have left out one of the essential ingredients of the 2,4-D, 2,4,5-T mix,' I said.

'No, I don't think so,' he said.

'According to my sources, you have. That mix does in fact create a dioxin.'

'I couldn't test for that,' he said.

'Why not?'

'To obtain enough of it to test would be a very hazardous process.'

'So, it doesn't all just turn into a dioxin?' Finally I wanted him to support all the information I had and then write a report for our politician Nick Harris.

'Only a fraction of it.'

'You can't test for that?'

'We don't have the facilities to do it safely.'

'You mean *you* don't?'

'No one does. Not in this country. There was a lab in Western Australia, but that was owned by the company importing the stuff.'

'2,4-D and 2,4,5-T is in fact Agent Orange, isn't it?'

'I couldn't comment on that.'

'Why not?'

'I've never tested Agent Orange. I would have to test the stuff before I could say it was identical to your mix.'

'A matter of interest,' I said. 'Are you getting any chemicals to test from the ship in the bay?'

'Not yet,' he said.

'Are you expecting to?'

'Well, we should.'

'Would you be prepared to write a letter for a politician spelling out what you know about Agent Orange, and what the problem is testing for any dioxin it might produce?'

'No,' he said. 'Any letter to a politician would have to go through the director of this institute. And we'd have to have the request from him, the polly.'

'I understand that,' I said. 'And you'll have an official request from him. But I'd like to follow up a bit on this. Those samples you have of Agent Orange were taken from a truck dumping the stuff in the Yarra River.'

He was silent for a moment. 'Are you there?' I asked.

'Are you certain?' he said.

'I collected it,' I said.

'Have you reported it to the Environment Protection Authority?' He firmly believed that the bureaucratic institutions could handle everything. Didn't these people ever ask themselves why we're in the mess we are? I had been reporting the leaks from the Point Gellibrand wharf for two years and no one was ever fined. Thousands of people had been reporting air and water spills for years. Nothing ever happened, perhaps a pollution fine on a company, one that could be paid out of the social club's petty cash tin.

'I'll tell you about the EPA,' I said. 'They're totally toothless. People have to do their investigations and metre out their own punishments.'

He was silent again. 'I know,' he said, in a voice without strength, accepting my allegations as if they were something he had known for a long time and had now allowed to rise to the surface.

'Can I have your number?' he said. I gave him Willa's. Also the number of the farm and the address there.

'If you were prepared to do anything on this,' I said, 'you'd lose . . . '

'I didn't say I'd do anything,' he said quickly.

It seemed to me, though, as I hung up, that here was an individual who could be called upon for some moonlighting in a good cause.

I called Nick Harris's office and was told he would be at Parliament House this morning. I rang Parliament House and, after a few minutes' delay, I got through. 'Can I see you later today?' He seemed slow on the uptake, so I reminded him that he had promised to take relevant evidence to the Parliament.

'I want real evidence,' he said. 'I mean documented.' He was very unhappy.

'It looks as if we'll have the evidence you need.'

He didn't like it. He didn't answer until he had run it through his analytical mind. I knew his logic was prompted by questions that went something like this: will the damage be worse if I ignore this offer of information? or will it catch up with me down the track?

He obviously decided that my track record indicated it was possible he would be hurt if he ignored it. 'I'll leave a message that I'm to be called out of the House when you arrive,' he said.

I watched Willa dressing through the bedroom door. She was talking to me as if she were quite unconscious of her body. I hadn't seen her dressing before. To me, she was dressing to meet another suitor.

'I hope Peter is sincere about the manifest,' she called, as if I weren't watching her. She thumbed her pants up over her hips, took the bra from the bed and leaned forward to encase her breasts and then straightened up again to apply the hooks at her back. 'It's possible he won't be. He dangles things like that.' She slipped on a shirt and buttoned it at the full-length mirror. One leg was slightly cocked, and the smoothness of her inner thighs was very inviting.

'I'll come with you,' I said.

She turned and looked at me. 'I'm safe with Peter,' she said.

'Yeah,' I said. 'You're right. Where are you meeting?'

'At Provisions. It's up the road.'

'He doesn't want to come here?'

'I don't want him here.' She slipped the Ruger into her bag, swung it on her shoulder, smiled at me and headed towards the door. 'You'll have to drop me off, though. I don't have my car.'

I checked the breech of the Glock, slipped out the magazine, hefted it for weight, even though I knew it carried a full load, and then slipped it back into the butt. I followed her to the lift and put my arm around her.

Eighteen

We waited for Bresler, but he didn't arrive. The morning was bright with a thinnish sunshine, not far off cold. Willa rang his numbers, but no one knew where he was. 'He's playing it very carefully,' I said. The coffee was strong and rich and the cafe was warm.

'Do you think he's gone?' Willa asked.

'Gone where?'

'Have they killed him?' she said.

'I doubt it, he's just in a funk. I know the type. You've only seen him once under any sort of pressure.' I was jealous and liked staking Bresler out like this for Willa's examination. I continued. 'Things are catching up with him. His social life is jeopardised. He's one of those people who pretend they know it all, have influence, and really they're running around picking up crumbs. They're never really playing the game.'

'He's a bloody jerk,' she added, exasperated. It seemed a quaint description of him, but the vehemence was appropriate.

I thought we should go back to the dock, where everything had started. The thought of the tall, lanky bloke hiding around the corner of the shack on the chemical dock when I had first approached them had stayed with me. It was almost as if he had been sprung. He had thrown his head back against the wall, hard, as if he was punishing himself for his own stupidity.

'Let's go for a drive,' I said.

Linda called. A truck coming through from the Adelaide races could pick up the horses. She would have them bedded down at Caulfield tonight. There was a feeling of relief. She would stay with us overnight and find lodgings nearer the stables in the morning.

I peeled off the Westgate Bridge to the south and then headed down towards the river.

'Where are we going?' Willa asked.

'Coode Island,' I said.

On the island, I slowed the car. The checkpoint was manned, but there was very little traffic. Beyond it were a few tanks farms and the chemical dock. I stayed far enough away from the checkpoint to be indistinguishable, and took my field glasses and focused them.

'What's this for?' Willa asked.

'The manifest. I just want to follow one of these blocks from the dock. See what we have.'

'They're not going to hand it over.'

'I dunno. They must be feeling uneasy about now. They know a co-worker is dead. It's amazing how friendly that can make people become if they don't really know why it's happened.'

At lunchtime a battered old car moved up to the checkpoint from the other side. I put the glasses on it. It was lanky, alright.

'Get down,' I said, sliding low myself. I glanced at Willa's legs, revealed in their dark stocking as her dress rode up. She flicked her eyes skywards, as it to say does this have to go on all the time.

The lanky bloke didn't even look at the car, despite it being unusual. When he hit the end of the street, I U-turned and followed him. I hoped it was his lunch hour and we didn't have to follow him home and knock on his door. He drove to the old Graham Hotel in Footscray. The counter lunches had a sort of rural bent to the menu. Heavy soups, casseroles, roasts.

I stayed in the car while Willa went in to talk to him as a sympathetic journalist. I watched her walk. Upright, broad shoulders, that something appealing I couldn't place in any category except style. This thing with her was becoming serious. The lovemaking was so tantalising, so novel, that just seeing her leg appear for a moment against her skirt as she stepped up into the hotel, hardened me.

I left the car and followed her into the pub. The chemical worker had his back to me and she was talking to him at the bar, explaining to him in a way that could only be listened to—deep and sincere eye contact—exactly what she had in mind for a story. When she glanced across and saw me, there was a flicker of annoyance, but then she was back in the role.

'I can do this story keeping your involvement to a minimum,' she said. 'But if I don't get your cooperation, I'll have to drop the human approach and do it as a solid investigation.' She stopped, took the drink she had ordered, and looked at him, wondering if he had taken on the full implication.

'Somebody is going to have to wear this,' she continued. 'If we do it as an investigation, we will have to use the words of the company. You know what they'll say as well as I do. They'll say it was a mistake in loading procedures, something like that.'

'I wasn't the foreman,' he began.

'I know that,' she said. 'He's dead, so someone else will have to wear it. You.'

'They're not saying that to me.'

'Of course they're not. They'll keep you quiet until the timing is right to drop you in it. Then it will be too late for you to complain. The press will be saying, why didn't you say this earlier?'

I was totally taken by her ability. She would have made a great muckraker, except they would have sent her out on boring human interest stories until they had blunted her edge.

'I don't know about this,' the lanky bloke said. I caught his face in profile. He was a worrier. She followed up. 'All we need to do is blame it on the chemical mix,' she said. 'I know it was the mix. You know it was, but we can't prove it until we have the manifest, a copy of it at least.'

He was won. 'I can't get it to you until tonight.'

Willa had arranged to meet him on the Melbourne—Werribee road. She would follow his car the moment he left work and then catch him on the highway. I would be driving, and she would reach for the manifest. That way, she explained, it cut down any opportunities for violence. And once the manifest had exchanged hands the lanky bloke would be comparatively safe.

'You have a talent for this,' I said.

'I'm beginning to think I could be very nasty,' she said.

We'd had the windows on Willa's car fixed by a garage on Nelson Place. We drove to pick up her car in the carpark there. I checked beneath it for any recent additions, checked the interior before opening it, and then went under the dash for a further look. No bombs, but it paid to be careful.

It was mid-morning and there was very little traffic about, so we walked across to a coffee shop and watched the traffic and the carpark. In fact, I wanted to rid the area of the juggler's presence. I didn't want him playing around in my imagination, hovering here in one of my favourite areas. I loved the glints of sunlight off the flat sea around the marinas. It was like that magic act of getting back on your horse a moment after you've been thrown. The action gives you back your nerve. Just his presence had got very close to breaking me.

A few people walked along to use the laundromat, but it was a decidedly slow morning. No one looked remotely suspicious. The Glock was very reassuring, though, resting lightly against my back muscles.

Willa left the shop first. She would take the road around the water and I'd follow a few moments later. We were headed to Parliament House in Spring Street.

Although Nick Harris was a Federal politician, we were going to meet him at the State Parliament buildings where he had a previous meeting. We drove up Collins Street and swung through the traffic lights to the carpark behind the House. We were asked who we were seeing, then pointed to parking areas on soft grass. We walked up to the back door, the entrance through which the politicians avoided the public. The guard rang through to Nick and, instead of giving us ID cards, told us that Nick was on his way down to see us.

He came down the corridors of pretence with big strides, putting an arm out to shepherd me back outside. He looked impressive, his Armani giving him the image of some wealthy and stylish entrepreneur. I didn't think it was a good look for a working politician. I stood fast and his arm fell to his side. I introduced him to Willa and he lost the quality of urgency which he had imagined was going to get him out of this one.

'We'll talk outside,' he said.

We walked out in front of him. He didn't seem to know how to handle Willa. 'This is getting into something quite big,' he said.

We didn't say anything.

'I received a call from the prime minister,' Nick began, ducking slightly in deference even to the title. 'He wants this thing played down.' I gave a grunt of laughter. I was supposed to be impressed.

'What?' Nick asked me, knowing he had missed something.

'It can hardly be played down,' I said. 'The crew all died, and the bay is turning into the closest thing around here to dead water.'

'It'll blow over.'

'Not without people talking it through, promising things,' I said.

'It'll ruin our trade if people begin to suspect we have a dangerous port.'

'Bullshit,' I said. 'The PM wants it hidden for other reasons. There's a lot of filth going on down here.'

'No evidence, though?' Nick said, looking hopeful. His face had a phoney look of anticipation, as if it were saying, you've got something for me, haven't you? But it was an old look, the fire had gone out of it, like an old footballer in a bar making a move on an old mate, offering a shoulder to bump, stylised and with no strength.

'It's forthcoming,' Willa said in an impressive tone.

'Let this one go,' I said, 'and you'll lose your electorate next election.'

Nick turned away for a moment. 'Tell me the worst,' he said. He didn't bother to hide his resignation. He really hated having to do anything at all.

'The worst is that you have one of the world's deadliest dioxins sloshing around in the bay. That's a little thing your children will inherit down the track when their livers refuse to work. And those chemicals appear to have been going to Syria; that should be good for our international reputation.'

I stopped and looked at him, waiting for a response. Nothing. I continued. 'The worst thing for you is that it will be discovered that the PM manipulated you on this, and you will be remembered in history as something putrid. You had a chance to make a difference and you did nothing. Of course, there'll be a lot in that category by the end of the decade.'

He laughed nervously. 'No wonder you're a good journalist,' he said. Suck, I thought.

'Meanwhile,' I said, 'there are people trying to kill us. The same people who killed Evans. We don't know who they are.'

'I read that this morning,' he said. 'I thought that might be how we could make it low profile.

The person responsible for the ship going up is now dead.' He was refusing to see any reality at all.

'Yeah, murdered,' I said. 'Very low profile.'

'What have you got?' he said suddenly, putting his hands out for the envelope of photographs, and the information from Willa's friend, Germaine, and then just as suddenly withdrawing it. 'I don't want to know just now. I have to make some decisions today and it would be best I didn't know.'

'Fuck you,' I said.

He grabbed me by the arm, but spoke to Willa. 'I'll look at everything you have at the weekend. I'll meet you . . . somewhere. Not at my place. I have party people coming all the time.'

Nick took our numbers and swore he'd get back to us.

As we walked away from him, Willa said, 'How depressing.'

'What part of it?'

'All of it. His positively crawling deference to the prime minister was terrible.' There it was again. On some levels the wealthy by inheritance barely knew how the world worked.

Back at her apartment she asked me if I knew the prime minister. 'Yes,' I said.

'Could you ring him?'

'For what?'

'His help.'

'He can't help us. If we approached him with what we've got so far, we'd be overrun with federal cops. I'd be raided; you'd be raided. We'd get nothing done. The whole thing would be covered up. How would it look if the government was forced to announce that Australia had been providing weapons to terrorists? The gutless bastard would paddle down shit creek before he would do that.'

Linda rang about three and said she would see us later in the evening. Willa spoke to her and I realised from the warmth of her voice how much she liked Linda. She handed me the phone. 'They're perfect,' Linda breathed. 'Haven't been troubled by the journey at all. Fantastic temperaments.' I arranged to meet her in the morning, early.

'What time is early?' Willa asked.

'Any time from four-thirty on.'

Willa shook her head. 'Dark time.'

I asked her if she liked Linda. 'Yes,' she said. 'She has developed the confidence to get what she wants. She's battled. She knows she deserves some success and is going after it.'

At four we headed out to Coode Island again. We parked in an area usually reserved for trucks and waited for the lanky bloke, Dick Scullard, to leave the chemical dock. Ten minutes after we settled, his battered vehicle hove into view and headed through Footscray to Old Melbourne Road and the ramp onto the freeway.

He didn't appear to look in the mirror, there was no shifting of the head, but he was prepared when I drew alongside him in Willa's BMW. He handed her a brown manila envelope. I kept pace with him until she had slit it and pulled out the manifest. It was headed Cargo and Tankage status. I eased back, found a firm place to cross the nature strip in the middle of the freeway and headed back to Melbourne. Old Nick wouldn't be able to squirm out of this one.

'It's the right date,' Willa said. 'The right ship, the *Dana Rose*, and the right chemicals. It's not marked as Agent Orange, just its numerical identification. Same with napalm.'

We drove to a Pink Panther copying outlet and ran off fifty copies. At the South Yarra Post Office, I sent myself and Willa and a lawyer I knew several copies each. Willa sent some to friends. If anyone was watching us during this activity, and I hoped they were, they would have understood that the game was close to over for them. The relief of having evidence and distributing it made us a little crazy, a little happy.

It was marred by the message from Linda on the answering machine that she wouldn't stay with us tonight but would see us in the morning at the track.

'Not me,' Willa said.

Nineteen

They say that no trainer with an untried two-year-old in their stable ever committed suicide. The reason for that is the euphoria and wealth that temporarily descends on you when your horse wins.

Willa and I walked down the darkened corridor of corrugated iron to the training complex. The trainer's office spilt a pool of light out over the saddling courtyard.

I doubt if suicide had ever entered the mind of Frank Big, the trainer Linda had found. He was wide open to offers. I said I had some more horses to be trained and I didn't think Linda could handle more than the couple she had.

'If they're any good, I'll train them,' Frank said. 'If they're shit, they're out. Do you want Linda? She's here now. I'll give her a call.' He looked at Willa. 'Got any horses?' he asked her. Willa shook her head and Frank lost interest, walking to the door of his office.

'Don't call her,' I said. 'I'll see her later.' I told him that Peter Bresler had once mentioned him. 'Shit, that's strange,' he said. 'He's never been sighted around here, although over the years I've had a couple of horses that have beaten his.'

'What's he got running around at the moment?'

Frank tossed me some marked-up race books before he left the office to tend his horses. Willa stood in the door absorbing all the horsey sights, sounds and smells.

I found that Bresler was racing Devastator. The horse was an average sprinter who, with the right weight, could win the better-class handicaps. He was a five-year-old, so he was well tried and tested. He would hold no surprises, unless in later years they found he could suddenly gallop in the wet. And then if he could get a mile, they would try him over jumps. There was a theory that a horse in the air, not using his galloping muscles, was no longer under stress and, for a second, was refreshed. So, a horse that could sprint over a mile, freshening up over jumps, was a better proposition than a slow but proven stayer. This theory was yet to be supported by laboratory tests.

None of the race books were well thumbed, twisted or battered, so Frank wasn't a nervous or losing gambler. There were no old form guides or a gambler's hieroglyphics on the back of anything.

I went outside with Willa and caught up with Frank. 'What's Bresler's interest in racing, Frank? What'a you reckon?'

'Meet people, do business, impress clients.'

'Yeah, I suppose,' I said. 'Say he was paying off people and laundering the money, how would he work it?'

'Got good horses have you? As good as Linda's two?'

'Young stuff coming up, same breeding. Two geldings that could win you a sprint in the city if you set them right.'

'Good enough,' he said, grinning at me. He explained how it worked. If you wanted untraceable money, you paid the jockeys riding the good horses in a race to allow one horse to win. Then, for the individual you owed the money, you put a bet on the winner at something over six to one. To be able to do these things, you needed to have a racing *in*. Hence the horses owned by Bresler and Evans. They could even arrange the race fix for those buying from them. For huge amounts of money, they could arrange many races.

'Have a look at his horses,' I said. 'Is there any sort of pattern there?'

'Hah,' he said, scanning quickly. 'They ran Devastator out of his distance. You know, didn't need to pull him up. He'd get a flying fuck before he got two thousand. So here they've got the odds up because he doesn't look so good now. Then they run him the same distance so that when they pulled him back to a mile, his real distance, he looks a dog of a horse. That's when they make sure he wins. They wouldn't have to pay out much at all.'

'And that's how they launder the money?'

'It's usually the business partners who do that. They keep a gap between owner and operators.'

Around us, strappers were hosing down animals that had already worked out. The horses were steaming in the morning air. The water was scraped from their hides with steel bands or hoops that squeezed the water from their coats.

Then came the best part for the horses, the towelling. They were never dried completely, but the horses loved it. I noticed Frank had learned some lessons from the old school. Hay was placed along the horses' back before the coats were thrown over them again. This allowed quicker drying because of the air circulating through the hay. Later in the day, they would be groomed until they gleamed.

As I greeted Linda, who was saddling our two in their boxes, she jumped. 'God, you frightened me.' She rested her forehead against the high saddle flaps for a second, as if she were about to give up. Willa gave her a quick hug. I stroked Apple's velvet muzzle.

The jockeys who were to ride were young blokes who already had the clock in their heads, knew to the second what time the horse was doing as it pounded home down the straight, could limit that horse to any time Linda asked. As we walked with the horses out onto the sand tracks, the morning gloom gave the figures hanging around the track a shadowy, ephemeral appearance.

Willa, Linda and I walked on as the jockeys rode the horses out onto the track. 'How's it been?' I asked Linda.

'Haven't done much but stay with the horses,' she said. 'They're working even better on this surface.'

As the horses bounded eager onto an outside track, I sensed danger. There are some people who can sense the wrongness of things even though they can't put their finger on it. It is the sense of a hunter who, quite unconsciously, has hooked into the trace of a smell of a wild boar or the rutting scent of wild cattle. I've ridden stock horses who know instantly when there is a renegade in the herd, and they refuse to go near it. They'll stay fifty metres away and balk at any attempt to press the animal further.

I scanned the vast shadows of the stands as we moved out to the centre of the track, where Linda could time the horses coming away from the six hundred. Anybody could be in those empty stands, crouching behind rows of seats ready to blow us into the turf.

Linda had field glasses and watched as the horses did some steady pace work in the back straight. It would take them several minutes to make their way around to the six hundred.

Behind us was the small shelter for the trainers, who had so many horses they would freeze if left to the elements while their horses flew past.

Linda nudged me as the horses neared the six hundred, slipping into another gear. The sky was still dark, the horses were flying. Art Shy seemed to toss his head as if he wanted to slip under the bit, but he took it up again and settled down to the hard work over the last two hundred. I watched them coming to the line, fast, a shade quicker than I had seen before, ever.

If they came in at thirty-six, it meant that the jockeys had held them back over the first two hundred. It was harder to check their time accurately that far out. As the horses came bouncing up, blowing, excited with themselves, Linda said, 'The pricks,' under her breath. I looked at her and she raised her eyebrows. I understood. She had timed them over the first two hundred, found it slow. They'd come home way too fast. The secret of the horses' speed would be well and truly out.

'You brought them home too fast over the last two hundred,' Linda said.

'They were pulling hard,' Art Shy's jockey said.

'Bullshit,' Linda said. 'If you want to ride this horse, don't spoil him.'

I took Linda's glasses as she bent down to check the front legs. I swung them up onto the stands. I couldn't shake the feeling that someone was watching us, waiting for a shot, waiting for anything.

As the horses were about to move off at a trot, I called them back.

'I want to check their recovery,' I said to Linda, and the jockeys walked the horses across the sand tracks, a barrier between us and the stand. I was bent over, my fingers on the pulse on the inside of the knee. The horses were fit. The rate was already no more than forty-five, and dropping.

Then I heard a horse coming hard down on the outer sand track, too close. I had a strong urge to run the horses across before it arrived on us, but there was no time. The jockeys looked at each other. You didn't ride so hard in this deep sand. We risked being trampled if the horses were spooked. The galloping horse didn't slacken speed. My skin crawled like hackles rising on a dog's back.

I grabbed Art Shy's bit and pulled him around, keeping us hidden from the rider as he rocketed past. The jockey on Art Shy's back looked down at the gun in my hand.

'Do you know him?' I asked.

He shook his head. 'Fucking amateur. He'll break that horse down.' His answer was automatic. The gun held all his attention.

The horse slowed three hundred metres on and continued around at a trot. I didn't want him coming around again——that frightful dream feeling of being unable to move while it all happened over again. I had to break the thought. I felt the adrenalin rush. It was the sort of madness that had saved me before. It rose as a bright rage. I left the group, running over the outer sand track.

I watched the horse and rider as I ran. He leaned forward as the horse broke into three-quarter pace. I had a couple of minutes. He wouldn't push the horse as hard this time or it would drop from beneath him. I ran hard to get around behind the grandstands.

Here was the wide expanse of the betting ring. Once over the iron fence with its Victorian spikes, I ducked up the stairway into the members stand, and waited.

Half a minute later I heard the sounds of the horse on the asphalt. There was a slight ding to one of the racing plates—it was loose. The horse stopped. The silence tempted me to look or run. Just check, I told myself; that's all I'd be doing. Stay, stay, I repeated, smothering the temptation. If he comes around the corner, I have him.

I strained for the sound of the horse. Most horses would be moving around fidgeting, after a run. I broke cover then, for he could have come up other stairs and might be descending the tiers behind me. I ran from the stairs. There was a flash of movement behind a bookie's odds frame. I fired and the empty frame spun.

He was gone behind the fence, behind . . . behind what? I was leaning over the cyclone fence, looking down the row at nothing. It was a cleared area and he wasn't there.

I ducked back quickly as a burst of bullets hit the fence, snapping iron and ploughing asphalt. It was a silenced weapon. The rider was above me, miraculously clinging to the roof there. I fired as he dropped. My reflexes were nowhere near like his. It was the acrobat. This fucking freak, probably saw everything in slow motion as well. I began pulling off shots. I hit his arm and the machine pistol dropped. Another bullet plucked at his leg. Then I was hit in the side with a force that tossed me backwards, ripping at me. As I fell, I kept pulling off shots in the freak's direction. When I looked, the area was empty.

Where is he? I thought, my mind curling with fear. I felt a warm liquid flowing across my stomach, and my head was light enough to float away. 'Keep at it, keep at it,' I said aloud. 'Keep watching. He'll be back, get the bastard.'

'What are you saying?' Frank's voice said, and I opened eyes that I had thought were already open and searching. Frank was examining the wound. I looked out towards the Glock, it was held by a very small fist a very, very long way away.

'They were here,' I said.

'I can see that,' Frank said. 'Just don't tell me about it. The ambulance is on its way.'

'Show me,' I said to Frank. 'Show me where. I want to see it. It's better if I see it.'

Frank pulled my shirt away. The hole was in my side. It was a strange thing, because it had tendrils of white fat splaying out of it and against my skin. The fat had refused to absorb the blood that was flowing there.

'Did it come out?' I asked, meaning the bullet.

'Yeah,' Frank said, 'underneath you.'

I lifted myself, shifting on to my left side, to show the hole beneath, on the right. 'How bad is it bleeding?'

'There's been a nice flow,' Frank said. 'It's clotting, closing off.'

'I don't want to go to hospital,' I said. 'The bullet's gone.' I thought that all I probably needed was one of those plastic air-tight bandages they have now, so the wound heals in its own juices. They leave them on for a week, and everything's healed. In a hospital, I would be an easy mark.

Frank brought a car around and drove me to his complex. 'I can fix you up a bit,' he said. 'But someone will squeal to the racing squad. I'm going to say I bound you up and put you on your way to hospital.'

Willa and Linda were at the entrance to the complex. I staggered into the ensuite off Frank's office. 'I want pethidine,' I said. 'This is going to hurt soon.' All trainers have a stock of pethidine, synthetic heroin. It quietens a horse until the vet arrives, helps the trainer deal with the anxiety, live a few more years into old age. 'It's not a problem,' I said, looking at the wounds front and back. 'It's just gone through the fat.'

'We don't know that.' Willa and Linda had come in with wadded cotton wool and bandages. Willa sprayed the entrance and exit wounds with iodine and bound the wound quickly, then sponged off the blood. She dressed me, pulling on my jeans, pulling on a shirt Frank handed her, giving me a pair of strapper's socks, wiping the blood from the shoes.

Linda handed me a bottle of antibiotic. I looked at the instructions. It was for a broad spectrum of bacteria, it needed shaking, and it recommended 20 ml for a horse. I thought 5 ml would do for me. I attached needle to syringe, shook the phial, held it bottom up in my hand, pushed the needle through the rubber membrane and sucked out 5 ml, then thought, 6 to be on the safe side. I pulled the shirt up on my arm, swabbed the flesh at the back of the upper arm and whacked the needle in. The antibiotic was bulky in the muscle. I slipped out the needle, capped it, rubbed my arm for several minutes and then swabbed it again. Nothing like playing it safe, I thought.

Frank handed Willa a syringe with pethidine. 'I dunno about this,' he said. 'It says only for animal use. Don't give it to him unless the pain gets too much.'

'If you can get up,' Willa said. 'I'll take you.' There was no pain as I stood up, but I did it by numbers anyway, so the bleeding wouldn't start again. I realised the bullet had been a heavy calibre one because it had stayed intact to exit.

Linda brought the car over and she and Willa helped me into the passenger seat. We bumped over to the carpark, down over the steep guttering and onto the road. At a chemist shop in Malvern Road, we stopped for plastic dressings.

'Tell them they're for your grandfather's bed sores,' I said. Fuck it, I thought, as Linda walked into the pharmacy, there has to be an easier way for me. I should have started out with a kill policy. I'd be better off now. In case we were being followed, I held the Glock in my lap, scanning the street ahead, and then the rear vision for activity behind me. I realised Willa was watching my tremors.

'I think you need a hospital.'

'Only if infection sets in,' I said.

Linda was back in a moment. 'He told me there's some controversy about them,' she said, as she slipped behind the wheel and eased the car out into the traffic. 'Some doctors swear by the method. It's revolutionary. Others opt for the old iodine methods.'

We took a room at the Windsor Hotel under a bogus name. I felt strong again, but the movement of the lift left me nauseous.

I lay on towels Linda had placed on the bed. My side was bleeding, an oozing flow. Linda sprayed the entry and exit wounds with a clear, odourless liquid, and Willa smoothed the adhesive plastic into place. 'These have to be good,' she said. 'They were twelve dollars a pop.'

The dressings were comforting, they held my flesh firmly. I felt too fit to sleep now, and I didn't feel right in the hotel. Willa wanted to be home, but we would need protection. I gave her the number of a security firm and half an hour later we had it. Four young men, obviously moonlighting from the police force, drove two in a front car and two in a rear, to Willa's apartment. Two stayed outside in the hall and two remained in the wide entrance hall. They checked the rooms and the windows. The blinds were drawn, and I felt easy. I wouldn't worry again until a change of shift. That was the time for unknowns to appear suddenly on the scene.

When I woke, feeling the pain and the stiffness. I asked Willa for a hit of pethidine. My temperature wasn't too bad. There was a rise, but no more than could be expected of a body rushing all the emergency fluids in to save itself. I imagined for a moment how it would feel to be dying. There would be no one to mourn my disappearance. I thought of Evans's death, swift and merciless. A quick way is always the best way of going, no matter how horrible it might be to an observer. I remembered that a paragraph of his obituary had indicated he had no family.

I rang the Coroner's Court while Willa was preparing the pethidine shot. I spoke to a friend who had helped me with information on many occasions. He gave me the name of the individual who had identified Evans's corpse. Peter Bresler.

'Bresler,' I said to Willa.

Willa shot the pethidine into my lower thigh muscle. I felt a distinct freedom as the pain miraculously disappeared. I drifted into a long, apparently dreamless sleep, and when I woke, evening was coming down in the western sky.

Willa and Linda were talking out in the living-room. The bedroom door was open.

'He's fine,' Linda said. 'The wounds aren't hot and his temp is normal, well only just up. It's always higher at night anyway.'

Listening to their voices, I found there was no friction in them. They were two people trying to work out the best thing for the invalid in the house.

'Ring Nick Harris,' I called. 'He'll be in Canberra.'

Willa brought the phone in. She looked fresh and remarkably beautiful. Her hair fell down against her cheeks as she smiled at me. Her lips were a deep red, the teeth shining. 'You ring him. The drama will have a more valid ring.' Linda stood behind her, leaning against the door jamb. She smiled at me.

'The wounds are probably closed,' she said.

Beside me on the table was a half-empty jug of water and a full jug of orange juice. 'You've been drinking a lot,' Willa said.

'What?' I asked, forcing my memory. It seemed like the first glass of water to me. But then the memory returned and I knew I had been reaching for this glass forever.

'It's been two days,' Willa said.

'Where are our people?' I asked.

'The last shift left, there's a hold-up with the next.'

'We have to get out of here,' I said, dialling Nick Harris's number.

'As soon as you're able to move,' Willa said.

'I can move,' I said, speaking with my hand on the mouthpiece.

'We've got all the evidence you need,' I said. 'Send someone for it.'

I realised that was a bad idea. A dead staff member would hardly raise a protest. A dead MP was another matter. They'd think twice before they killed Nick Harris. 'You've got to pick it up yourself,' I said.

'Make up your mind,' Nick said. 'But I can't do it until the House rises, then I'll have to catch a flight. It'll have to be in a couple of days.'

'I'll have to ring you back. How does a country trip sound to you?'

'Not good. Why not the city?'

'We have to move. We're being watched. And Nick, has anything I've given you been wrong?'

'No,' he answered. 'But it better be worthwhile.'

Willa was sitting on the bed listening. Linda had gone from the doorway. After I hung up, Willa made a suggestion.

'I've got a beach house,' she offered. 'It's only an hour away.'

Twenty

I quickly applied new dressings while Willa and Linda threw clothes into a bag. There was a solid block of immobility in my side, but it didn't seem to be too hot and the pain wasn't too bad.

Extreme movement still made me nauseous, and there was a touch of self-pity as I thought of what had to be done. It was similar to the nausea of self-loathing. The way to dispel it was to make decisions and act on them. The first thing was to get away from Willa's place clean. The watchers had to be either fooled, distracted or removed.

We left the apartment and walked to the stairwell. I took my shoes off. I was the only one without rubber-soled shoes and if they were waiting, they would hear me. Willa was tense and held tightly to her bag, pulled out of shape by the weight of the gun. Linda was preoccupied. In the stairwell I eased up to look down on the watchers from a window. Where the garden foliage was high, a car was parked on the roadway. Willa squeezed my arm as I started down the fire escape beside the lift well. They were to give me three minutes before they followed.

In the foyer, I walked out the rear exit, ran for the bushes that lined the back of the building and then angled off to the carpark. Adrenalin had taken the pain away. I came up behind the waiting car. I swore silently. There was only one inside, his attention fixed on the foyer.

I plunged my Gerber knife into the rear tyre. When his car sagged the driver turned, opening the door. I hit him along the side of the head with the Glock, and then turned back to the building to see where his friends were. He had to have friends. Already Willa and Linda were heading down in the elevator. I was feeling pretty good, my movements easy. There was a feeling of high anticipation.

I saw a young bloke come around the corner of the building. He saw me approaching with the Glock at my side and he froze. 'Fuck off now,' I said. He looked at his friend's head hanging over the steering wheel and ran. A second man headed round from the side of the building. He ran past the doorway of the foyer where Willa and Linda were exiting the building. I showed him the Glock and he stopped. He was one of those smart arses who get pleasure from his skills. I could tell because he didn't believe that he had lost the edge in this. His eyes were moving rapidly, searching for an escape. I waved him towards me with the Glock. 'You want to run, do you?' I taunted him. 'You can if you want to.' I was still waving the Glock.

I wanted to shoot him, and would at the first opportunity. As he came close, I pointed the gun at his cock, pivoted slightly and smashed his leg with a kick down on the side of his knee. He screamed, too loud, so I slapped the side of his head with the gun barrel and lifted him into the foliage.

Neither Willa or Linda looked at me as they came towards the car.

'That was shocking,' Linda said as I slipped into the passenger seat.

'At least we're alive,' I said. The adrenalin rush felt marvellous. I lay back in the seat and prepared to enjoy the drive.

Through Geelong, and then after a fast twenty minutes of driving, we swooped down through the forests of stunted gums growing in the light grey, sandy soil, towards the sea.

In the distance the ocean moved. We came out of the hills and passed the Anglesea shopping centre, over the bridge that forded the river where in my youth I had rowed in the clinker-built regatta boats. Then we were veering around the right-angled turn that had once held a cafe called the Four Kings in its inside turn, and on up the hill to a major scenic delight, the Great Ocean Road.

I looked back on the town where I had had my first sexual experiences. If anyone had known that town in the dark, it was me. I had roved the dunes and the beaches with my cousin, a great surf swimmer at fourteen—the bastard had won senior surf races at that age—and his friend with a hat made from a black cat he had shot. The friend had become an artist of considerable talent, but nothing had impressed me more than having been capable, in his youth, of wearing a cat skin on his head when he was wooing girls. I'd known then he was destined to make a living in some unlikely way.

We saw some great times together in various caravan parks and home barbecues where the girls thought we were older because we were members of the Anglesea Surf Club and had muscles from swimming and rowing. I felt at home on this coast.

At Aireys Inlet, the holiday houses in the tea-tree were exposed to the ocean winds. We stopped at the small store and Willa and Linda bought bread, groceries, vegetables and fruit, while I walked across to the pub and bought wine. I hadn't seen the new pub before. Hadn't in fact been down since before the Ash Wednesday fires that had wiped out thousands of houses and several pubs along the south coast of Victoria and South Australia. They had claimed eighty-odd lives in one blistering day, thirteen of them fire-fighters, several asphyxiated from dense smoke while trying to hide in the ocean.

Returning with two bottles of red, I found them still discussing recipes and what each other liked and how much, and what they could cook well. I didn't hurry them. This being such an out-of-the-way place I was relaxed and even enjoyed their shopping.

We drove down close to a long sandy beach. The big waves were cracking just off shore on a full tide, a slight breeze from the mainland stiffening them to a good height that meant they dumped before beginning a roll. Further on was Willa's place, a two-storey shack at Eastern View. Beyond the scenic windows at the front of the house was that marvellous stretch of dangerous beach just before the Great Ocean Road begins its high turns over dark rocks encircled by a raw and rolling ocean.

The gravel drive and courtyard was raked in a Zen sort of moment and movement. It had started to spring weeds. It still looked spectacularly neat, though—no footsteps or tyre tracks spoiling the pattern. We would be alone here.

I followed Willa and Linda as they carried the food up the stairs to the back door of the place. I was painfully aware of their legs and buttocks in their tight jeans. I couldn't believe the feeling. Here I was wounded, yet nearly out of my mind with lust.

I cut some wood for the fire from the pile of driftwood Willa had around the side of the house. Evenings grew chilly here even in summer. The fireplace drew well and the fire started without filling the room with smoke the way many of the chimneys along the coast tend to do.

I watched Willa and Linda working together.
Two very beautiful women who had found they
had similar ideas and respected each other's experience. It was a pleasure to be around them.

We kept the curtains closed and the lights low,
but the food was superb. The pasta sauce had
tomatoes, olives, garlic, capers, anchovies, mush-
rooms and a good virgin olive oil. The wine was
a cabernet sauvignon from the Margaret River.
Linda produced some grass she had grown on the
shores of the lake and saved from the rabbits. I
considered refusing because too much wine prior
to smoking can be disastrous and I thought that
the wound would make me feel paranoid and
vulnerable.

Linda prepared the massive joint, making it a
work of art.

I felt the warmth and excitement instantly. The
first physical thing I was aware of was the waves.
This sea was flooding the coast lines of the world.
It was benign. The waves were cracking occasionally, but they were only surface breaks that had
no effect on the life beneath them. And then it
was totally natural that these huge waves were
dragging at the earth, helping it re-create and
replenish.

I felt Willa's hands on my shoulders, around
my neck, and I stretched out, a shuddering
stretch rippling the length of my body. She unbut-
toned my shirt and lowered her face over mine,
her lips cool, her tongue hot and soft, her hair

falling over my face. She touched the plastic dressings. 'Healed,' she said.

I nodded, feeling the softness of her beneath her shirt. I touched the soft skin of her arm, sliding my fingers across it. I saw her throat swallow. Her lips were moist.

She turned and looked across at Linda. 'I don't need to be selfish about this,' she said to Linda.

'I'm not so sure about this,' Linda said as she stood up, unbuckled, and slid her jeans down her legs. She was slender, her movement perfectly balanced, resembling a ballet dancer removing woollen warmers. As she came forward, Willa lowered her head, kissing me with remarkable gentleness. She stood up to remove her clothes. Linda knelt beside me, her shirt slipping from her arms. She looked back at Willa.

Willa's fingers caressed Linda's breasts and Linda leaned forward to kiss me, her arms back around Willa's legs.

'Bed?' Willa said. They eased me gently to my feet.

On the bed, Willa's legs slipped together with Linda's. A slow sliding of limbs, each holding the other's thigh tight with her own, moving slowly against it. When we had reached that state of trance where everything is possible, I savoured them as if they were one.

We were asleep before nightfall, but as we turned in the bed for comfort, Willa murmured that she would never have considered anything quite so spectacular. The circumstances in which we were living at the moment demanded exaggeration, she said. As I drifted in a sea of exhaustion, I remember wondering what she meant.

I woke around five. I was uneasy. Guilt, I told myself. No one can enjoy themselves so much without feeling it was wrong. Hell, I can't think like that, I'm not even Roman Catholic. I glanced across at the women. Linda had gone. I remembered her stirring much earlier. She had an hour and a half's drive to Caulfield. Willa was smiling, her eyes covered by her hair. 'I know why the dangerous life appeals to you,' she said.

Around six, as the sun was lighting up the sea, I took her coffee, orange juice and toast. I had spent the time since I'd woken attempting to work out what to do next. Why had Evans and Bresler felt so much confidence. I had looked out on the ocean, a deep green in the sun, watched it slop around into a crescent of sand banks just below the surface. My bare feet on the floor were gritty with sand. I turned on the video.

It seemed as if these characters expected to walk away from the exploding ship without repercussions. The media had gone easy on them because of the media proprietors' commercial interests in chemicals. But surely they would have to have something more concrete than that. I took the problem into Willa with breakfast.

'It's easy,' she said. 'It all comes back to the warning to Nick Harris from the prime minister. Isn't that what you said?' She had seen the warning for what it was, a meeting of very commercial minds behind the scenes.

'That doesn't make it easy.'

'It shows where their power source is. I mean it doesn't necessarily mean the prime minister is involved; it might just mean he has the same attitude to things. It's like belonging to the establishment. It's not a meeting of conspirators, it's a meeting of minds and attitudes; whatever they're faced with, their responses are the same.'

This made me uneasy. Did Evans and Bresler have serious backing, or was it just that an investigation of the ship's purpose would embarrass the government?

Would knowledge of the ship's destination enable me to play the game at a higher level? I knew the prime minister, but we had never been mates—the opposite, in fact—so he was unlikely to speak to me on such a sensitive matter. He had been a backbencher when I had dealt with him as a journalist and had questioned him once about the rumour that he had altered the recording of parliamentary party meetings.

However, I did know an influential member of his staff. A press secretary with whom I had spent many hours in country bars. He had wit and a discriminating conscience, although the latter was becoming increasingly difficult to maintain.

Ned Duffield. An individual of inordinate energy and great creativity. Listening to the prime minister sprout material that enabled him to decimate the opposition verbally, I often detected the mind of Ned. In fact it was Ned we should have voted for, not the prime minister. The PM only showed the good taste to use Ned's material.

It was not a good idea to ring Ned before eight. He wouldn't have finished the papers and his mind wouldn't have been with me.

Willa turned on the bed as I took her tray out. I washed the few things and then stood looking out at the sea. It had an undulating motion this morning, as if there had been a storm far out and we were only now getting the result. There was no wind and the sun was coming up bright in a cloudless sky.

Looking along the sand, I saw movement at the high tide line. It was a fox. It scuffed through the seaweed there, dragging at something. It seemed totally preoccupied with its job. It stopped and checked the wind, its nose high, and then it went back to its work. A fox in the open doesn't like anything within a radius of six hundred metres of its work, so things were cool on the sand this morning.

I went back to Willa's room. She had kicked off the bedclothes as the sun warmed her room, and was lying face down. Her body was strong and lithe. Her French pants lay loose over her firm buttocks, inviting. Thoughts of last night's activities swamped me. The pliant and eager limbs, the warmth of lips. I was lost.

I rang Ned about eight-thirty, just before Canberra's ten-minute rush hour. He didn't seem pleased to hear my voice. He was even colder when I mentioned the ship and my predicament. What happens to old friendships? If they demand effort and difficult work, they tend to disintegrate.

'Ned, tell me why the PM would be warning a little dipshit like Nick Harris to stay away from this information.'

'Nick is a highly regarded politician, and the PM always gives such people access.'

'Jesus, Ned, you're talking to me. I don't want a fucking quote. The PM rang Nick.'

'Did he tell you that? Seems unlikely to me.'

'Well, let's put it this way. During a conversation they had together, Nick was told not to pursue a certain line. And the thing is he has to, because his electorate is seriously affected.'

Ned knew this was true. He was a minor numbers man, so he knew the grassroots fights over serious local issues. As I turned away from the window, I noticed the little fox trotting back along the beach. He had obviously been to the far point. Such confidence meant there were very few people in the houses along this stretch. 'Ned, I need some help here. You know if I get the right story I can stop feeling like there is some bloody conspiracy of silence behind this whole thing.'

Ned laughed. 'You were always one for conspiracy theories,' he said.

'So were you, before you landed that cushy
fucking job up there in never-never land.'

Ned laughed. It was a form of flattery that he
appreciated. 'So how can I help you?'

'Why is the PM soft on what looks like a total
fuck-up by some shonky operators?'

'Any student of politics would know instantly,
if they had been looking at our arms export
figures lately.'

'I haven't,' I lied.'

'Well, we've spent billions of dollars trying to
get an arms industry up.'

'The great small l liberal government.'

'Yeah, well it hasn't worked. So, I suppose, and
don't quote me on this . . .'

'I've never quoted you on anything . . .'

'. . . that the government wants the private
section of the industry to begin barking. In fact,
they would like to see some export figures
coming from arms. They could claim it as some
of theirs.'

'Hey, they export a heap, look at those small
arms to Indonesia. They train officers from all
over Asia.'

'Yeah, they're hoping that once they become
senior men, they'll recommend their governments buy arms from us. Can't you argue against
that sort of shit?'

'I am,' I said.

After I hung up, I realised how sick the government had become. It was prepared to cover up a catastrophe to protect a crook because he might be a potential moneymaker. I sat on the sofa opposite Willa and told her my thoughts.

'Why bleed about it?' she responded. 'You've known it all along; that's why you do what you do.'

As she spoke, I watched the fox flipping along close to the ridge of seaweed. Suddenly, he cut off from the beach at right angles, a red streak through the beach grass and across the road.

'We've got to go,' I said. 'Now.'

I knew that absolutely anything could have frightened the fox, but we had to heed a warning.

Twenty-one

I began sweating halfway up the slope of the hill behind the house. It wasn't pain. More a body reaction—from having been used so continuously so soon after trauma. Close to the top, I began to feel light-headed. On a ridge above the house we finally rested. The dry bracken was comfortable and I went to sleep immediately, leaving Willa to watch the house.

My shoulder was pushed several times. 'There is someone down there,' she said. My consciousness came with bitter physical recriminations. My hands were shaking, the arm of my shirt was wet through from my dribbling with fatigue. My other arm was gone, the circulation cut off. No feeling at all. I could have turned quickly, broken it, and not felt a thing.

Willa was lying with her head down, slightly behind me, and I felt exposed. Behind us was the beginnings of a rainforest that really began about fifteen hundred metres further north. It had huge trees that reached thirty metres and were wide enough to live in. I wanted to be there. Slowly the feeling in my arm returned. I was watching the house now, but couldn't see anything.

We elbowed and kneed our way back from the lip of the small cliff that was the centrepiece of the hillside. When I thought of our position like that, I knew, if they were there, they must have seen us; they would have been amateurs if they hadn't scanned such an obvious place as the lip of a cliff.

Willa pointed. 'They're there.'

'Where?'

'Over to the left. A car parked in behind the cypresses. No one got out. I often watch the sea, everyone does, but if they were doing that, they would have parked closer to the beach.'

'Lovers?'

'Perhaps,' she said. 'But we're being cautious, aren't we?'

We crawled back and walked to the fire trail that wound its way east, parallel to the beach. Taking this course meant we could descend behind them. 'What condition are you going to be in?' Willa asked.

'Fine,' I said, showing the Glock.

If they came for us while we were on the fire trail, we'd have plenty of cover between us and them, until the moment we descended. We rested many times under the guise of listening for pursuers approaching through the bush. At the height of the day, we lay in the shade of some big trees. I was glad of the rests. I felt a pleasant exhaustion as I rested with my back to a tree trunk. Gradually I began to feel right within myself.

Just on dusk we heard them blundering along and moved off the trail. If we were being hunted, we were seriously undergunned.

'They're not into bushwalking,' I said, listening to the sounds.

'If there's enough of them, it doesn't matter,' she said.

'We have to see,' I said.

Where the foliage was thin and silhouetted against the sky and sea, we crawled into a thicket of ground-hugging shrubs. There were three of them and we let them pass. They had serious weaponry with either flash suppressors or small silencers.

We kept close to the timber on the east of the trail as we descended to the beach. We heard our hunters occasionally. They hadn't discovered the trail and were pushing through thick scrub. Now the light was fading from the sky, I was tempted to take them as they blundered past. But I reasoned I wasn't strong enough and any energy that I could summon I was counting on for crisis time.

Descending the face of a hill, we moved through the tea-tree at the back of the neighbouring houses, careful to keep a bank of it between us and Willa's house. We didn't have to worry about our noise too much—in front of the house the waves were booming in.

We moved into the garden space of the house next-door to Willa's place. There was a fibro shed, and then a wood heap, and we walked next to them.

Willa pinched my arm. 'Listen,' she said, gesturing uphill. My ears were filled with rushing blood and rolling surf, and my breathing was a pant. But I listened through that noise. Up on the hill it sounded suddenly like a platoon coming down behind us. We had been seen.

'We'll move,' I said. She pointed east, to the next house. Lying on the roof was a sniper, and there was another on the water tank behind the house. I couldn't believe my stupidity. We had been the subject of an old-fashioned rabbit drive.

'The beach,' I whispered.

'What the hell are you talking about?'

'It's the only place left,' I said.

From the neighbour's house we looked down on to the beach. The foliage beside the path to the roadway and then across the sand was only about a metre high. We would have to crawl rapidly and stay off to one side at the bottom of the track until the light faded completely, before making a dash for the sand. I didn't think we had time to wait.

They saw us before we reached the bottom of the track. An eagle eye from the hill behind us fired too early, the bullet whining off through shrubbery. We ran, across the road towards some low rocks on the beach. The sand was amazingly kind to our feet. It was still firm after the high tide. We flopped behind a rock, no more then sixty centimetres and two metres wide. We saw our pursuers running. They didn't have to fire again. There seemed to be a dozen descending through shoulder-high tea-tree. In two minutes they would have us surrounded, and dead.

'The water,' I said.

The surf was big, but it was rolling. No chop. It had a soft evening gleam to it. It looked like a chance. In another few moments the surface would be dark, and cold. They wouldn't expect us to try. The ocean rolled in here from Antarctica.

'We run and dive,' I said. We dive sideways, every which way, until we get beyond the first break. They may follow us in.'

'Oh shit, shit, shit,' she said rapidly, as she raised herself into a crouch. And then we ran for it, barrelling across the sand and into the water. The killers behind would have to stop running and cope with their rapidly beating hearts to get a shot at us. I had been there myself. It would take about three seconds. We were in the water at that point, diving.

The shots came as we emerged for breath. We were up to our waists. And down again, swimming under water now, only our heads coming up. We were close together. I could just see her shape. The bullets hit the water as if it were a wall and made silver threads through the sea around us. Below the surface there was no accuracy. I began to feel the cold, but my wounds had no pain.

Beyond the second break, we waited, our heads close as we took stock of what was happening on the sand. I was blowing heavily but I felt alright. There were three men with rifles standing waist deep.

They were unused to water, because they didn't rise with the first break waves, but stood as they were dumped on. They wouldn't be coming any further. In the shadows on the beach, though, somebody or something was being carted from a car perched on the beachside shoulder of the road. Three figures had converged with some-thing heavy.

A sudden ballooning of flame came at us over the ocean, lighting the sea as we ducked below the surface. A flame thrower. Under the water we could see each other perfectly, illuminated in orange as the flame stayed burning on the surface. Tendrils of burning phosphorus sank towards us from the lake of fire and we swam further out to sea. I had been saved from fire once before, when a northerly had pushed flame from a bushfire out across the tongue of the lake where I was holding horses. I had led them into deeper water, but not before my back had been burnt.

We moved east with the current and came up twenty metres from the fire that was pooling on the surface. Laughter came faintly over the sound of the surf. They squirted more jellied fuel over the first break, until a larger wave picked up the fire, broke in the midst of it, and took a wall of flame towards the operators as they struggled through waist-high water. One was caught, swallowed by flame. He struggled in the shallows screaming.

They were going to be wary now and this gave me hope, and an idea.

'We take the run-out to the big waves out the back,' I said to Willa.

'We'll drown out there.'

'Christ, no. It disperses about three hundred metres out.' I was whispering close to her face, her skin golden in the light from the flame dying on the beach. 'But I'm going to have to leave you out there for about ten minutes, unless you want to come in further along the beach.'

The men on the beach were huddled around their burnt companion. They dragged him out of the water onto the sand, trying to see how bad he was.

We took the run-out to the west, submerging and clinging to the sand as the white waves rolled over us. The flame was flickering along the water-line, spreading but dying.

To strip off my clothes, I pushed the Glock into my underpants. The lightweight Glock nestled against my cock, and I placed my hand on the gun to check if it was secure. My skin was goose bumped, and I felt the dressing, surprisingly smooth. I looked further out to sea. The sky was black and a thin wind riffled the surface. A dark line grew further out—a wave beginning to grow as it moved into shallower water. A monster. It began sitting up strongly, its sloping surface taking the hues of the lights from the beach. I looked across at Willa.

I left Willa and, taking the Glock in one hand, sprinted fifteen metres towards it before turning to roll onto the dark-glassed surface for a slicing ride down its face. My underpants were stripped away instantly. I angled back towards the bloke with the thrower. He was pumping squirts of flame over the first break close to the beach, more to light a target than burn anything.

To get in front of the broken water, not be engulfed by it, I raised one leg behind me and then the other, my head down. Raising my hand, I cleared the ejection port of the gun to empty the barrel of water. That's the good thing about Glocks, they could be immersed in mud for a year and still fire. Now, firmly propelled by the wave, I was closing on him.

I felt the wave lose the break and dropped away from it, the Glock held down close to the surface. I was no more than thirty metres from my target.

I went under the water, only the gun above the break in two hands. I would have to come up fast, ignoring water in my eyes, and fire, accurately. A miss would mean he could incinerate me.

I emerged from the water directly in front of him, firing. I had triggered away four shots—the first shedding the water from the gun—before I realised I was hitting him. He was turning the thrower towards me, and the flame flared heat twenty metres away as he began to pan towards me. I hit him in the face with the fifth shot, and he went down, the flame falling beneath the water, boiling a huge swathe of it. I ran west along the beach to avoid it, jacking off several shots towards figures running towards me. Suddenly they stopped and began running away. I couldn't believe it.

Behind me a scream hit the air. I turned, and saw why they were running. The marksman was burning in the jelly his machine had released. He staggered for the sand, the flame still scorching the beach to the east. He stopped moving as he reached the beach, refusing to drop, becoming a motionless pyre before toppling back into the sea of flame.

I went into the ocean again. In the light from the huge bonfire burning on the surface, I saw Willa catch a mountain out the back, straight in towards me. I went to meet her. I lost her for a moment, but she came up beside me breathing hard.

'The house,' she said, as she ran to the beach. I thought she was as unhinged as I'd been, but then I saw what she meant. The remaining car was pulling out. They were leaving the house, panicked by the fire and the burning. The fire would have been visible fifteen kilometres away in Lorne and no doubt the locals were already on their way.

We ran for the house. It was clothes and warmth and freedom. They'd left the doors open, the lights on.

'The lights,' I said, and she turned them off.

Twenty-two

And that was all I remembered until I woke some time later. My hands and feet were bound. I was covered with a blanket, but the floor was cold, I was still wet and I was shivering. I rolled until the blanket was under me. The back of my neck had a long-distance ache, the pain coming to me from a bank of fog it was threatening to break through.

The smell of smoke arrived first. It switched me into gear, bringing pain with the alertness. The house was burning.

'Willa,' I screamed. 'Willa.' I struggled with the bonds and despair flowed through me. If she was in another room, I'd never reach her.

The flame was burning the hall door, catching whatever oil or polish was used on the floor, it approached in a ripple scorching as it went. The flames were dancing higher with every square metre of floor that was claimed. I could hear the fire behind the hall door now, it was growling.

I grabbed a chair between my feet, wedging it up against the bonds at my ankles so they'd take the weight of the thrust, and tossed it hard at the floor-level bottom window. It went through easily enough, leaving a large jagged border. Breaking the stuff with bare feet was out. But I could use the firm, broken glass to sever the twine around my ankles. The heat was now a dangerous blast and I couldn't take the time to cut the twine on my wrists. I was burning from the reflected heat and the closeness of flame.

The kitchen alcove was suddenly hidden by a wall of flame. I rolled onto the soles of my feet, pushed myself upwards and dived through the hole in the glass, landing on my shoulder in low tea-tree. Rolling down the low rise to the track up from the ocean, I lay there in the heat, not caring about anything. Laughter was trickling through my throat. I was alive.

After at last catching my breath, I realised I could no longer feel my hands. I couldn't move them. The blood was cut off and they were no longer capable of working. It was then I heard the car, and cursed that I hadn't headed for cover earlier.

I rolled onto my feet and stayed in a crouched position. In my precarious crouch, I swayed alarmingly, the pain and the bonds making me dizzy. I sank to my knees. The heat across my shoulders was insistent. I'd stay like this forever. I was tired. I didn't even think. If someone had offered me a quick death, I probably would have accepted.

A black Merc came to a stop on the gravel track. The windows were dark and reflected the flame.

Turning, I tore uphill through treacherous undergrowth, knowing my tied hands would mean injury. I didn't look behind, although I strained for sounds over the roar of the fire. I heard nothing. The running became a compulsion; bending low through the shoulder-high bush, I couldn't have stopped if I had wanted to. I changed direction several times on the hill face and finally, near the crest, I walked into some lignum and sat down, panting deeply, wanting to have my breathing controlled before I got close.

I sat there for what must have been a couple of hours, the branches digging into my back and arms, but I didn't want to move. Several fire brigade units attended the blaze, but with my hands tied, I had no wish to fall into the wrong hands. In my mind's eye, I could still see them moving up the hill to take me. When the crickets started after the trucks had left, their sound moving in waves over the night, I knew I was safe. At the first footstep they would have stopped abruptly, only to start again when the footfalls had moved on. I decided to move down to the houses along to the west. I needed my hands back and something to wear.

Minutes later I was standing at the edge of a clearing at the back of a house. I stared at the back door. I knew there was no real safety in breaking in, but being so close to a symbol of refuge lifted the spirits.

I saw my 'lifesaver' placed beside the back step. It was a device for removing mud from shoes before entering the house. The blade gleamed. I lowered myself to the ground and slid over to it. I sat with my back to it and felt the positioning of the blade with my forearms. It was pretty blunt, but I worked at what I thought was the sharp edge of the thing. I didn't know if I was cutting my hands or not. I suspected my hands were bound with the same twine as my legs. It was synthetic and susceptible to the heat of friction. Minutes later my hands were free, but useless. They hung lifeless in front of me. I began rubbing them on my stomach, willing circulation to come.

Behind me there was a crunch on the gravel. I turned quickly, uselessly. It was the French 'journalists from *Le Monde*'. They spoke English with only the slightest accent, charming. 'We see you again,' the tall one said in the suede coat.

'Obviously,' I said.

His short friend kicked me in the ribs. It left me gasping. 'We have the advantage.' Each of them had a handgun. They appeared to be Walther P38s.

I nodded, trying to remember the name of the one in suede. Marc. Marc Paris.

'You can do nothing. But we can do much.'

'*Rainbow Warrior*,' the short one said, and kicked me again. I struggled to my feet: if you're on the ground, people always feel they can kick you.

'Your woman,' Paris said. 'They make love to her, very much.' He moved his hips suggestively. 'And then they take her.' I thought only, she wasn't in the house. She's alive.

I leaned back against the weatherboards of the house. 'Now, we ask the questions, oui?'

I nodded. There would be no need for them to torture me. I wanted to tell everything I knew. That's all I had ever wanted to tell anyone.

'Your Mr Evans, what do you do for him?'

'Nothing.' I was punched in the stomach. Not the correct answer.

'He's dead,' I managed to gasp.

'Non, non, he's not dead.'

'I saw it. It was in the newspapers. You saw it, you must have. It was everywhere.'

'You always believe newspapers?' the little bloke asked.

'No,' I answered.

'Mr Evans wants to leave a country, he does. He has himself murdered and everyone is happy. He has done this before.'

'All I know about Evans is that he appears to be selling chemical weapons to several countries, and he has the government's backing. The ship on the bay was his.'

'This we know,' Paris said.

'He killed a relative of my client. I've been hired to expose him for what he is.'

'So you're a journalist too?'

'Yes. Where's Willa?'

'She is with him.'

'You saw her leave with him?'

'Yes,' Paris said.

'You didn't follow them.'

'They have chopper.'

I began to feel the blood returning to my hands. The pain was severe, but I still couldn't make the fingers function. It was as if I had blocks of wood at the end of my arms.

The smaller man held his Walther close to my head and looked at his companion.

'Have you ever killed anyone?' Paris asked.

'Yes,' I said.

'Why did you not kill Evans before?'

'Why didn't you?'

He waved his gun dismissively. 'We will get him.' Considering they had no idea where he was, it sounded somewhat arrogant.

'If I find him for you . . .'

'You kill him. We will come with you,' he added. 'To make sure it is done.'

'Fine,' I said, 'let's go.'

In the gardening shed in the house next door I found overalls and a denim shirt and a pair of rubber boots.

I used the phone to call Nick Harris. I'd convinced my captors that I needed to keep my investigation going so that Evans would hear I was still alive and come for me. All Nick would say was that I had better be sure the evidence was good.

Twenty-three

I was at the pub at five. Nick was due at six. Marc Paris and his mate had parked their black car behind an abandoned church about four hundred metres from the pub. I took a beer from the front bar and walked outdoors. I was feeling like your average alcoholic bashed by youths who'd used a cigarette lighter on your clothes in the hope they were flammable. I had no idea why Paris and his mate were trusting me, or me them. It was enough they hadn't killed me. We had something going.

The pub is a two-storey bluestone relic, tucked into the base of a small hill. The peppercorn and eucalypts shade it in the summer. A short distance away is a bluestone bridge that crosses a trout stream that is a raging current come the summer storms. Apart from the pub, Darlington boasts several houses and a school, and a fast driver doesn't notice its existence. The nearest small town is over thirty kilometres away. But the pub has a life.

This is the meeting place of reprobates. Several country racing trainers have made it their watering hole, along with the local graziers, farmhands and a cop. It is such a tightly knit little town that the drug squad didn't tell the local cop they were raiding a grazier for several hectares of marijuana. On weekends the polo and advertising crowd descend. The fox hunters mid-week. On these occasions upstairs rooms are used to pursue frantic lust. If they're filled, the odd car will speed out onto the backroads and park in small stands of gum trees.

The evening breeze was warm as it moved across the paddocks from the north. The beer was chilled and delicious. In overalls and rubber boots, I didn't feel out of place drinking in the front bar. This is not a tarted-up pub. The old wood is still there, and the intimacy created by a small and crowded drinking space is still there. On the walls are shots of winning horses owned by the publican; in the back room, the large hot plates where dinner guests cook their own meat.

Around five-fifteen the locals began turning up for an evening's drinking. I was still nursing my first beer in the bar. Jamie Scott, the publican, was out with a delivery truck, the barrels donking down the ramp. He'd told me to help myself if I wanted another.

Lurch and Dog were two of the first. Lurch was a fencer, around fifty, who would now drink until midnight. He'd be at work at eight, and despite the grog put down, he would drive fencing spikes with brutal accuracy, the sledge hammer moving with easy speed.

Dog was a poacher. He took all game out of season, but only for his own needs, and those of his friends. Lurch was tall, raw boned, the type of physique a city bloke would try and hide. Too many angles. Dog was short, plump, but a huge capacity for heavy work. The short back meant he would work into old age.

They had constructed the railing fences on my place. Now they were working on an Arab stud to the east. 'What's the bloke like?' I asked. 'Is he making any money?'

'He's a fuckin' prick. Hauled us out of the pub Satadee to finish a paddock. I'll tell you, those wires are hummin', strained 'em right up, the first frost and he won't have a fuckin' fence on the place.'

'Is he making any money?'

'It's gotta be a tax dodge. He wouldn't know a horse from a two-tooth.'

I looked at Dog. 'You wouldn't have a gun would ya?'

'In the ute. Why?'

'Need one for tonight.'

'There's an old Breda auto.'

'What size shot?'

'Sixes. Got some twos to get the hares right out.'

We went out to his ute. He pulled the case out of two black garbage bags. The case was scuffed but the gun inside was spotless. 'Picked it up at a clearin' sale from a widow. Her old man hardly fired it. It's old, but have a geezer at it.' He pulled back the breech and I slipped my thumb in so that light would be reflected up the barrel. No pit marks, a glistening oiled silver.

'Put it in ya car?'

'My ride's not here.'

Next to turn up was Rob Goings, the grazier drug grower. He was out of the slammer because he had dobbed in some drug-dealing mates. Lurch filled me in on how they caught the bastard. 'Come in here after his first deal, right, in Geelong. He had a white suit, a white panama hat, and them big sunglasses. He'd been givin' Jamie's wife one, right, so I reckon the word got out, you know.'

I gave Rob a nod and he headed down the bar. 'What's doing?' I asked him.

'I've still got the place,' he said. It was a major preoccupation of his. It had been in the family for a century and he didn't want to be the one to lose it. He was market gardening now, illegally taking water out of the trout stream.

A white chauffeur-driven limo pulled into the carpark. It didn't attract too much attention. The locals were used to the habits of the wealthy, and although they watched everything, they reserved their comments for significant happenings.

I was the one who was more concerned. I thought it would be Nick Harris, but it was Peter Bresler. He and his driver were laughing as they headed into the bar. They were very confident, enjoying themselves. At my expense, I thought. So, Nick Harris had to be an informer . . . or someone he had spoken with?

Jamie wasn't in the bar, and I knew I could depend on the three men drinking not to interfere. Bresler came in first. I kept my back to the door, knowing he wouldn't see too well in the badly lit bar. As the door swung open a second time, I punched the driver in the back of the neck. He hit the floor hard and I pulled the .38 special from his waistband.

Bresler didn't want to turn. He moved his head back, hands out, feigning resignation, giving up. But he was reaching for a weapon. Lurch hit him on the side of the head with a wine bottle. He had been fast but soft, and Bresler folded slowly, supporting himself with one hand on the footrail as his head drooped. Slowly he looked up.

'Hey, Peter,' I said 'What are you doing down here?'

'What? What?' He gestured at himself with his free hand, as if to ask, why this?

His driver stirred at my feet, so, with a kick to the lungs I warned him to be still. He began to gasp for breath. I looked at Rob, the weak link in the bar. 'Go and keep Jamie occupied, would you?' I said. He left.

'Is Willa alright?' I asked Bresler.

He dropped his head, like a boy caught out in a shameful act. Looking up, he said, 'Yes, yes, she's fine. He said he wouldn't hurt her.'

'They've abducted a friend of mine,' I said to Lurch and Dog.

'Give it to them,' Dog said. 'Shit like that deserve to die.'

'Where can we take these two?' I asked Lurch. 'I want to talk to them.'

'Real serious, like?' Dog asked.

'Yeah,' I said, 'But I'm meeting a friend here any minute, and he won't want to know about these two.'

'I'll back the ute up,' Dog said.

He shot out the door. He roared the ute across to the side door and came in with a roll of baling twine. He and Lurch tied Bresler and his driver and we hefted them into the back of the ute. It took about two minutes. Dog pulled the canvas across the back of the ute and snapped it down. 'Any noise,' I said to the canvas, 'and I'll kill you.'

I drove the ute over to the church, parking it out of sight near the black Merc. 'Here's someone who knows where Evans is,' I said. The French military were renowned for their torture schools, started during their Algerian crisis. Let them do the dirty work. Paris pulled back the tonneau and looked in on the two. 'Another friend,' he said, smiling across the ute to his companion, who had a silenced Uzi pointing at the ute. Paris looked at me. 'We know this one.'

'Don't go easy on him,' I said. 'He knows everything.'

I walked back to the pub, crossing the highway to walk up to it under the peppercorn trees.

Nick Harris's government car reached the pub about the same time I did. Nick had changed into casual gear, all new and crisp.

'I want you to keep me out of this' was how he greeted me as he walked into the bar. He was either an excellent actor, and politicians have plenty of time and practice to perfect that art, or he genuinely wasn't surprised to see me. I had to give him the benefit of the doubt. He wasn't edgy or looking around, anticipating the furtive arrival of Bresler. Jamie and Rob came in from behind the bar. Lurch leaned on his elbows, staring down at his beer. They all heard Nick.

'Don't see how I can,' I said. 'If anything comes out of it, one way or the other, I'd have to say I'd been talking to you.'

Dog walked back into the bar. As he walked past Nick, he said, 'Ain'tcha the bloody dickhead who put the power lines through here.'

'The government did,' Nick said.

'Nah, I seen ya on telly. You reckoned it'd have no effect on animals. Those birds nest'n on the towers, the young'ns can hardly fly.'

'I'll look into that,' Nick said.

'Gunna take the towers down, are ya?' Lurch called out.

'Think we better talk outside,' Nick said.

Outside, we leaned on the limo.

'Where's the evidence?' Nick asked.

'In my post box,' I said.

'We better go,' Nick said, anxious to be away as quickly as possible. I looked at the back of the ute, took him by the arm and walked him over to the trees bordering the highway. I quietly told him everything that had happened over the past few days. Mostly he just shook his head and commented that he didn't want to know this. 'The reason I'm telling you this', I said, 'is that although you have ambitions to be a cynical bastard, and are practising hard at it, once you know about a scam like this, it'll worry you.

'Now my post box number in town here is 407. If I haven't contacted you in the next few days I'm dead, and you just lift the evidence. There are other copies around, and if you don't use them, the other people will.' I saw a slight relief in his eyes. 'It'll look bad for you, because I've told them I've been to you for help.' Politicians understand blackmail. 'By the way, mate, have you told anyone about our meeting here?'

His eyes flickered.

'I need the truth,' I said, taking a good hold of his arm.

'My phones are bugged,' he said. 'A lot of people would know.'

'Why are they bugged?'

'I've been getting threats,' he said. 'Over the ship.'

'Okay,' I said, 'wait here.'

I walked to the churchyard. The Frenchmen had broken into the building and had Bresler and his driver seated in the pews, facing a faded and torn altar. Bresler was missing a tooth. He was unaware of it resting on his lower lip. He was dribbling blood. The smaller Frenchman was wearing tight gloves. As I watched, the tooth fell onto Bresler's lap. He didn't even look down.

'Anything?' I asked.

'This Evans knows you are here, and he is coming for you. We will deal with him. But you have a lot of aaah . . . trouble, you say.'

I walked to Bresler and smashed the side of his jaw. It unhinged and began to tremble. 'Where's Willa?' I said.

'Farm,' he said. I backhanded him.

'Where?' I asked.

'Your farm, she's there.' Bresler's eyes were still firm, the pain hadn't unfocused them. He still had mental resources.

I looked at Paris. 'If you don't need these two, I'd like to keep them,' I said.

Paris gave a dismissive shrug: who would want these two anyway? I walked them to the back of Dog's ute and clipped them in.

Back at the pub, I stopped the ute near Nick's limo and took the Breda in its aluminium case from the shelf beneath the rear window. Nick looked at it, but didn't ask what it was. I opened the case, took the oiled weapon from inside. There was nothing to pull through the barrel to remove the oil, so the first shot would have a sharper, headachy jolt and smell of burning oil. I put one cartridge in the breech and three in the magazine and replaced it on the shelf.

As a further precaution, I snapped back the ute's canvas top and let Nick look at my captives, and them look at him. 'These bastards came for me, here,' I said. 'So whoever is listening to your phone has a direct line to the people involved in the burning of the ship.' It would keep his mind focused. Nick backed away as if he had been shot. I snapped the canvas top down again.

'Jesus Christ,' he said as we walked away, 'what did you do that for? Let them see me.'

'Because if I don't win on this, Bresler will come after you.'

'Don't they kill hostages?' He meant, didn't I?

I laughed. 'You mean I should?' I looked at his face. 'You were just thinking aloud, weren't you?' I added. 'Of course if they were to die, they could never identify you.'

He was in shock. He had never been close to violence of that type. A country pub, way from anywhere, and two men bound and gagged in the back of a ute. And he had seen it and wasn't going to do anything. Take the bastards to the edge all the time, I say.

'Heard from the prime minister?' I said, my tone denying anything he had just witnessed.

'He just wants to be kept informed. He wants a very positive resolution on this one.'

'I think he's going to get it,' I said, 'whether I win or not.'

Nick was emerging from his shock. 'If you don't have the evidence; if I don't see Evans, you'll be in the slammer for life. I can't let that go, whoever they are?'

He meant it. He'd seen a way that he could survive the circumstances. I couldn't see it. If you see a person bound and gagged, you report it immediately, unless you want to be an accessory to the crime.

'They came to kill me,' I said. 'I want you to remember that.'

Nick nodded. 'Even if that's so it can't alter my position. The law happens to be something that has to be followed.'

It wasn't that I disagreed with the law, it just didn't take in exceptional circumstances.

'I want you to take a room here at the pub,' I said. 'Sleep with your mobile on, and hope I get to call you.'

I opened the door to the front bar and he hesitated, wanting to go to his car and leave, but as I looked back, holding the door open, he glanced at the ute and quickly followed me.

'Dog,' I said, 'can I have a loan of your ute for the night?'

'Sure, mate,' he said. Dog owed me. While he'd been fencing on my place, Dog had tuned the motors on my convertible and had even borrowed it a few times to head to the Warrnambool pubs his hair slicked back like Elvis and in an expensive leather jacket, for good times away from his poaching grounds.

'Nick's a friend of mine,' I said to Jamie, who was wondering about the undercurrents at work here. 'You can put him up for the night?' I looked at Rob. He made a sign to indicate he had told Jamie nothing. Jamie nodded hesitantly.

Dog tossed me the keys and I left the bar. The ute was battered, but the engine was smooth and powerful. The evening sky was darkening rapidly. I walked into the hall and rang the farm, there was no answer. If Bresler had lied, I would kill him.

Twenty-four

I flew down the deserted backroads. The police only visited them after ten p.m. when the local pubs closed and the local farmers and graziers tried sneaking home blotto. I was filled with dread at the thought of finding Willa hurt. The ride was rough for my passengers. The softening up process.

I came down the track to the farm around eight. I killed the engine and the lights and drifted down towards Charlie's dairy farm. It was peacefully sleeping. The lake was a mirror in the moonlight. I entered his drive and coasted down to the house. His living-room light was on and on the blind I could see his silhouette as he watched television. I knocked on his window. The light was turned off and a few minutes later he called from the wire door of the verandah.

'It's Jack,' I answered him. 'I need to know if anything's happening at my place.'

Charlie stepped out into the dark. 'I wasn't sure how much oats to feed the horses,' he said. 'I think they've put on condition in the last few days.'

'Anyone been past tonight?' I asked.

'No one,' Charlie said. 'But then I didn't hear you.'

'Have you got any binoculars?'

'Sure, bought them for the missus to watch the birds on the lake.'

'Nothing strange happening? No one hanging around?'

'No,' Charlie said. 'The Mahoneys have kept their eyes open too. No one lurking.'

'I've got Dog's vehicle here,' I said, pointing. 'Can I leave it over by the old dairy?'

'Sure. That foal's a healthy little bastard. Tried to stand up ta me tonight, box me like an old roo. When she saw me retreatin' like, she turned round pigrooted, wobbled down the paddock, the old mare chasin' her.'

I decided to take Charlie into my confidence. 'A friend of mine was abducted. I've got two people in the back of the ute who know where she is.' I looked at him straight. After all, Lurch and Dog had gone along with me.

'You're in a lot a trouble, seems to me,' Charlie said. 'I don't want to hear anything, right. I'll go inside, shut the doors and winda's, but if I hear anything, it's off. Right?'

I drove the ute through the gate at the back of the house, around the new dairy with the steel fencing, and headed down to the fibro building with the timber cattle yards. I was feeling pretty sick. I wanted this over as quickly as possible. I stopped the ute on the red gravel, swung open

the wide gate and drove up on the cement apron
that led into the dairy proper.

Out of the ute, I snapped back the canvas.
Bresler and the driver had, rolled up together,
back to back, trying to undo each others hands.
Impossible with baling twine tied tight. I dropped
the back of the ute and pulled Bresler out. I made
him hop to the cow bale and tied him there. I
was filled with an appalling rage. It was impossible to contain. I drove an elbow into his face,
loosening more teeth. I pulled the gag away.

'Who's with Willa?' I said.

'I'll help you,' he said, his eyes running around
the dairy. At night, a dairy looks as if it might be
the place in a nightmare where you stop living.

'You're not answering the question,' I said and
hooked him in close with a left and right.

He was panting hard. 'I don't know,' he said.

'Why did you come down here?' I asked.

He was silent, a quick, rasping breath the only
sound. 'You don't want to answer that one?' I
asked. I drove a right over his ribs, there was a
dull, far-away thud as ribs broke. 'Oh Jesus,' he
said. I chopped at his face. 'You better change
sides now, mate, or you're going to die.'

'She's with him, Evans. I told you.'

'Why the fuck are you down here?'

'He's coming to get you.'

'And so were you, right?'

'My people want to know how it works out.'

'Come on, you had to make sure I was dead, didn't you? Who were you going to tell?'

'My clients. I'm bound to secrecy.'

'Bound to secrecy? What bullshit.' I laughed. 'Listen, the only people who really can betray their country are all bound to secrecy. And then they go and trade their information. They sell what they have for what other countries' spies have . . . So what's supposed to happen to me?'

'I just had to make sure you weren't going to talk about it. That's all we came down to do, talk.'

'Bullshit. I'm to be killed, right?' I punched him with the heel of my hand, in the way big Jack Johnson used to jab, saving fingers and knuckles. You need to be well balanced and in close so it's accurate.

'You're going to die,' I explained, 'unless you tell me who you're working for.'

'The Indonesian military.' He said it like a threat, and if he could have smirked, he would have. The information pushed me right back. The Indonesians bought napalm, Agent Orange? What about Syria, the Hamas?

'You didn't know the ship was bound for the Middle East?' I said.

'It was to scorch East Timor, all that high country. There'd be nothing left to fight over.'

'Except the oil in the Timor Gap,' I said. 'It's the reason the Indonesians invaded, and Australia went along with it. An unholy bloody alliance.' I walked up to him for eye contact in the bad light. 'So, where's the Middle East in all this?'

He didn't answer. I hit him hard, because he thought he was going to win no matter what I could pull out of the hat.

His body was unresisting now. I pulled a knife from my pocket and cut the waistband of his trousers. They dropped slightly. 'Now tell me, you piece of fucking vermin, where's Willa?'

'Christ,' he gabbled, 'I don't know. No, for Christsake. Not that.'

'Where?' I said, moving the knife close.

He was speechless, he shook his head, was having trouble breathing.

'If I don't find Willa at the farm, and if she's hurt, you're going to die, because she trusted you once and you betrayed her.'

Before leaving, I checked the bonds on the driver. I slipped a twine noose around his neck, tied a knot in the style of one for a fish hook, to make it look like it would slip, and the other end through the arm on the tailgate. I gagged Bresler now he was breathing normally again.

I slipped the Breda from the case and, holding it in the crook of my arm, I headed across the paddocks beside the lake to my place. If my captives were still there in the morning, I would be dead. Charlie could let them go.

In the dark, I walked over the crusted and dried algae from last summer, high above the lake's waterline. I had been meaning to collect it, but I didn't want to draw the horses attention to it. They had left it well alone until now, but they're very curious buggers and if I tried to move it all, they'd find a small piece to play with and within a day their livers'd be shot, and I'd be down half a dozen brood mares.

I approached the box thorn warily, but then walked around it and looked at the farmhouse. I knew the farm as if it were a part of me. Animals moving in a paddock, dust in the air, a dog's pricked ear—all were things only a farmer would notice and know the reason for.

Two minutes later, as I moved up on the stallion paddock, Sacco found me. His huge wet mouth was around my hand, licking it. I was sure no one was here before me, unless they had been in the house for days. Sacco wouldn't have eased up on them.

I kept a long watch on the house and then moved up through the yearling paddock. The donkeys running with them knew I had come from Charlie's place, so there was no disturbance.

Finally, I headed to the house across six hundred metres of good level country. I crept up to the old pine tree, its huge trunk still growing despite lying on the ground, struck by lightning in a big summer storm several years ago. It took me to within twenty metres of the house, and I walked from there across to the cement water tank that was filled by the mill close to the house.

The house was filled with solitude. I walked along the weatherboard wall, opened the verandah door, which squeaked with alarm, and stepped inside. I was alone. A timber house can tell you that better than any other. It had ceased to do anything but rest. I relaxed and walked through the living-room to the kitchen. Nothing had been disturbed.

Some time later I walked to the back of the house and onto the verandah. A quick glance wouldn't show you the cellar entrance. You would have to be looking for it. It was a small place. I examined the ancient gun collection. The only really serious weapons were a Lee Enfield .303 and, remarkably, a Martini Henri .45, because I had the ammunition for it. It was a single-shot lever action, made before they could accurately calculate the strength of steel, and so the action was way over the strength required. This rifle was from the Boer War. It sent a lengthy .45 slug on very long but slow journeys. It was cumbersome, as the barrel was long, but it was much lighter than the Lee Enfield from the Second World War was. I ran a pull-through down the barrels of both to clean out the preserving grease.

The phone rang as I was working the action on the Lee Enfield. Like the Glock, you could drop it in the mud and it would still come up functioning. It was Evans—why wasn't I surprised?.

'You had a very fancy fucking death,' I said, cold and hard. 'And your mate Bresler's about to have a real one.'

'Let's talk about this.'

'If Willa's dead, there is no talking,' I said, 'only dying.'

'She's alive,' he said. 'I'm bringing her down.'

'I don't believe you,' I said.

Incredibly, I heard Willa's voice. 'Jack,' she said, 'I'm alright.'

'Where are you?'

'I don't know,' she said.

Her voice was cut off by Evans. 'We're bringing her down now,' he said. 'And I want Bresler.'

The exhilaration was unbelievable. But it lasted about a minute. It might well be the last call to keep me happy while they disappeared forever.

I was surprised he wanted Bresler. There was no loyalty among thieves of this calibre. I was sure if they did bring Willa, it was only to kill me. She was the bait, the hostage to have me surrender. I had two hours to plan.

I made my preparations. First I changed my dressings. I stood in the bath and stripped them away. I took the hand shower and washed myself. The holes in my side were filled with puckered flesh. The splayed fat had been pulled inside as if a sea anemone had retreated. When I moved, only the small fold of external skin had nerves to produce pain.

I was careful leaving the house, but Sacco was at the back door and that reassured me. His hearing was honed enough to hear my car approaching the house five kilometres away. He would investigate any other sound.

I climbed the windmill and settled down behind the sail ten metres above the ground. The sail was only just visible from the house, over the roof of the stables, so if I began firing when they arrived at the house, I had considerable cover from the front——none from the rear.

The Breda I'd put on the ground below me. The rifles were laid out next to me on the maintenance shelf. I lay down beside them, staring up beyond the sail I had braked so that it wouldn't turn with a wind change and tip me off.

The night sky was bright with millions of pulsing stars. I had forgotten the window to the heavens that was denied city dwellers. When I found myself beginning to doze, I knew it was time to leave my high perch. If I turned in my sleep, I would end up in the tank below me, or worse, straddling the edges. Sacco was lying below me. The way the water was moving in the breeze, it looked like a giant saucer of water would be slopped on him. He was oblivious to its movement.

Lights from the cars swept into the driveway. Two cars equipped with spotlights running off their generators. I watched as several figures jumped from the rear doors and spread out across the approach to the house.

I turned the round sail of the mill so I was hidden from their view. I looked through the fans of the sail.

It wasn't Evans who stepped from the lead car. I hadn't seen the bloke before. I debated whether to slip a .45 through the back window of the larger car where I expected Evans to be. I held back. I was glad I did.

Willa stepped from the back seat of the car, followed by Evans. He held her very close to him. I put the front sight of the Martini Henri on the back of his head, but refrained from shooting. The slow bullet would keep its weight as it ploughed through both of them.

'We've come to barter,' Evans yelled out. 'Her life for Bresler's.' I didn't answer. I moved down the windmill behind the tank, out into the lucerne paddock, and whenever the spotlights came my way, I lay down in the sixty centimetre high growth.

It took no more than two minutes to reach the side of the house, and the sound of Evans's voice was becoming too strident. He would have to do something very soon. Sacco was with me. His anxious breathing was too loud. I motioned him away. He streaked off.

No one could have drawn aim on him in the time he took to reach the driver of the first car. The driver squealed, and it turned into a full-on scream. I ran from the side of the house, fast through the shadows. Evans tried to put a bead on me, but Willa ducked to one side, leaving his right flank exposed. I couldn't risk a shot. I kicked him hard in the chest, bringing the sole down with all my weight behind it. I felt bones give. The brass butt of the Martini Henri glanced off the side of his head. He went down. As I fell forward over Willa, I twisted to bring the Martini Henri to bear on the second car. I could see nothing behind the tinted windows. I fired into the engine block. It was a Japanese job, it cracked like an egg. 'The garage,' I yelled at Willa.

The doors opened on the other side of the car and two people spilled out of it, firing under the chassis. I couldn't believe we were still alive. But they had been firing to miss Evans's slumped body. I put two shots from the Breda under the car. There is nothing quite so commanding as the sound of an automatic shotgun. The two began running. I could see only shadows, but I caught one near the fig tree in the middle of the garden. As I swung on the second, he merged with the darkness.

Sacco's guttural gobbling sounds ceased and he flew after the retreating figure. I grabbed Evans by the collar and stepped back into the garage.

I was worried about the men they had dropped off coming down the drive. The garage had a rear entrance across a courtyard to the house. I pushed over a work bench made from red gum five centimetres thick, but I didn't want to be trapped behind it.

I looked at Willa. She was in a dark shirt and jeans, and we could fade just as easily as the others into the darkness, except I knew the ground.

Evans stirred at my feet. I grabbed a bridle from the wicker basket full of old leather and bound him. My hands were shaking. The adrenalin was coursing. I forced myself to breathe normally. There seemed to be a lump rising in my chest and I forced calm. I didn't want to die.

I motioned to Willa to open the house door. As she went for it, I emptied the Breda out into the night. I scooped Evans up in a dead man's lift and ran with him bouncing over my shoulder. I fell through the door with him. His head hit the wooden floor and a handgun slithered across the floor. I had no strength to hoist him inside. He lay blocking the door. It was then the red laser beam came through the darkness like a fine, red torch light. I lurched backwards to avoid it. But it wasn't for me. It came to rest on Evans's side and there was the merest stutter of sound as his body twitched under automatic firing. I grabbed his legs and hauled him across the shiny, wooden floor onto a rug. I rolled him in it quickly, carried him to the cellar and lowered him in.

I had to fight back a rising hysteria. The laser sighting beam came from the roof of the stable, wandered over the verandah, me, and then it was gone. Willa was waiting by the verandah door. I reached into the cellar for a weapon and came up with an old German bayonet. 'Get out of here,' I managed.

We tumbled out the verandah door, rolled under a railing fence and were loose in a forty hectare paddock. It was like freedom. The moon had gone and no one could see more than a metre or so in front of them. I was the only one on the place who would know where I was. Willa grabbed my hand.

'We walk out of here, right?' she whispered.

I didn't say anything. I looked back towards the house. There were no lights there, but a slight gleam where the stables were. We walked towards the low ground and circled back towards the stables. There was a strange scuffling. It was more than just a stabled horse being restless. The night was quiet now. Coming up from the low paddock behind us was ground mist and I thought it might give us silhouettes. We dropped into the long grass. The sound continued from the stables.

We wormed our way forward slowly. The stable door was white and I saw a single shadow stark against it. I motioned Willa to stay put. When I got to the railing fence, I saw the shadow was in fact a horse's leg over the stable door. The fire fight had panicked it at first and it had tried to jump from the stable. Now it was trying to keep calm, but it was losing the battle, moving on its

back legs, making half circles. In a moment it
would lose it, turn into a berserker.

I slid under the fence and waited a few
moments. I stood up. It stopped moving. It knew
I was there, and knew I had brought help before.
Hard earth caught the sound of my footsteps. It
was looking at me, ears pricked. I had to frighten
it, have it rear off the door. I punched it with a
right hook and it stood on its hindquarters, rising
off the door and into the dark of the stable. I
dropped to the ground and rolled. Off behind me
to the left, a machine pistol opened up and the
bullets plucked at the corrugated iron above me.
Willa emptied the magazine in that direction and
I crawled back into the grass.

A second man ran around the side of the stable.
He was only a moving shadow but I drove
upwards with the bayonet. He fell to the ground,
flopping there. I grabbed his weapon, rolled
under the rails and waited.

The horse began barrelling the stable walls
with both hind feet. Nothing more. I moved back
to where Willa had been. Only flattened grass. I
didn't risk a whisper. She was on her own.

I headed in the direction of the lake. I checked
the weapon and found the safety. I slipped the
magazine. It was heavy enough to be full. I
slammed it back, checked the breech, saw there
was one in the spout. It was a Heckler and Koch
machine pistol.

In the front paddock some horses were moving up towards the house. One mare was snorting and looking back over her withers. Her tail was raised in the style of an Arab colt, so she was frightened, ready for flight. Someone was down there.

I moved forward, crouched low. It was misty and I could only see for ten or so metres. My foot touched something that moved like jelly. I had found the Frenchmen. Paris had his throat cut, and his friend had been garrotted with barbed wire. A nice touch. The laser beam had shown Evans as a target and had also shown their hiding place. Whoever had killed them had taken pleasure in it.

I walked away noiselessly. There was a gleam from the water and I was coming out of the darkness of the rising ground behind me. I had a chance if their killer moved against the water. I saw the legs of three or four horses against the line of the lake. They were up to mischief. They had decided whoever it was they were following was not dangerous. One reared and pigrooted. They were going to follow him up, innocently.

For them to behave like that, the bastard had no scent of fear, and he would be no further than twenty metres from the animals following him. I squatted down to watch. But there was no sign of a figure.

I headed down towards the boat and walked into the water. Lake water is not as cold as the

ocean, but late at night it doesn't feel any different. I submerged myself. I knew straight away he
had located me, because by the time I was fifty
metres from the shore I saw the horses gambol-
ling around, heading towards the boat, frolicking
as if they had found a friend.

I lowered my head beneath the surface and felt
the freeze. My teeth began to shake, but I held
to the mud of the bottom with one hand, the way
a body surfer digs in to avoid the turbulence of
the big wave overhead. Acclimatised, I raised my
head to the surface, only my eyes and nose out
of the water. My jaw was still shaking. I prayed
the cops hadn't sprayed the boat, at least not too
thoroughly, just in the normal cop fashion.

I saw a figure sliding the boat towards the lake.
He pushed it out then, walking beside it. If the
spiders were gone, I'd have to rise and face him,
firing across the water. By that time I would be
cold and, compared to him, barely able to move.
I needed him closer to be certain of a hit.

For a moment the moon burned through lighter cloud and whitened the mist. I saw the face
of the freak. It had a perpetual taunt to it, as if
he were still teasing children. He moved towards
the boat, poised, balanced, his wounds obviously
healed.

He was about knee deep in water, trying to
locate me. I coughed to lure him on. He pushed
the boat and jumped in. He allowed it to drift
with the push. He was kneeling in the bow,

watching. He began to paddle there with the butt of his weapon.

I would have to empty the water from my weapon if I didn't want the first bullet to blow the barrel apart in my face. He was twenty metres away when the fangs of the first spider found his skin. He yelled, began firing in my direction and jumped from the boat. He ran backwards in the shallow water, towards the shore. I shook the water from the machine pistol and began firing. I didn't see him for a moment because water streamed in my eyes. The weapon was jerking, but it was making phht phht sounds that I didn't trust. Then I heard Sacco.

The dog began to growl, a sound that is pitched so ferociously most animals run the second they hear it. Hyenas must have that sound when they're fighting over the guts of the freshly dead. I ran forward.

Sacco was fastened to the freak's face, pulling and jerking as he levered with his feet on the chest. The acrobat didn't go down. He knew he was finished if he did. His face was finished anyway, even before the bite finally began to close. He shot Sacco then, but the dog held on. The acrobat dropped to the mud, Sacco still attached.

I grabbed Sacco's collar and began choking him off, pulling the metal ring of the leather slip collar with one hand, the other palm down against the back of his neck. It was a tricky business, I didn't want a dead dog. The pressure had to be just enough so that his wind pipe closed but wasn't crushed. Finally he came away, the man dropping backwards to the ground.

I had to hold Sacco back. I think the freak died of a heart attack, although maybe his breathing had closed down. He just turned away as if he were finished with life and its horrors, and one long breath slipped through the mashed tissue like a deep sigh. I searched Sacco for the wound. The shot had smashed his back leg in the muscle above the hock. He'd live. I shot the acrobat in the back of the head.

As I carried Sacco towards the house, Willa joined me. She pointed west towards the road. Four cars were approaching. Jesus, I thought, this is the end.

Twenty-five

The cars came up the drive evenly spaced, the dust rising in their headlights. They stopped behind the wrecks in the drive. The wrecks looked like birds shot on the wing. Six men in casual jackets leapt out with weapons low and positioned themselves behind the stationary cars. They were facing the garage and the house. Bresler was helped from the third car. He was slightly stooped, but his damaged face was eager.

Five metres away I laid Sacco on the ground. He wasn't even whimpering. The pain threshold of a dog bred for fighting must be enormous. I was shivering uncontrollably. I lay low. Willa lowered herself across me, a warm weight. From the lead car, a bloke stepped out with a loud hailer. 'This is the federal police,' he called, and the loud speaker whined and crackled. He began again.

I watched the driver's side door on the last car open. Nick Harris stepped out. It didn't make sense. A state politician bringing federal police. And then, of course, it did. A free flow of trade between states, said section 92 of the Constitution, and in this case that meant only information and influence.

One of the young assault types began discovering bodies. The police retreated quickly, one swinging protectively in front of Nick. Bresler jogged back to a car, holding his chest. The cars were backed up outside the gate, their dust rising above the house in the glare of the headlights.

Willa and I crept over to the tackroom at the side of the stables. The dark wasn't a problem, I had often grabbed gear before sunrise. I laid Sacco in the corner, bound his wound with a pressure bandage, and gave him 2 ml of pethidine.

I grabbed some dry riding clothes that were hanging just inside the tackroom door, and in the dark we bridled the horses. Outside the stables was still quiet. We walked them into the forty hectare paddock next to the house. Sacco was riding wrapped in a saddle blanket.

Hidden by the night, Willa rode beside me as the horses strode down to the low ground near the water. A mist was now rolling off the lake as the surface cooled in the chill morning air.

An hour later two vans pulled up at the gate, and the cars moved in again. This time it was a SWAT team of a dozen who assaulted the house. They found nothing. All the lights in the house were turned on. We carefully moved the horses in closer, dismounted, and kept them between us and the house. They were grazing naturally, and occasionally Sacco moved in the blanket. I watched the house as I leaned on the horse's wither. Willa leaned her back against the shoulder of her horse, facing away from the house. They knew it was a horse farm, they would expect horses.

I flinched when a powerful spotlight flashed out from the verandah, but it was someone looking down into the cellar.

They saw Evans and someone went down after him. 'He's alive,' the bloke called up, and Willa clutched my arm. I saw Peter Bresler stagger out onto the verandah. He had to lean back against the verandah and he touched his face with the back of his hand, as if wanting to keep it together.

A stretcher was brought onto the verandah and lowered carefully into the narrow cellar. Several minutes later six men were involved in lifting Evans out. It was a surprise to see Bresler confront Evans. He pushed himself off the wall and gestured for the stretcher to be lowered to the verandah floor.

Bresler was tough. He spoke through his battered mouth and dislocated jaw, the voice rasping from the back of his throat and carrying clearly in the still night air. He waved the men away, and it was a further surprise that they obeyed him. 'Leave us,' he said, and the special forces left the verandah. The senior officer said, 'He's dying; he needs attention.' Bresler didn't answer him but took his sidearm and turned back to the crumpled figure on the stretcher. The officer walked off through the house following his men.

'You were playing two parties, right?' Bresler said to Evans. He held the sidearm out unsteadily for Evans to see. 'You blew that ship?' Evans was obviously beyond answering.

Bresler snapped the breech with difficulty, wobbling on his feet—now there was one in the spout. Willa and I were astounded.

'You sold the cargo to two buyers,' Bresler said. 'To the Indonesian's through me, and to the Syrians. The ship had to disappear. If it reached either port, you were dead. Am I right?'

Evans was obviously unconscious, neither his head or body reacted. Not even when Bresler raised the gun to his head. Bresler shot Evans, the gun bucking his hand, and he was forced to step back. Christ, I thought. Who is Bresler that he can do that.

Bresler left the verandah and walked through the house, out to Nick Harris's car. I left my horse with Willa and moved up to the fence at the front of the house. Bresler had the driver side door open and was using it as a prop as he leaned down to talk to Nick Harris. 'It's all over,' Bresler said. 'Evans is dead. The bodies of the others will be around here somewhere. They'll clean up in daylight.' Nick Harris didn't say a word. I could see him looking through the windscreen, frightened.

Taking care that there was no clink of bridle bits, Willa and I walked back through the mist towards the gate onto the backroad that led to town. We began to talk about the things we had witnessed, keeping a wary eye on lights that approached our road. We only had to open the paddock gate to disappear. Now we had the answer to why we had been chased by different parties.

I was beginning to understand the moves behind the deals. Bresler was one of those individuals who was given carte blanche by the government to trade and deal and solve problems. It had happened in wartime, and it was still happening now. During the Second World War certain industrialists working with BHP had been given the power to make decisions for the government, spend millions of dollars, make decisions on key personnel.

Now, it seemed, the government had been double-crossed by one of its key people—Evans. The government had thought the cargo had been bound for East Timor, not Syria. It was plain that the government backed Evans's sale of chemicals to Indonesia because they didn't want to lose the oil in the Timor Gap. The government would do anything to appease the Indonesians in order to become a serious oil nation.

We thought of abandoning our horses and catching the morning train to the city. But it would have meant taking money from an ATM, and that would immediately give our presence away to the authorities. That was unsettling, even if they had given up on us. I decided to leave

Sacco outside the vet's surgery if we made it to town and wake them to operate immediately.

We would ride our horses to Melbourne. We could leave them in those Altona paddocks where the kids agist their pony club horses. It was time to disappear. Move beyond the machines that recorded our habits, our allegiances, our whereabouts. The Breslers of the world required removing. We would see what we could do about it.

The smell of the lake and the spring grass rose around us. I heard tiny thumps on the turf and Shy Bride's filly appeared beside us on the other side of the fence. She snorted at us, challenging us, throwing her head high in the air, a tiny long-legged replica of her mother. The big mare arrived beside her out of the dark, neighing softly, anxious for her young'n.